CW00922627

Patricia Bevin was born and raised in Northamptonshire where she still lives. She is married to Keith and has three grown-up sons and two grandsons. In 1977, she qualified as a state registered nurse. Apart from breaks to have her children, she has spent her working-life working in nursing homes where she was a registered manager for over thirty years until her retirement, in January 2021.

She has always been an avid reader of crime novels. This is her second novel.

To Mum and Dad. Thank you for believing in my writing. I wish you were both here to read my books.

Patricia Bevin

# A CAREFUL DEATH FOR SOME

AUSTIN MACAULEY PUBLISHERS™

LONDON ★ CAMBRIDGE ★ NEW YORK ★ SHARJAH

Copyright © Patricia Bevin 2022

The right of Patricia Bevin to be identified as author of this work has been asserted by the author in accordance with section 77 and 78 of the Copyright, Designs and Patents Act 1988.

All rights reserved. No part of this publication may be reproduced, stored in a retrieval system, or transmitted in any form or by any means, electronic, mechanical, photocopying, recording, or otherwise, without the prior permission of the publishers.

Any person who commits any unauthorised act in relation to this publication may be liable to criminal prosecution and civil claims for damages.

This is a work of fiction. Names, characters, businesses, places, events, locales, and incidents are either the products of the author's imagination or used in a fictitious manner. Any resemblance to actual persons, living or dead, or actual events is purely coincidental.

A CIP catalogue record for this title is available from the British Library.

ISBN 9781528998079 (Paperback)
ISBN 9781528998086 (ePub e-book)

www.austinmacauley.com

First Published 2022
Austin Macauley Publishers Ltd®
1 Canada Square
Canary Wharf
London
E14 5AA

Thank you to my family and friends who have been so supportive to me as I am discovering a new career as a writer.

# Chapter One

Wednesday evening at seven thirty, on a warm May evening, five people arrived at Julie's house. It was the three-monthly get-together for discussing the next village fundraising event. Julie was a primary school teacher and welcomed the other five committee members with coffee and cake.

"Been baking, I see!" said George, a local parish councillor, who owned a haulage business, rubbing his hands together when he spotted the large cherry cake on a tray with the coffee cups. He was a large man in his mid-sixties who, judging by his figure, enjoyed his food.

"I think some of the cherries sank to the bottom, though!" Julie replied with a grin as she started slicing it. "I'm not the best of cake bakers but thought I'd have a go!"

"It's very nice," said Mary taking a bite after Julie handed her a slice on a plate. Mary was a retired accountant. The others in the group were Celia, a housewife with three young children, Simon a local farmer, and Beverley who was a retired nurse.

They all lived in Merrydale, a small village on the outskirts of the town of Olehampton. The population was about seven hundred. It boasted a primary school, a shop, a butcher's and a pub.

They had been meeting once a month for the past three years. Each committee member took turns in hosting the quarterly meetings and providing light refreshments. They had held several successful fundraising events over the past three years and had raised a total of eight thousand pounds for their village to improve amenities. The village hall had benefitted by having the lighting updated, a skateboarding park installed, the primary school had received some new play equipment for the children, and the elderly now had a community bus service twice a week and the church had new hymn books. All the money raised had been wisely spent and was much appreciated by the recipients.

Beverley had been the latest recruit six months ago to the fundraising team, after the previous member had moved out of the village.

They all settled down in Julie's comfortable sitting room. There was a three-seater settee and two armchairs which easily accommodated five people with a coffee table in front. Julie sat on a dining chair. They all had been served their slices of cake and cups of coffee.

"Now, any ideas for the next fundraising event?" said Simon looking around at the others.

"What about a duck race in the stream?" suggested Beverley.

"We did that a couple of years ago," replied Simon. "The kiddies liked it and it raised quite a good amount."

"What about a fancy-dress event then?" asked Beverley.

"We did that too, in the first year of this committee getting together. It didn't raise as much as we had hoped but it was our first fundraiser and I don't think we advertised it as best as we could have done," said Julie.

Beverley sat back against the back of her chair feeling a bit rebuffed. *I don't think I'll suggest anything else,* she thought to herself. *I'll keep my thoughts to myself.* She was aged forty-nine and even though she was a retired nurse where she had dealt with many people during her nursing career, she was still quite shy.

Simon suggested a barn dance saying he could hold it in one of his barns on his farm.

"Fire regulations won't allow them to be held in barns anymore," said George. "Hay bales are a fire hazard and it wouldn't be the same in the village hall."

"Crikey, I don't want my farm burned down so we'll forget that!" said Simon.

"What about a raffle, then?" suggested Celia.

"We can hold a raffle with whatever event we decide on," said George.

The living room door opened and in walked Julian, Julie's husband. He was a mechanic and had not long showered and changed after returning from work. "Sorry to interrupt, but what setting on the microwave do I need, and how long do I reheat the casserole for?" he asked Julie after saying a general hello to the room.

Julie got up excusing herself to the others. "Come on, I'll show you." She laughed.

"You know I'm not a cook!" he grinned.

She returned after a couple of minutes laughing and saying how hopeless he was in the kitchen.

"Have you ever had a Safari Supper event?" asked Beverley. She had intended to keep quiet but couldn't help offering another suggestion. "There was one in the village where I lived before and it was very successful."

"What a cracking idea!" bellowed George. "There's no great outlay as it's held in people's houses so there's no booking halls or anything. I think it's brilliant. What do you others think?" He looked round at the others who all beamed at Beverley. She blushed and didn't say anything. She was quite reserved and didn't like to be the centre of attention.

Simon asked Beverley what a safari supper actually involved.

"Different houses offer a different course of a three-course meal and then a coffee course," she explained. "All is meticulously planned beforehand. We had three houses that hosted the starter course, another three that did the main course, another three that did the puddings, and then a couple of houses offered coffee and mints. The diners paid a cost upfront for the whole meal, obviously booking up in advance, and had an arranged amount of time at each house before moving on to the next course at a different house. The host or hostess at each house prepared and served the courses. It has to be carefully planned and not too elaborate as each course needs to be served quickly as the diners only have a certain amount of time there before going to the next house."

George clapped his large hands startling the room. "Well done," he congratulated Beverley who blushed. "I'm all for this. It's something we've never held before. Are we all agreed?" Everyone raised their hands. They looked over at Beverley and smiled.

So, it was unanimously agreed that Safari Supper would be the next fundraising event.

"We will need to have a list of people willing to offer their houses and which course they would be happy to provide. We can offer some expenses, but bear in mind, it's a fundraising event so we don't want too big an outlay," said Simon. "I am more than happy to offer my house for a course. I also have some trestle tables and chairs that can be used for extra seating at mine and any other houses that need them, too."

"I can accommodate quite a few diners as I have a conservatory as well as a dining room," said Julie.

Mary said she had room for several diners as well but would need to borrow some extra tables and chairs. "If it's nice weather I can have some people seated outside," she said.

"No problem," said George. "I must have at least a dozen tables in one of my barns and they each seat six comfortably. I have quite a lot of chairs as well."

Celia said she would probably need to cater for the coffee course as she was not a Delia Smith or Mary Berry!

George suggested that the committee start asking friends and neighbours in the village who would be willing to offer their houses. "We probably need about eleven or twelve in all. There are six of us here so we need five or six more."

Julie said she was sure her sister Heather would offer her house. She lived only two houses away so it would be convenient for diners to get to. "We don't want people having to drive to the houses as we don't want them drinking and driving," she said.

"We could provide wine and beer or shall we ask people to bring their own?" said Simon.

Mary said, "My brother Ned works for a cash and carry in Olehampton, so I'm sure he would be able to supply alcohol at a discounted price. That way, we would make more money as we would sell it for a profit."

"That's great, Mary," said George. "I know some supermarkets give glasses on loan if alcohol is bought from them. We can purchase a small supply of drinks from them in return for the glasses, but the majority of the alcohol can be bought at a discount price from Mary's brother, if he agrees."

Julie was making a list of everything that was discussed.

Each committee member would have a job to do to get the idea off the ground.

"Let's have a recap," said Simon. "Mary, you ask your brother about some discounted alcohol. I will speak to Tesco's about the glasses and buying a small amount of alcohol. Julie, you ask your sister if she is willing to be on board with one of the courses. Beverley, do you know anyone who may provide a house?"

"I have a friend, Sheila, who lives in the same road as me, Celia, and Mary. I think you all know her. She is an excellent cook and loves entertaining. We have many evenings when we cook for each other. I will ask her tomorrow. She will be up for it, I'm sure."

"Great," said Simon. "My sister Frances lives just off the High Street so I'm sure she will be happy to help as well. That's ten houses. Who else can we ask?"

"What about Sarah?" said Celia. "She's a good friend and neighbour of mine. I'm sure I can persuade her!"

"That's eleven houses, if they all agree, and are within walking distance of each other. We need to decide a date now," said George.

"Today's May 12$^{th}$ so how about the middle of June before school closes and families start going away for their summer holidays. That also gives us a good month to organise it," said Simon.

Julie looked at her phone, scrolling to a calendar. "What about Saturday, 15$^{th}$ June?"

"Right, that's decided. Let's meet again in a week once everyone has been asked and are available for the date and what courses they could do?" said George. "Have a think about menus, and discuss it with the various people."

"Meet at mine next Wednesday at seven thirty?" offered Simon. All agreed to meet at Simon's house next week.

Julie got up to make another cup of coffee for everyone. "There's still some cherry cake that needs eating!" remarked George looking at his empty plate.

Julian wandered into the room. "Successful meeting?" he asked.

"Very successful," replied Simon. "A Safari Supper! Eleven or twelve different houses offering different courses. I think Julie's nominated you to make a coq-a-vin!"

"No way!" laughed Julian. "If I'm cooking, they will get beans on toast."

He sat down in Julie's seat. Julie entered with a tray of coffee. "Oi you, that's my chair, get your own," she grinned.

Julian got up and brought another dining chair over. "Anything I can help with?" he asked. "Apart from the cooking!"

"I will need help with setting up trestle tables in houses that need them on the night," said Simon.

"Count me in," said Julian.

They all drank their coffee and the remaining cherry cake was eaten.

The meeting finished at nine thirty.

"See you at Simons house next Wednesday," said George as he put his cap on, ready to leave. The others followed him out. It was a fine evening, and hopefully, the date of the supper would be as good.

Julie cleared up the cups and plates and stacked them in the dishwasher. Julian followed her into the kitchen and said he thought the supper was a great idea and should raise quite a bit of money.

"It was Beverley's suggestion," replied Julie. "Apparently, there was one held in her previous village."

"I don't really know her," said Julian. "She always appears very quiet, so it's nice that she should come forward with this idea."

"She used to be a community nurse, so she must have met many different people in her job, perhaps she feels different now she's retired, and is in a new village. She's quite friendly with Sheila. She is quiet and a bit shy, but appears to listen to what's going on. I felt a bit sorry for her as her first two suggestions were knocked back as we had done them before she was on the committee, but of course, she wouldn't have known that."

"Has she got a husband?" asked Julian.

"She's widowed, which is apparently why she moved. I think losing him and then retiring made her want a fresh start. She's only in her forties which is young for being widowed and retired. Perhaps, she'll return to nursing sometime in the future. I think I will try to befriend her more. I don't like to think of her being lonely."

"You are a kind soul," said Julian. "You already have a lot on your plate with being a full-time teacher and looking after me!"

"Yes, I do," she laughed, "and guess which is most difficult!"

"Come on, let's watch the news together and go to bed."

# Chapter Two

The following Wednesday evening, five committee members made their way to Simon's farm. It was a lovely warm evening and everyone walked. Julie met Celia along the road. They had a chat about school and Celia told her how much her eldest daughter, Freya, enjoyed being in Julie's class. "She tells me it's fun and you are lovely with them even if they do something naughty!"

Celia's two younger daughters went to nursery but would be going to primary school next term.

Julie laughed and said it was a pleasure to teach such young minds. "Their brains are like sponges; they soak up information!"

They arrived at Simon's farm house at seven thirty. The house was adjacent to what were obviously barns. They could see the back end of a tractor poking out of one barn. Cows were grazing contentedly in a nearby field, the ripe smell of cattle accompanied Celia and Julie up the path to the front door. They knocked and it was quickly opened by Simon, who welcomed them inside,

"Come in, everyone's here now!" he exclaimed. "Follow me."

Julie closed the front door and she and Celia followed him into the lounge.

Beverley and George were sitting in large armchairs. Mary was sitting on a two-seater settee.

"Sit yourselves down and help yourself to coffee," said Simon, as he pointed to a second two-seater settee. Celia and Julie did as he asked. Simon sat by Mary.

A tray with filled coffee mugs was on a coffee table with some chocolate biscuits arranged on a plate.

"Sorry, there's no cake, but Marie is away at our son's for a few days and I don't think you would want any cake I would attempt to bake," he said. They all laughed and said chocolate biscuits were fine.

Simon asked who wanted to start off.

Mary said, "I've spoken to my brother Ned and he can get alcoholic and soft drinks at a discounted price from the cash and carry where he works."

"Excellent," said George. "I've spoken to Tesco's and as long as we purchase some wine and beer we can have as many glasses as we like."

"We will have to decide how much to get from them before we ask Ned what to get for us," replied Simon.

"The village hall kitchen will be able to provide plates, cutlery, cups and saucers which I can collect the day before and distribute around the houses," said George.

Beverley said she had spoken to her friend, Sheila, who was very happy to open her house to people and would serve a main course.

Simon said his sister, Frances, was happy to do a pudding course at her house.

Julie said she had spoken to her sister, Heather, who had also agreed to host a main course at her house.

She said she had also spoken to her neighbour, Sarah, who had also agreed to host a main course.

George asked if ten houses were enough to host all the courses.

"I think it might be," replied Julie. "We could have two starters, three mains, three puddings, and two coffees. What do you think?"

"I suppose the starters may take less time to eat so there would be time for a quicker changeover," said Beverley.

"But we don't want people queuing to get into the houses for mains," said Julie. "I think we need to find another house for the starters and also for the coffee course."

"Does anyone know anyone else who may open their house?"

"I do have another neighbour, Kerry," said Celia. "I don't know her quite as well as Sarah, but she's friendly and nice, and may do it. She lives next door to me so it would be convenient for diners as well."

"Ask her anyway, and we'll presume she says yes. If she doesn't, I'm sure we'll find someone else between the six of us," said George. "I really think we need three houses for the starters rather than just two."

Everyone agreed with this.

"Menus now," said Simon. "Any thoughts, anybody?"

"I think there should be two choices for all the courses," said Julie. "Should we ask people to choose when they book?"

"Definitely," replied Celia. "Whoever is cooking needs to know what quantities to cook."

"I thought some rice with either lasagne, or bolognaise and a chicken dish, we could serve garlic bread or French stick with it rather than vegetables," suggested Celia.

"That's what I thought as well," said Julie. "Not everyone eats red meat but most people generally eat chicken. Rice is better as vegetables can go mushy if left heated for too long. We would need to ask if anyone has a food allergy so we can cook theirs separately. Perhaps each house can choose which two mains to cook and then the diners assigned to that house get a choice!"

"Ok, good point about the allergy, though. We need to make sure about that," said George. "What about starters?"

"Soup, and perhaps a prawn mayonnaise?" suggested Mary. "They are easy to prepare beforehand."

Beverley said she was severely allergic to prawns, but as she was hosting a pudding course, it shouldn't matter as she wouldn't be in contact with any prawns.

"Do you carry an adrenaline pen?" asked George.

"I carry one in my handbag all the time," she replied, looking down at her small, red handbag by her feet. "I also have an allergy alert bracelet on all the time," she replied as she held her left wrist up for them to see.

"Ok, so the starters and mains sound good," replied Simon "Pudding ideas anyone?"

"Cold sweets are easier to serve quickly, what about a fruit cocktail and some sort of pastry tart and cream?" asked Mary.

"I think we have our menus," said Simon "It sounds good. Is everyone in agreement?"

All agreed and Celia suggested there be raffle tickets on sale at each house to pump up the profits.

"How much do we charge for the meal?" asked Mary.

Simon looked around at everyone. "How about twenty pounds a head? This is for a three-course meal with the proceeds going to good causes."

"It's still forty pounds for a couple which may be a bit expensive for some people," said Beverley.

"How about thirty-five for a couple but twenty for a single person?" suggested Celia.

"Agreed everyone?" asked George. Hands were raised as six members agreed on the price.

"What time do we start serving?" asked Celia. It was agreed the starter courses would start at seven o'clock.

"Right," said Simon. "We all need to sell as many tickets as we can, and the week before the supper, we can order the meat from our butcher in the village. I will see him this week and tell him of the event. He's sure to give us a discount as it's for the village. I will also ask the local shop and pub for raffle prizes."

"Where will we be getting the other ingredients from?" asked Beverley.

"I suggest whoever is hosting the starters, puddings, and coffee get the ingredients from wherever you shop and keep receipts," said Simon. "I hope we can do some deals with shopkeepers when we say it is a fundraising event. As we are the committee, I will leave it up to each of you to speak with the hosts."

"I can buy the rice and bread when I know how much is needed," offered Mary.

The coffee and chocolate biscuits had been consumed by now, so Simon went out into his kitchen and replenished the refreshments. He returned with a tray. George reached for the largest chocolate biscuit, not unnoticed by the others.

"I can print the Supper tickets out," said George. "I will deliver them to your houses before the end of this week along with a book of raffle tickets."

"Let's hope we sell enough to make this a good event," said Mary.

"Well, the villagers have always supported us in previous events, so hopefully, they will with this one, too," replied George. "Shall we meet here in two weeks with an update on which houses are definitely hosting which course and how many tickets have been sold?"

"Agreed," they replied.

"Then get selling those tickets!" said George.

They finished their coffee and biscuits.

The committee left and made their way home. Celia walked with Mary as they lived in the same road.

# Chapter Three

The following week was quite busy for all the committee. Each committee member consulted with the people who had offered their house to host the evening. Tickets were also being sold at a good rate.

Friday evening, Celia knocked on her neighbour Kerry's door at seven o'clock and was invited in. Kerry was a single mum with two teenage sons. She worked in the local estate agent's and finished work about six o'clock. She had lived in Merrydale for about two years.

"I'll be happy to be included with this," she said after Celia explained about the Safari supper. "I want to be more involved with the village activities." She made Celia a cup of coffee as they sat at the kitchen table. "It will be nice to meet more people. Being out at work all day, I don't know as many people as I would like to."

Celia explained what it involved and Kerry agreed to host a pudding course.

"I'll suggest the boys go out for the evening or they may start bothering us!" she said with a laugh.

Celia thought how nice she was, and perhaps, should have made more effort to be a friendly neighbour. She would do in future, she decided.

They had a good chat and felt they had each made a new friend.

Celia returned home and spoke with her husband, Luke. "I've had a really nice conversation with Kerry," she told him. "I think she's quite lonely from what I can tell, although she works. She's really nice and I think we'll become friends. I don't know why we haven't seen more of each other considering she only lives next door."

"You are a good person, that's why I love you," He replied with a grin. "Go on with you," she retorted. "Let's get the dinner on now, it's getting late."

Celia went upstairs to have a shower after preparing their meal and putting it in the oven. Macaroni cheese and garlic bread tonight. The children had been fed earlier and were in bed.

Over their meal, Celia told Luke about how many tickets she had already sold. "Most people I've asked are keen to get involved," she said. "That new, young couple at number nine said it was a daft idea and too expensive, so I just left without further comment."

"Their loss," replied Luke. "You would think they would want to become involved with the village now they live here?"

"You'd think so, but it's up to them. Perhaps when they have children they may do so," said Celia.

She was pleased that she had managed to sell quite a few tickets. She needed to make sure her three, young children were in bed early on the Safari supper night as she was going to be very busy cooking and serving, and having youngsters running around would not be acceptable to the diners. Luke would have to deal with child care as well as well as helping out!

She made a list of all the people she had sold tickets to. There were fourteen in all. Most were fellow neighbours who lived in their road. She knew a lot of them as they had children at her school. Tomorrow she would go to Martin Close, which was just off their road. It only had around ten houses, but at least three had children who went to her school so she hoped they would participate. She realised that quite a few couples would need babysitters on the night but she knew there were quite a few teenagers in the village that regularly babysat, so she hoped it would be the case on the night.

She would make an effort to ask older people as well, or there wouldn't be enough babysitters to go around!

She went up to check the children who, thankfully, were all asleep. She called down to Luke she was going to bed as was feeling tired.

After their evening meal, Julie rang her mother, Jane, for a chat. She lived in a village the other side of Olehampton. She was a maths teacher in a secondary school. She had lived on her own after a divorce from Julie's father eleven years ago. He had remarried, and had a second family of two young boys. Julie visited him often and got on very well with his wife, Barbara, and her half-brothers. Julie's mother was dating a fellow teacher at the school and was happy with her life which pleased Julie. It hadn't always been as harmonious as the divorce had come out of the blue and tensions had run high at the time, but eventually, all sorted itself out.

Julie told her mother all about the plans for the Safari Supper. She invited her to sleep over at her house for the event weekend so she could participate. "I can help you out with the cooking and serving. I'll enjoy that," said her mother. "Great, thanks," replied Julie. "I've sold twenty tickets."

Simon was also pleased to have sold ten tickets. He and his wife, Marie, were popular around the village. They had lived in the same farmhouse for over thirty years and had raised their family of two sons and a daughter there. He could always be counted on to help anyone out who needed it. Last winter, at two in the morning, he had used his tractor to pull one of the village teenager's car out of a ditch after it had skidded on an icy road. He was always cheerful and after a couple of drinks, was the life and soul of a party!

He made a list of the people he had sold the tickets to. Marie, who was hosting a starter course, was on the phone with George's sister while he was totting up his sales.

"Frances says she'll host a pudding course. She'll tell George," she called out to Simon.

Simon and Marie got on very well with her. A couple of tickets had been sold to his fellow farming neighbour. He had actually been surprised at this as Roger and Fay were not known much for joining in village events. They were a quiet couple in their sixties and ran an arable farm rather than livestock like Simon. They were not particularly friendly with people in the village; a nod of acknowledgement rather than stopping for a chat when they met anyone. He wondered who they would sit with on the Safari night and if they would contribute much to the conversation on the table. *Never mind*, thought Simon, *as least they have bought two tickets contributing to the proceeds.*

Marie was still visiting their younger son, Gary, and his wife, Georgina. They lived in a village about twelve miles away. They were expecting their first child and Georgina was not having an easy pregnancy, so Marie was helping out for a week or so. Simon missed her and hoped she would be back soon. He was very competent cooking for himself but she had left some prepared dishes in the freezer for him. He wouldn't starve!

He made himself a coffee and sat in front of the television to watch the last bit of the news and weather. He had one of Marie's cottage pies heating in the microwave. He was anticipating a lazy evening. He liked the spring and summer as he was not quite as busy around the farm as he was in the colder months. The animals were in the fields and after a wet, early spring, there was plenty of good grass for grazing.

The microwave pinged to tell him the cottage pie was ready. He took it out and put it on a tray and returned to the lounge. The news was finished and the One Show had begun.

His eyes started closing after his meal. The telephone suddenly rang, startling him awake with a jerk. The tray and empty plate nearly fell off his lap, but he caught it all before it fell on the floor.

He got up to answer the phone. It was Roger.

"I've just chased an intruder off my farm," he told Simon. "I thought I'd warn you in case he comes onto yours. Goodness knows what he was after, there's not much to pinch here."

"Thanks for the tipoff, Roger," replied Simon. "What did he look like?"

"Young, by the way he scarpered when he saw me. He had on a green, army type jacket, and blue jeans, and a cap. He may be looking for somewhere to hide. We've both got barns which he could doss down in," said Roger.

"I will check mine out. Thanks for ringing me, Roger," said Simon as he put the phone down in the cradle.

He put his tray in the kitchen and went outside. He went into the nearby barns but saw nothing amiss. Some of the cows wandered over to the fence and started lowing when they saw Simon.

"I haven't anything for you and you're not due to be milked till the morning," he told them with a grin.

Simon employed a man called James, who came in twice a day to help with the milking. He was about forty, and lived on his own in a rented cottage in the village. He had worked for Simon for over twenty years. He was totally reliable and you could set your clock by him. He was never late and rarely took a holiday. He had a collie dog called Jess, who accompanied him everywhere. He arrived every morning at five for the milking and again at four in the afternoon. He didn't mix much, and didn't appear to entertain anybody in his cottage. He didn't say much when working, just got on with the job in hand. He was a perfect employee for Simon, who thanked his lucky stars that James had approached him for a job all those years ago.

Simon also employed Stan, who worked from ten till four and did general work around the farm. He was now seventy and Simon wondered when he would retire. He would miss him as he was a grafter and helped Simon out with all sorts of things around the farm such as maintenance, cleaning the barns, and helping out with anything else Simon asked him to do. He lived with his wife in the village.

Simon had asked both James and Stan if they wanted tickets for the Safari Supper but both had declined saying it wasn't their sort of thing.

After thoroughly checking all his barns, Simon went back into the house. He rang Marie, and asked how everything was with Gary and Georgina.

"Much better, Georgina had a scan this afternoon and all is well, thank goodness. Another couple of days and I should be back," Marie replied.

"Good. Send them my love. I miss you, hurry back!" said Simon.

"How's the Safari supper sales going? I'm happy to provide a starter course."

"Great, I'll tell the others. See you in a couple of days, love you," replied Simon.

"You too, see you in a couple of days," said Marie.

Simon didn't tell her about Roger's intruder as he didn't want to worry her. He would tell her when she returned home.

He put the phone down, locked the front door and had a long soak in the bath and then went to bed. He was never late to bed as he was up at four thirty every morning for the milking.

# Chapter Four

Mary was also doing well with her ticket selling. She had sold six pairs to various friends and neighbours. She lived in a detached house in Main Street. She loved gardening and her back garden had plenty of flower beds – always a mass of colour. She had a small lawn at the front of her house, and one flower bed which hosted spring blooms of begonias. Their heads were heavy and the colours superb. She had lots of people stop by and compliment her on them. She invited many to come and see her back garden as she was very proud of her horticultural achievements.

When the village had Open Gardens every two years, Mary's garden always was the most admired and won her Garden of the village every time.

When she had worked full time, she hadn't had much time for the garden, but since retiring ten years ago, she had found green fingers and spent many happy hours tending to her plants. She had a shed at the bottom of her garden where she had all her gardening equipment and various chemicals and fertilisers she needed to maintain her perfect garden.

Mary lived alone. She was sixty-four and had retired early as she had had enough of calculating numbers and pouring over business accounts. She had earned enough to retire early and not wait for her pension. She lived quite simply with a black cat called Ebony, for company. She had a son, but they hadn't seen each other for a while. Her son's marriage had split up a few months ago and he had moved away and not kept in touch. She had no address or phone number to contact him which made her sad. She hoped one day he would get back in touch with her. She wasn't sure where her daughter-in-law moved to after the marriage failed. That also made her sad as she had liked her.

Her friend, Lorna, was a regular visitor to her house as Mary was to hers. Lorna and Mary often had day trips out together and enjoyed car boot sales where they competed to find the best bargains! Lorna was widowed and had a son, daughter-in-law, and two grandchildren who also lived in the village. She also had a married daughter but she didn't live locally.

Mary checked her list of ticket sales. She had been surprised at some of the takers and non-takers. A couple at the end of her road had bought two. Mary hadn't met them before; they were a young couple who worked in Olehampton, so were out all week and weren't seen much over a weekend. Judging by the smell of paint when the front door was opened, Mary supposed they were busy decorating.

"It sounds like a nice evening out!" the wife exclaimed. "Count us in for two tickets."

Another neighbour further up the road, who Mary had assumed would want to have tickets, said, "Not for us, thank you." and quickly closed the front door.

Mary was not a great cook so would offer her house for a coffee course.

Her brother, Ned, had bought two tickets but said they may not attend as it wasn't "his thing". He was single and lived alone in a nearby village but had a lady friend called Wendy, who also worked at the cash and carry warehouse in the office. They had "walked out" together for over five years, neither wanting to commit themselves to living together. It suited both of them to remain just good friends. Mary said she would let him know the week before the supper as to how much alcohol and soft drinks the event would need. He had assured her that his manager would let them have a good discount on the drinks as it was for a good cause.

Mary and Ned didn't see each other very often, they weren't very close, but spoke on the phone every couple of weeks or so. There was fifteen years difference in age between them. Ned had been a big surprise to his parents. Being fifteen, Mary was usually out with her friends rather than being at home with a crying baby brother, although, she liked to show him off to people when she took him out for a walk in his pram.

Beverley looked at her list of sold tickets. Twenty! Her friend, Sheila, had offered to host a main course at her house. Beverley would host a pudding course. She was pleased with her ticket sales as she had called on people who she didn't know and wondered what their reaction would be, but she had been pleasantly surprised. Beverley really liked living in this village. Thank goodness she had found this one, far away from her previous one. She was quite shy so had appreciated being asked to be on the committee. She was also pleased to have made a good friend in Sheila.

George lived in a large, detached house in the centre of the village. He had been a village resident for near on fifteen years. His haulage business was very successful and he was proud to serve on the parish council. He had been married to Anne for thirty years and was very grateful for her support. She didn't work and hadn't for a long time. She had been at home raising their four children who were now all married with children of their own.

She told George she was happy to host a pudding course.

"I've sold fourteen," he told her. "If we all sell that amount, we should be laughing."

The next committee meeting was set for the following Wednesday so he hoped everybody sold well and had a good number for the event.

# Chapter Five

The following Wednesday, the committee gathered at Beverley's house. It was a nice, warm evening and all had walked there.

Beverley opened the door to greet them and showed them into her lounge. It was a small room but she had set up additional chairs alongside her two-seater sofa and two armchairs. She served coffee and cheese and biscuits. She handed a plate to each person who helped themselves to the various cheese and biscuits set out on a coffee table in front of the sofa.

It was a bit of a squash in the room but all managed without bumping each other's arms as they held plates and coffee mugs.

George asked how everyone had done with selling tickets.

All six members consulted their individual lists and related their sales.

"Ninety sold. Well done everybody. That's brilliant," said Mary.

Everyone congratulated each other.

"We should do really well out of this," said George. "We obviously have expenses to pay out as well but with selling raffle tickets it should bump up the final amount raised."

"Shall we each contribute a raffle prize?" asked Simon. "This will keep our costs down."

All agreed to this suggestion.

"Now, whose house is hosting which course?" asked Simon. A discussion started, lists scrutinised, and continued for ten minutes.

"I think we've got it," said Celia. "Starters are being hosted by George, Julie and Simon. Mains are being hosted by Sheila, Sarah and Heather. Puddings are being hosted by Frances, Beverley and Kerry, and coffee by me and Mary. Is everyone agreed? Have I got this right?"

"I think so, if you believe we don't need a third coffee house," said Simon. Julie said that the committee members, once they have finished hosting their courses, could go around to Mary's and Celia's and offer to help out with the coffee courses.

"Right, it's just two weeks to the event so shall we all order our own ingredients depending on which course, and keep receipts. Liaise with whoever you have asked to host a course and ask if they want us to get the ingredients or would they prefer to get them themselves. We also need to post a flyer through the doors of everyone who has bought a ticket saying which house they are allocated to for each of their courses. If we don't allocate then we could have everybody turning up at the same house!"

They looked at their lists and finally got it sorted as to whose house everyone would be eating at. Beverley went to the kitchen and replenished the coffee. There was still some cheese and biscuits in front of them. George took some more, crunching the crackers loudly which caused some smothered laughter from the others.

The meeting ended at nine thirty with another one arranged to be held at Mary's house the following Wednesday with updates from everyone. After that, they would re-convene at Simon's the Wednesday before the Safari Supper date on the Saturday night.

The committee members left thanking Beverley for her hospitality. "Nice to have you all," she replied shyly. *It was nice*, she thought to herself. *No one knows me very well here and that's how I want it to stay.*

It was still light and a fine evening. The members departed to their own streets calling cheerio to each other. Mary and Celia walked home together as they lived in the same road.

Beverley cleared up the cups and plates. She was really happy to be part of the village and pleased to be involved in the fundraising committee.

She was making new friends here. She was getting to know Sheila well. Beverley had had acquaintances before in her previous village over fifty miles away and tried to join in with activities and events, but had made no lasting friends, but now felt part of a community.

The move to Merrydale was a fresh start where no one knew her and what had gone on before she moved here. She could walk around with her head held up without people pointing a finger at her.

She locked up, had a bath and went to bed.

# Chapter Six

Marie returned home from her son's house. Simon was very pleased to have her back home. They caught up on each other's news. He told her about Roger's intruder and said to keep a careful eye out on their farm in case he turned up there. "It may be something or nothing," he said. "Probably someone wanting shelter in a barn for the night."

Marie agreed to watch out.

She unpacked her case and put a wash on. She changed into old clothes as she was planning to do some gardening. They had a plot at the back of the farm house which Marie called her own little sanctuary. She had a bench, bird feeders, and a small shed where she kept her gardening equipment. After morning coffee, she hung the washing out on the length of line, pleased that there was some light breeze to dry it. She didn't believe in artificial drying and although Simon had offered to buy a tumble drier, she much preferred the outdoors for drying washing.

Simon had brought her up to date with the Safari Supper preparations. She went into one of the barns to see how many trestle tables and chairs they had. They had a good stock that they lent out to the villagers for the various village functions. Simon would lend them out to the Safari Supper houses that needed extra seating. The chairs were quite small, fold-up ones so fitted nicely around a table.

Marie counted twelve trestle tables and thirty chairs. That should be plenty she hoped. She would ring around and ask who needed any for the event so Simon could drop them off on the day.

She noticed there had been some sort of disturbance in the far corner of the barn. She walked over. There were some cigarette stubs and a couple of squashed, empty beer cans. The floor which was always dusty looked as if it had had something dragged on it. She would tell Simon and also James and Stan.

It looked as if Roger's intruder had been here as well. She looked around the barn. There wasn't much in it at this time of year. In the winter, there were lots of straw bales.

She went out closing the large doors behind her. She went into the next shed where Simon kept his tractor. He was using it today so the barn was empty. Nothing appeared to have been disturbed in this barn.

She left the doors open so Simon could drive the tractor in at the end of the day.

She saw Stan who was sweeping up debris in the yard. "Nice to see you back home. How's the family?" he asked.

"Doing well, thank you," Marie replied. "I shall be glad when the baby's here safe and sound."

"When's it due?" he asked.

"A couple of months, not too long to wait now," smiled Marie.

She offered Stan coffee who declined saying he'd got a flask of tea. She told him what she had found in the barn.

"I will keep my eyes and ears open," he promised. "Best tell Simon to keep the barn doors shut and locked overnight. We're too trusting around here," Marie agreed with this.

She went into the garden and began to weed some flower beds. It was an enjoyable task, especially, on such a nice day. She had put pansies in before she had left to go to her son's and they were growing well, a real splash of colour in each of the flower beds.

"Do you want me to mow the lawn for you?" a voice asked.

Marie turned around and saw Stan.

"If you don't mind, that would be great," she replied. It was a manual push mower and she found it rather heavy.

Simon kept on at her to have an electric one but she hadn't yet got around to buying one.

Stan went to the shed and retrieved the mower. *He is such a nice man*, Marie thought. *We shall really miss him when he decides to retire.* But as yet, he hadn't mentioned any plans, so Simon and Marie hadn't brought the subject up in case it got him thinking about it!

The rest of the day passed pleasantly. Stan mowed the lawn. Marie's back was aching a bit after bending down weeding. The washing had dried and been ironed and put away. She just needed to prepare their evening meal now.

Over supper, she told Simon about the findings in the barn. He said he would go out in a bit and lock all the barn doors. "Must keep a look out, we don't want to lose anything. I'll give Roger a ring and tell him about it, too."

He finished his meal, got up from the table, and went to make the call.

# Chapter Seven

Celia was relaxing after a busy day. Having three young children under the age of ten wore her out. The eldest girl, Freya, who was almost ten, had one more year left at school and the two younger ones went to nursery each weekday morning. She had had the younger girls within the space of fourteen months so both were able to start in the same school year which pleased them. She loved them all dearly and enjoyed their young company, but was happy when evening came and they were all asleep in bed. Luke was pottering outside in the garden shed. He kept an array of tools and gardening equipment in the shed. He also had an electric socket in there for a light so he could use the shed any time of year. In colder months, he plugged a small heater in. Celia called it his "Man Shed." "Having three daughters and a wife, I need man space," he grinned.

Celia turned the television on. She had missed the local news as she had been upstairs with the children. Had she heard a report on the news, she would have been quite alarmed.

She watched a programme about cooking. That reminded her about the Safari Supper. She would go to the supermarket on Saturday morning when Luke could mind the children and purchase some good quality coffee and some mints and chocolates. She also needed to buy a couple of raffle prizes.

She was looking forward to the event. She planned the tables and chairs and seating arrangements in her head. She had quite a large lounge and a kitchen diner and could move things around to accommodate people. She would need to be able to seat probably thirty altogether. If it was a nice, warm evening, some people could sit at the patio chairs and tables in the garden. She would need to borrow a couple of kettles. The village hall kitchen had a few so she would ask George.

Luke came in about nine o'clock. He asked Celia if she wanted coffee but she yawned and said she would be going up for a shower and then going to bed.

"I think I'll do the same," he said. "It's been really busy at work; everyone wants a piece of me. I can't turn around without someone calling my name."

Luke worked at a medical centre on the outskirts of Olehampton as a maintenance person. He had worked there for over ten years and enjoyed it very much but he was the only maintenance person for a very large practice so he was busy all the time as there was always something going wrong that he needed to sort out.

They retired to bed. They missed the local news again; they were fast asleep.

# Chapter Eight

Mary had an early night, too, so also missed the local news.

She had been over to see her brother, Ned, and his lady friend, Wendy. She didn't meet up with them very often. Wendy lived alone in a bungalow a couple of miles away but often stayed over at Ned's. Wendy had cooked a lovely fish pie and they had sat talking around the dining table all evening without turning the television on. Mary was telling them about the Safari Supper arrangements. She said she would ring Ned with a list of how many bottles of wine, beer and soft drinks they would need. "We have a meeting on the Wednesday before, so I will ring you after that."

"Fine," said Ned. "As long as I've got twenty-four hours' notice. I can bring them over in my van on Saturday morning, so tell me the addresses and how many bottles to drop off at each house. Wendy can help me!"

Wendy volunteered in a Heart Foundation charity shop in Olehampton. She enjoyed it very much and got on well with the people who worked there and liked chatting to the customers.

She often brought items to his home, much to Ned's amusement. "Do I really need that?" he was often heard asking her.

"Of course, you do!" she would reply laughing.

George and Anne had been out to the local pub for dinner. They served a good fish and chips and a lot of villagers congregated there each evening for meals or chatting over their pints.

The couple who ran the pub were popular and made everyone welcome. Quiz nights were held monthly with the proceeds going to local village groups.

This evening had been busy and the young waitress was rushed off her feet serving meals and drinks. George gave her a five-pound tip and her pretty face lit up as she said thank you.

"Thank you as well," said Anne. "It was lovely."

Their empty plates were collected and George strode to the bar to pay for the meal and order another set of drinks.

"How are you, Stan?" he asked clapping him on the back. Stan went into the pub every evening at nine thirty for a couple of pints and always sat by the counter. If ever he didn't go in, if he was poorly or away, there was a space left where he would normally sit.

"I'm good, thanks," Stan replied. He had been telling people standing drinking around the bar about the intruder on Roger's farm and the disturbance in Simon's barn.

"What's this?" asked George who only heard the tail end of the conversation.

"Young lad who scarpered when Roger spotted him but we think he ended up in Simon's barn for the night." he recounted.

"That's quite unusual, we haven't had any trouble with vagrants for a long time," replied George. "We must be on our guard; he could be looking to steal from houses."

Everyone nodded and agreed to watch out for strangers in the village.

George ordered his drinks and returned to his table. He told Anne about the intruder on the farms.

"Keep the doors locked when you are on your own in the house," he warned her.

They reached home just before eleven o'clock and went straight to bed without turning the television on, so they, too, missed the news.

# Chapter Nine

The following day, Julie arrived at school at eight thirty. She loved teaching children and had a good set of fellow teachers with whom she got on really well. They congregated in the staff room for a quick coffee before going into their respective classrooms and then to assembly which started the school day. Julie heard part of a conversation and asked what was going on.

"Someone's on the loose around here," she was told. "It was on the local news last night."

"A youngish man released on bail has run away and the police are looking for him in this area. He's been spotted in a couple of villages near to Merrydale."

"What was his crime for which he was bailed for?" asked Julie.

"It didn't say on the news, but it must be something quite bad for it to have been on the news, asking folk not to approach him but to ring the police immediately if he's seen," said one of the other teachers.

"Did it say what he looked like?" asked Julie.

"He was wearing a green camouflage jacket, jeans, and a cap when last seen," she was told.

"We must all keep a look out then," said Julie. She looked worried hoping he would not come near the school. "We should warn parents and children about him."

"Yes, I'll do that in assembly, without frightening them. We must tell all the children not to talk to anyone they don't know. I will also send a letter home with them telling their parents to impress on their children not to speak to strangers," said the headmaster.

They could now hear the children arriving for school. Lots of laughter, chat, and hugs for Mum or Dad. The teachers went to their classrooms apart from two designated teachers who went to the school gates and opened them, admitting the children so the parents knew they were safely in school.

The headmaster spoke in assembly about the need for not talking to anyone that they did not know.

"We know all about stranger danger," said Freddie sticking his hand up. Other children nodded and agreed with Freddie. Freddie was a ten-year-old, red haired, little boy. He had a mischievous nature and was very popular with teachers and his school friends.

Freddie said he would hit a stranger on the nose and run off screaming if anyone tried to get him. The other children laughed.

"You must not do that, Freddie," admonished the headmaster. "You should not be going anywhere near a stranger in the first place."

Freddie looked crestfallen and muttered he would still like to punch a stranger on the nose if he was coming for him or his mates. His fellow classmates giggled.

The assembly finished with a rousing edition of "All things bright and beautiful."

At the end of the school day, Julie and another teacher saw the last of the children off the school grounds into the care of their parents. They went into the staff room and put the kettle on to make a cup of tea. She sat down with a sigh of relief. She had enjoyed the day and never underestimated young minds. They were so funny without realising it. She smiled thinking of Freddie in assembly, stating he would punch a stranger on the nose!!

She had her cup of tea and went back to her classroom and collected her bag. Most of the teachers had left by now. She called cheerio to the headmaster saying she would see him tomorrow.

She walked home. It was great having a job where she didn't need to drive to.

Once home, she sat at her kitchen table and made a list of the ingredients she needed to buy for the Safari Supper. She was making a starter course.

She completed her list and started to prepare dinner. Julian usually arrived home from the medical centre about five forty-five.

They always ate in the kitchen about six thirty for their meal and enjoyed talking about their day.

Julie told him about the stranger and how the police were looking for him. "Apparently, it was on the local news last night but we missed it. Young Freddie said he would punch him on the nose if he came near him," said Julie with a smile.

Julian laughed. He knew Freddie as he lived next door and was always asking questions!

It was a lovely evening so they went for a walk in the village. Julie pointed out the various houses that were going to be hosting a course for the supper. "It's going to be really good; no one needs to walk far to any of the houses. It was a really good idea of Beverley's. I hope it's going to be a success and raise a lot of money."

They walked by Simon's farm house. He was driving his tractor towards a barn. He saw them and waved. He leapt down from his tractor and came over to them.

"Hi, have you heard about the police looking for someone in the nearby villages?" he asked them.

"Yes, we have," replied Julian. "We've warned the children yet again about not going near any strangers."

"He might have been here in Merrydale the other night," said Simon. "Roger chased an intruder off his farm and Anne spotted some cigarette stubs and beer cans in one of my barns."

"Crikey," said Julie. "I hope he's gone somewhere else now and the police catch him soon. It makes you feel very uneasy thinking he may be about."

"I wonder why he's in this area? From what I've heard, he comes from quite a distance away," said Simon. "Do you think he's trying to locate someone, or perhaps, has family in this area?"

"Surely, he would know where his family lived," pointed out Julie. "I know where all mine live."

"I really don't know. We need to watch the news tomorrow and see if there's an update. Hopefully, the news will say he's been caught."

Julie and Julian said goodbye to Simon. He drove the tractor into the barn and padlocked the doors shut.

# Chapter Ten

The following Wednesday, the committee met at Mary's bungalow. It was a lovely, warm evening, so Mary thought they could sit outside at the table and chairs on her patio. The garden was looking lovely. There were lots of colourful flower beds. She was really proud of her achievements and revelled in the compliments. She made them all a cup of coffee and arranged some chocolate biscuits and brownies on a plate.

As she walked out with the tray, she could hear them talking about how nice her flower beds were looking. She smiled as she was complimented on her garden.

They all had notes with them and George started with his.

"Right," he said. "We all know which houses are hosting each course. I have distributed flyers to each household that bought tickets so everyone knows which house to have each course. Everyone agreed. No one has objected as far as I know. Has anybody disagreed with their houses?"

All the committee said that no one they had sold tickets to had objected to the houses where their courses would be held.

"Good," replied George. "Has anyone with a ticket said if they have any allergies?"

He looked around the table at everyone. No one had.

Beverley said, "I told you before that I am severely allergic to prawns but I'm doing a pudding course and not going to any house for a starter course so it won't be a problem."

"I can't eat bananas, they make me feel a bit sick," said Mary, "but I am hosting coffee so that won't be a problem for me either."

Simon said he wasn't too keen on rice, but as he was doing a starter that should be fine.

George reminded everyone that although they weren't actually going to be eating at the houses for meals, if anyone wanted one, then tell the hostess at the house of their choice so one can be saved for them.

"There should be plenty of time to nip out and collect one. The houses are very local to each other," said Simon.

"We can go and help at other houses after we have served our courses and the diners have gone." suggested Beverley.

"Yes, good plan. Has everyone got a list of what to buy?" asked George. They all agreed they had. The houses hosting starters, puddings, and coffee were purchasing their own ingredients.

"I have ordered French sticks and garlic bread to collect when I pick up the few bottles of wine that we need to buy when I collect the glasses from Tesco's on Saturday morning. I will bring them around to each of the houses that will need bread, wine, and beer glasses.

"I have ordered the meat and chicken from the butchers, so will bring that to the houses hosting the main courses, Sheila said that would be fine as long as it was with her and the other two mains' houses by lunchtime."

Mary said Ned would be delivering the other bottles of wine and soft drinks that was being bought from the cash and carry to each of the houses who were hosting. "He just needs to know the amount. I've given him a list of addresses."

"I will give you the list of the number of soft drinks, wine and beer we need from him. I've calculated what I think we need in all," said George. "I have books of raffle tickets with me here so will give you all a book. Have we got enough prizes?"

All committee members said they would donate two prizes each. "The butcher has offered a couple of joints of meat vouchers, too," said George. "The shop said they will give a couple of boxes of chocolates and the pub said they will give a free meal for two people as a prize. We can keep the prizes at my house and do the raffle the next day. This all sounds good, don't you think?"

Simon interrupted and said he would call around at each house hosting starters, mains, and pudding houses with extra cutlery and plates and with cups and saucers for the coffee course.

"Good," said Mary. "I hope it goes really well. Well done, Beverley, for suggesting a Safari Supper in the first place."

Beverley blushed. She hadn't contributed much to the conversation this evening but was secretly very pleased that it had been her idea.

"I have twelve trestle tables and thirty chairs. Who needs some delivering?" asked Simon.

A discussion was held as to which house needed some. A list was made and Simon said he would deliver them on Saturday morning.

"Is there anything we've forgotten?" asked George.

"I think we've covered everything," said Julie.

"Let's hope the weather is warm," said Celia. June was being very kind so far and the forecast for Saturday was looking good.

Mary got up and went into her kitchen to provide more coffee and biscuits. The conversation turned to the missing man out on bail. He hadn't been found yet and there had been no further reports on the local news.

Simon said he hadn't seen any more evidence of him being on his farm "I lock my sheds up at night now," he said. "Roger locks his barns up as well."

Julie said all parents and children had been alerted about the stranger in the village.

The meeting finished at nine thirty. They thanked Mary for her hospitality and went on their way home saying they would no doubt see each other on Saturday during preparations for the evening.

# Chapter Eleven

Saturday morning dawned fine and sunny. The forecast was good all day and into the evening too.

The six committee members rang the people who were hosting the courses to make sure all was well. Thankfully, all were still on board and would be ready to receive the diners.

Simon delivered the trestle tables and chairs to the houses which needed them and later on in the morning, George delivered the village shop, meat, bread and wine, and beer glasses along with cutlery and plates. He also handed out French sticks and garlic bread to the houses hosting the starters and main courses.

Mary's brother, Ned, consulted his list and delivered wine and soft drinks to the various houses.

It was a busy afternoon. Hosts were preparing the dishes, setting up tables and chairs, and cooling wine and beer in their fridges.

Celia shooed the children out of the kitchen and asked Julian to take them to the park. "I need time to cook this afternoon and have them worn out and asleep this evening!" she told him.

She set up tables and chairs in her lounge and dining room counting them as she did it. Thirty, she counted, having accepted two trestle tables and twelve chairs from Simon.

Mary needed two trestle tables and twelve chairs. She set them up with one table outside with fingers crossed for the forecasted fine evening. She was hosting a coffee course so was not as rushed as the others probably were.

Heather, Sheila, and Sarah were hosting the main courses. They each needed two trestle tables and twelve chairs.

Frances and Beverley had some extra tables of their own and only Kerry needed one trestle table and six chairs.

It was a very busy afternoon in all the houses hosting the event. Celia and Mary called around to Sheila, Sarah, and Heather, asking if they needed any help.

Cooking the mains course was more time consuming than the other courses. It all appeared to be very organised.

Tables and chairs were in place and set with cutlery and napkins.

By six o'clock, every house was ready to receive the guests. Everything had gone according to plan. Wine and beer was being cooled, glasses ready, raffle tickets were ready for selling.

Seven o'clock saw guests arriving at the three houses hosting the starter courses.

George greeted his thirty guests and showed them to their seats. He had donned an apron and had a tea towel over his shoulder. Anne was in the kitchen putting the final touches to the plates of food. George served everyone with the dish of their choice. The prawn cocktail looked very appetising and the tomato soup was steaming hot. The French stick and garlic bread was ready on the tables. Lots of chatter and laughter accompanied the course.

The same was going on at Simon and Julie's houses. Guests were offered a glass of wine or beer. Some had a soft drink. The course was enjoyed by all. The prawn cocktail went down well, as did the hot soup.

After an hour, the guests vacated their seats, consulted their lists and went on to the next house for their main course.

Sheila, Sarah, and Heather were waiting for them in their houses. The main course of their choice was served, again with bread on the tables. The meals were hot and plates were cleared with lots of compliments to the cooks. Wine and beer flowed and chat flowed even more. Having thirty guests in a house made it noisy, but no one minded at all.

Pudding courses were served an hour later at Frances's, Beverley's, and Kerry's houses.

Warm apple tart and cream or fruit cocktail was enjoyed by all the guests.

# Chapter Twelve

At just after ten o'clock, guests descended at Mary and Celia's houses for the coffee course. There were around twenty-five to thirty people at each house because some of the diners had decided not to go as they had babysitters and it could be late if they stayed for the coffee course. It was bit of a squash in both houses but some people went into the garden at Mary's, so it was spread out. There was lots of laughter and talk. George, Simon and Marie were going to help Celia after first calling in at Mary's to make sure she was coping. George saw his sister Frances, said hello, and asked how her pudding course had gone.

"Very well," she replied. "It was a good evening. I enjoyed doing it."

Several of the committee members were already at Mary's before they carried on to Celia's to help with serving coffee and mint chocolates.

Each house had sold plenty of raffle tickets during the evening. The guests had been very generous.

George announced that the raffle would be drawn tomorrow at his house and he told people what the prizes were.

Beverley arrived at Mary's house to offer her help. She saw George and Simon who said they would shortly go to Celia's to help out there. There were people mingling everywhere, in the hall, lounge, and kitchen, all talking and laughing. She saw Sarah, Kerry, Frances, and Heather there heading for the kitchen to help.

"We've come to see if we can help out, too," Kerry said looking around the kitchen.

"Thanks very much, I could do with some help but Celia probably needs help as well," said Mary. "Beverley, can you start washing some cups up? Many want a second coffee and I'm running out of clean cups!"

They both went through to the kitchen. There were lots of used cups and saucers lying around. A pair of washing up gloves was on the work top by the sink. "I did start washing some up, but kept being called away," said Mary.

"I've brought a sandwich with me as I haven't had a chance to eat anything yet," said Beverley holding up her red handbag, "but I must use your bathroom first, if it's ok?"

"Of course, it's the second door on the left on the landing."

Beverley squeezed past quite a few people standing in the middle of the kitchen and took a look around. It certainly was messy with used cups and plates. She sighed and placed her handbag on a chair. Poking out her bag was her cling filmed sandwich. She really hadn't had time to eat anything earlier so she had made herself a cheese and pickle sandwich. She went upstairs to use the bathroom. Someone was in there so she waited on the landing for the person to come out. It was a lady but Beverley didn't know her. They smiled at each other. Beverley entered and used the bathroom and then returned to the kitchen. She met Frances and Marie coming up the stairs to use the bathroom. There were still some people in the kitchen. Sarah, Kerry, and Heather had washed a few cups up and she had to squeeze by them in the kitchen as they were busy talking to people. They apologised for not washing more up but said they had been talking too much! George, Frances, and Simon were just saying goodbye to Mary who, in the kitchen, was shooing them off to Celia's house to help her. They left the kitchen. Kerry, Heather, and Sarah left too, after a bit more washing up, to help at Celia's as she was hosting more people at her house. Marie came back downstairs offering to help with the washing up.

Beverley said she would manage the washing up here at Mary's. She admitted she preferred to stay in the background.

She sat down on the chair where she'd put her handbag, removed her sandwich, unwrapped it and ate it. *Peace*, she thought chewing. She frowned. She put a couple of uneaten crusts back in the cling film and put them in her handbag. She got up and moved her bag to a spare corner on the worktop near the sink. She then started the washing up. The kitchen was now empty of people. *They probably thought I'd hand them a tea towel if they stayed,* she thought with a smile.

A few minutes later, some people wandered into the kitchen asking for more coffee. "Won't be long, I'm just washing some cups up," Beverley promised them. They went out into another room.

It was noisy and busy everywhere but a happy atmosphere.

# Chapter Thirteen

After ten minutes, Mary went into the kitchen with some used cups and saucers ready to be washed. She saw Beverley at the sink, bent over her task of washing up. No one else was in there.

"Thanks a lot, Beverley, you're a star! I'll dry some cups up and take them through when I've made more coffee." Beverley didn't answer and she was making a funny noise.

"Beverley, are you ok?" asked Mary, when she didn't receive an answer. Beverley crumpled against the sink and onto the floor. Her eyes were wide open, her face was puffy and red and she was gasping for breath with her hands at her throat. Mary screamed. Guests came running into the kitchen when they heard Mary scream.

Beverley was lying on the floor. She was not moving.

"Is she dead?" someone screamed.

"Let me see," said a man rushing into the kitchen. It was Doctor Crowther from the Medical Centre. He was relatively new to the village but had settled in well and was liked by everyone, both in the village and the medical centre. He felt Beverley's neck for a pulse. He started resuscitation asking someone to call 999 for an ambulance. He continued to work on Beverley but then stood up shaking his head. "I'm sorry everyone, but she's gone."

He asked Mary for a blanket to cover her up. Mary shooed everyone out of the kitchen, her heart racing. She couldn't believe it. Beverley dead in her kitchen!

"Get everyone out of here," said the doctor. There was panic amongst the guests. Some had left the kitchen already but others were standing around gazing at poor Beverley on the floor.

"Everyone leave now, please!" shouted Mary. She found a blanket from upstairs and went back in the kitchen. Dr Crowther was staring down at Beverley's face. He took the blanket from Mary and covered Beverley's body.

He saw the allergy alert bracelet on her left wrist. He read it. It had the words "Prawn allergy" written on it. He looked at Mary with horror.

A siren was heard in the distance and the ambulance was outside the house in no time. Two paramedics entered and the doctor informed them that Beverley was dead but had not been moved. "Looks like an allergic reaction," he told them.

The ambulance crew rang for the police as it was a sudden death.

Simon and George arrived at the house as they had heard the siren and saw where it had pulled up. "What on earth's happening?" asked George. He saw a blanket covering Beverley. "Who is that?" he asked in a shocked voice.

"It's Beverley," said Mary in tears. "She was washing up and then just collapsed."

"How?" asked Simon in shock.

"I don't know, she came to help out, I asked her to wash some cups up and she just collapsed. It's awful," said Mary putting her head in her hands.

Simon put his arm around her and held her close leading her out of the kitchen.

Most of the guests had left. Dr Crowther remained and spoke with the paramedics telling them again it looked like she had suffered an anaphylactic shock. "She was allergic to prawns."

Celia and Julie quickly arrived after hearing the ambulance siren. They were shocked and started to cry after hearing the news.

"But she was fine earlier. I called around to see how the puddings were going at her house," said Julie. "The diners had almost finished and were ready to move on. Beverley said she was going to come over to Mary's to offer help with the coffee course. She was just clearing up pudding plates and stacking them in the kitchen saying she would wash them up tomorrow morning and then she was coming over here."

Beverley's friend Sheila arrived at the house. She was very shocked to hear the news and had to sit down quickly on a chair as she felt faint. Dr Crowther told her to put her head down to her knees and fetched her glass of water.

The police arrived. There was a young male and a female officer. "No one touch anything!" the young male officer ordered. He asked people to stay out of the kitchen except for the paramedics, Mary and Dr Crowther.

The female officer lifted the blanket and looked at Beverley, asking Dr Crowther what had happened. He told them what he suspected.

"This is Mary's house and she was here in the kitchen when Beverley collapsed. I heard her scream and came running in as did a few others."

"What's the occasion?" asked the male officer. "There's a lot of folk here."

"We have been holding a Safari Supper evening to raise funds for the village," explained Mary.

"Different courses were being served at different houses. I was hosting a coffee course and Beverley came over to help. She was washing cups up."

She started to cry. Dr Crowther put his arm around her.

"Is this her handbag?" asked the female officer seeing an open, small, red bag on the work surface near the sink.

"Yes, it is," replied Mary. She said she had seen Mary with the red bag at their meetings and said Beverley had arrived with it this evening.

The officer put on some blue vinyl gloves and looked inside the bag. She saw it held a purse, comb and a handkerchief. There was a piece of crumpled up cling film which obviously had held some kind of food as there were a couple of crusts and breadcrumbs evident. She asked Mary for a fork. She carefully lifted the crumpled cling filmed crusts out with the fork and sniffed it. "It smells of cheese, pickle, and fish," she said. "Prawns I believe, there's a bit of pink on a crust."

"But that can't be right," said Mary. "Beverley was allergic to prawns so she couldn't possibly have eaten any."

"That would explain what happened, if she had eaten a prawn," said Dr Crowther. "If someone has a severe allergy, death can occur in minutes, if adrenaline isn't administered quickly."

"Is there an adrenaline pen in her handbag?" asked Mary. "Beverley told us she always carried one."

"No, there isn't one here," said the officer peering into the open handbag without touching it. "I will bag this up with the crusts."

She asked the male officer to go and collect two plastic bags from the police car. He returned with them and the female officer, still wearing gloves, carefully placed the red bag inside one and the crusts in the second bag.

"I will need the names of everyone who was here at this house this evening and everyone who bought a ticket for the supper," said the female officer. "We need to know who would have access to the prawns. We will need statements. In the meantime, I will arrange for a private hospital ambulance to take the body away."

"It's 'not' a body, it's Beverley!" cried Sheila tearfully. "She has a name."

"Sorry," apologised the officer. "I will arrange for Beverley to go to Olehampton General Hospital. The coroner will need to be informed as it's a sudden death."

She made a phone call. She told the paramedics they were no longer needed. She and her colleague would remain with Beverley until the private ambulance arrived. The paramedics left.

# Chapter Fourteen

It was now eleven o'clock. Most people had gone home by now, shocked and tearful.

The female officer turned to Mary, "Can you let me have the list of names tomorrow morning? Come to the station in Olehampton at ten and I will have someone meet you there."

"Alright," replied Mary. "We have a list of who bought tickets for the suppers. Four people couldn't make it at the last minute but everyone else came for the evening."

"We will also need the names of the four that didn't turn up as well, please," the officer said.

"I will come with you tomorrow, Mary," said George who was standing in the kitchen doorway. "I have the complete list at my house."

"Thank you," whispered Mary.

"Do you want to come and stay at my house tonight?" asked Celia. She put her arm around Mary.

"Thank you. I don't want to stay here on my own tonight, but have you the room?" asked Mary.

"Yes. We have a spare room as the younger two girls share at the moment. Collect some stuff together and then we can go," said Celia.

"Simon and I will clear up here," said George as he looked around at the dirty crockery waiting to be washed.

He glanced at Beverley as he spoke.

There was a ring at the doorbell. Two dark suited men were admitted by George. The female officer explained why they had been called. No one spoke as one of the men fetched a trolley from the back of the ambulance.

They watched in silence as the men very carefully lifted Beverley and took her out of the kitchen and placed her onto the trolley.

"This is ghastly!" cried Mary. "I cannot believe what has happened."

Everyone nodded at her words.

The ambulance left for the hospital. The police officers said they would see George and Mary at the police station in the morning at ten. They then left the house after offering their condolences.

Everyone else left, with Dr Crowther laying a comforting hand on Mary's shoulder as they left the kitchen, leaving just George and Simon. She gave them her spare key so they could lock up when they left.

They looked at each other.

"How awful! What a terrible end to the evening," said Simon. "Poor Beverley."

"How on earth could a prawn get into what must have been a cheese and pickle sandwich?" asked George.

"I have no idea," replied Simon.

They rang their wives to say they were at Mary's clearing up, and updated them on what had happened. Both Anne and Marie were tearful and shocked when they were told what had happened to Beverley.

Simon and George told them they would be home as soon as they had finished clearing up.

They washed, dried and stacked up the crockery and cleaned the surfaces so the kitchen was restored to order. They went into the lounge and sorted the furniture so it was back to normal. They hoped they had put it back in the right position. They knew Mary was quite particular.

Simon stacked up the trestle tables and chairs that he had delivered to Mary's house only that morning saying he would collect them tomorrow.

He would come around tomorrow with his truck and take them back to his barn. He would also collect the village hall's cups and saucers which had been borrowed.

It was now after midnight so they locked up and left.

"We'll talk tomorrow," said George to Simon, "after Mary and I have been to the police station."

They patted each other on the back and went their separate ways home.

Anne was waiting up for George. He sat down with her and put his head in his hands. "It's awful," he told her. "Poor Beverley, it looks like she ate a prawn in a sandwich which she'd made for herself."

"She wouldn't have done that, no one would eat something if they knew they had an allergy to it," replied a tearful Anne. "There has to be an explanation."

"The police will investigate and the coroner will be informed," said George. "Come on, let's go to bed and try and get some sleep."

They locked up and went upstairs but found it hard to sleep.

# Chapter Fifteen

Next day, Mary and Celia were talking in Celia's kitchen. They had coffee and cereal, which both had to force down as they were not at all hungry. Her three daughters were in the lounge watching television. They had asked why Mary had stayed over. Celia told them that Mary was feeling lonely last night so had been invited to stay the night. Luke was in his shed. He had sat with them for a coffee. It was difficult to know what to say other than how awful it was.

"Has Beverley any relatives?" he'd asked.

"I don't know but I expect the police will find out," said Mary.

"She was quite a private person," said Celia. "She came to the village about a year ago, but I'm not sure where she came from."

"Perhaps, Sheila knows," said Mary. "I think they were quite friendly."

"Yes, they spent quite a bit of time together," replied Celia.

George rang up at nine o'clock. "Shall I pick you up in fifteen minutes?" he asked Mary. "I have the list of everybody who bought tickets for the Supper."

Mary went upstairs to put a bit of lipstick on. She looked in the mirror and saw how pale she was. She pinched her cheeks to try and get a bit of colour in them.

"Thank you for letting me stay," she said to Celia when she came downstairs.

"No problem, and if you want to stay for a few nights, you can," said Celia.

"No, I have to go home. I completely forgot about the cat last night. She'll wonder where I am," replied Mary. "He stayed out of the house last evening as he didn't like all the people there, so he's probably sitting meowing on the door step waiting to be let in."

"Don't you have a cat flap?" asked Celia.

"Yes, but I closed it up before everyone arrived, so he couldn't come in and get under people's feet," replied Mary.

"Shall I go over and see?" asked Celia.

"Yes please, George has my spare key so will give it me back when he comes. The cat food is in the pantry. He's quite a fussy eater."

"Ok," said Celia. "Luke can look after the girls."

George arrived and gave Celia the spare key.

Celia gave Mary a hug and said she would be thinking of her.

Mary got in the passenger seat of George's Range Rover and fastened her seatbelt.

"How are you?" he asked as they set off. "Silly question really but I don't know what else to say. Did you get any rest last night?"

"I kept dropping off to sleep but then kept jerking awake and remembering Beverley's poor swollen face," said Mary with a shudder.

George was a confident and careful driver. He switched the radio on to Radio 2 which played softly in the background.

They arrived at Olehampton police station at ten minutes to ten.

He parked in the car park and they got out. George locked the car. "Can't be too careful, even in a police car park," he grinned at Mary. She smiled back at him.

They went through the front doors and went to the desk. Mary looked around. There were a couple of men sitting on a bench but other than the policeman at the desk the reception area was empty. She had never been in a police station before so didn't know what to expect.

George gave their names to the policeman.

"Yes, we are expecting you both."

The policeman made a phone call and said someone would be with them shortly.

"Take a seat please," he said pointing at an empty bench.

George and Mary sat down but almost immediately a man appeared through a door behind the desk and went up to them. He shook their hands and introduced himself as "Sergeant Morris".

"Please follow me," he said.

They went through a door to the right of the desk.

He led them into a small room and asked them to sit down. The walls were painted light blue, window less and sparse other than a table and four chairs and a smaller table in a corner which held some equipment.

*A recorder probably*, thought George.

Mary looked down at the wooden table in front of her. It had some words scored deeply into the wood. 'Help me' was written in one corner. Mary wondered about the person who had written it and under what circumstances.

"I will be recording this interview," Sergeant Morris got up and switched on the recorder on the small table in the corner and said, "Can you state your names and dates of birth for the tape please?"

"George Bushell, 2nd February 1956" and "Mary Oliver, 16th November 1958" were said.

The sergeant continued after stating his name and rank for the tape.

"I am very sorry for your loss. I understand that the lady who died was a friend of yours."

"We did know her, but not very well," explained George. "She was part of our village fundraising committee."

"A Safari Supper, from what I have been told?"

George explained what the event involved. "Eleven houses hosting different courses."

"And the deceased hosted which course?" asked the sergeant.

"The pudding course," said Mary, "but she came over to my house to help me with the coffee course after her diners had left her house."

"Can you tell me what happened when she arrived at your house, please?"

"She arrived just after ten o'clock. She asked what she could do to help. I said that we needed some washing up doing. We both went into the kitchen and then she asked to use the bathroom. She went upstairs and then came down and went into the kitchen. After ten minutes or so, I went into the kitchen and found her collapsing at the sink. She was gasping, clutching her throat, and then fell to the floor. Her face was red and swollen and her eyes were almost protruding. It was horrible," said Mary putting her head in her hands.

"Take your time. You are doing very well," said the sergeant.

George patted Mary's arm. She continued, "I screamed and people came running. Dr Crowther was there and he started trying to resuscitate her but it was too late. She was dead."

George intervened "Dr Crowther suspects she died of anaphylactic shock. Beverley was allergic to prawns. The policewoman, who arrived, opened up a bit of cling film she found in Beverley's handbag. She said she could smell cheese, pickle, and fish and found a couple of crusts with a bit of pink on them which looked like prawn."

"Why had she got a sandwich with her?" asked the Sergeant.

Mary said, "When Beverley arrived at my house, she told me she had brought a sandwich with her as she hadn't eaten anything earlier."

"So the sandwich crusts were wrapped up in the cling film in her bag?" asked the Sergeant.

"Yes," said George. "But there's absolutely no way Beverley would have added prawns to her sandwich. She would have known what could happen."

"So, if Beverley's sandwich contained prawns as well as cheese and pickle it would have been deadly for her, so that means someone must have added the prawn knowing what could happen," said the Sergeant. "There will be a post mortem and that will establish the cause of death."

There was silence.

"Are you actually suggesting that someone added the prawn to the sandwich, knowing Beverley would eat it and could die?" asked George. "But surely, that would be murder!"

"That's the most likely explanation at this stage," agreed the Sergeant.

"But who would do something like that?" asked a very shocked Mary.

"That's for the police to find out. Have you got the list of everyone who bought tickets for the Supper?"

George took the list from his jacket pocket.

"We sold ninety tickets and eighty-six people turned up. Four pulled out at the last minute. There were also eleven other people who hosted a course including the committee."

"That's an awful lot of people. Do you know the names of people who were at your house for the coffee course?" the Sergeant asked Mary.

"Yes. We had allocated people to each house so we knew who was going where. It says on the list who was allocated to which house. There were thirty allocated to my house for coffee. The four who didn't attend the evening would have been there so that means there were twenty-six people present, plus myself."

"They will all need to be contacted," said the Sergeant.

He stood up and thanked them for coming to the station.

"We will find out who did this. We have your details so will be in touch," he assured them.

He opened the door and escorted them out of the room and into the reception area. It was much busier than it had been when they had arrived at ten o'clock.

There was a queue at the desk and all the benches were occupied. Sundays were obviously a busy day for crime.

George and Mary went over to the car. George unlocked it and they got in. He looked at his watch. "It's eleven thirty!" he said. "Let's go home."

"That was awful, wasn't it?" said Mary as George drove out of the car park. "I can't believe that someone may have murdered Beverley. It must have been someone who was at my house. That means the rest of us may not be safe until it's found out why Beverley was targeted. I hope they are caught quickly."

"Me, too," replied George. "We need to find out more about Beverley and her past before she came to the village. It must have something to do with that. We've never had a murder in Merrydale before."

"How do we find anything out and shouldn't we leave it to the police?" asked Mary.

"They will do their investigating and we will do ours as well," replied George.

Mary said she thought it should be left to the police and not George.

They arrived back in Merrydale and George drew up outside Mary's house. "I will come in with you," George said.

Mary opened her front door. Ebony rushed out and nearly tripped her up. George steadied her.

"I must open the cat flap for him. I closed it last evening so he wouldn't come in whilst everyone was there."

George followed her into the house. All was tidy and back to normal she saw. It was if the previous evening had never happened.

She hesitated before entering the kitchen. She opened the door and her eyes immediately went to the floor where Beverley had died last night.

George put his arm around her.

"I love this house and I really want to try and get over this," she told him. She went to the back door, bent down and opened the cat flap.

"I'll be fine now," she told George. "Thanks for your support today."

George collected up the cups and saucers neatly stacked on the kitchen table and took them out to his car to return them to the Village Hall. He would call round to the other houses that had borrowed some.

He said cheerio to Mary saying he would ring her later to make sure she was ok on her own.

"I've lived on my own a long time. Ebony and I will be fine, but thank you anyway," smiled Mary.

She saw George out and closed the front door. She went into the kitchen and put the kettle on. Ebony arrived through the now open cat flap. Mary picked him up, hugging him tightly. Ebony protested loudly so Mary put him down.

She made a cup of tea and took it into the lounge and sat down.

She was a strong person and would come through this, she told herself.

# Chapter Sixteen

George collected plates, cups and saucers from the houses who had borrowed them for the Safari Supper. It took a while because everyone wanted to know what the latest was on the terrible event of the previous evening. He had a coffee at Frances's house before moving on to the next.

Sheila was very upset. "We were really quite friendly. I will miss her a lot. I was getting to know her well. She didn't say much about her previous village," she said tearfully to George.

"Do you know if she had any family?" he asked her.

"I hadn't heard her speak of any really close relatives. She was married but her husband died but I don't know how. I think she mentioned a cousin who lived in the village where she lived before coming to Merrydale, but she didn't elaborate. I know she had been a community nurse around that area but again she didn't open up much."

"What was the village called?" asked George.

"Haleton, I think she said, it's about fifty miles away near the town of Burford."

Burford was a large town and George knew a couple of people who lived there. Being a parish councillor, he attended committee meetings and had got to know many people in many areas.

He would give one of them a call this evening and see if they knew Haleton and whether they had ever heard of Beverley.

He arrived home at three after he had taken all the loaned crockery back to the village hall.

Anne met him at the door. She had obviously been looking out for him and seen his car arriving back.

She threw open the front door asking why he'd been so long. He realised she presumed he'd been at the police station all this time. He reassured her and told her he had been collecting the crockery to take back to the Village Hall.

"You could have let me know you were back in the village. I thought you'd both been arrested and thrown into jail!"

"No, we weren't arrested!" he grinned. "Let me get changed and I'll tell you all about it."

Anne made a cup of tea and they sat at the kitchen table. She made him a sandwich as he told her he hadn't had any lunch.

George told her about the police interview and the theory behind Beverley's death.

"Murder!" she gasped with a hand on her chest "That's dreadful. Are we safe here in the village?"

"They believe Beverley was targeted for some reason. Someone knew about her prawn allergy and put some in her cheese and pickle sandwich knowing she would eat it," he told her.

"But who would do something like that?" she said in shock.

"It had to be someone who was at Mary's house last evening. Sheila said Beverley made the sandwich at her own house before arriving at Mary's saying she hadn't eaten all evening. She had it in her handbag which she left in Mary's kitchen when she went upstairs to use the bathroom. It appears someone must have added a prawn to the sandwich while she was upstairs."

"How absolutely dreadful!" exclaimed Anne.

"Also, Beverley's adrenaline pen was missing from her handbag. At one of our committee meetings, I remember her saying she always carried one," said George.

"This gets worse," said Anne. "It certainly appears that Beverley was definitely targeted."

The phone rang. Anne got up to answer it. "It's Simon asking for an update," she said as she handed it over to George.

"Hi, Simon," said George. He then related what had happened at the police station.

They arranged for Simon to come over after milking to discuss everything. Anne washed up their cups and plates.

Simon was telling Marie about Mary and George's visit to the police station. She found it very hard to hear that Beverley had been murdered.

"And by someone we probably talked to at some stage last night!" she said. "How absolutely dreadful."

George got up saying he was going to look for the telephone number of a chap that he knew lived in Burford.

"I met him a year ago when we had a council meeting at Burford. I can't recall what the meeting was about but I do remember meeting Jim. He was a nice chap who had some sort of business like ours. I remember taking his number to meet up again but we never have. I suppose we've all been too busy."

Anne asked George what he would like for their evening meal.

"Something substantial as I missed lunch!" he replied.

Being a large man he needed three good meals a day he was always telling her!

"I'd best make a steak pie then," she replied. She started the preparations of making pastry. She enjoyed cooking for George as he was not fussy and always appreciated and complimented her meals whatever she gave him to eat.

George went upstairs and looked in his council diary. He was sure he had written Jim's number down in it. "Yes!" he exclaimed as he found it.

He rang the number and a lady answered. George told her his name and asked if Jim was there.

"Just a minute," she replied.

He heard her call Jim. Jim came to the phone. He remembered meeting George at the meeting and apologised for not getting in touch. "Same here," said George. "But we're both busy people and time goes by quickly."

Jim asked what he could do for George.

"We've had a horrible incident in our village and a lady died. She's been here in Merrydale for the past year but used to live in Haleton so I wondered whether you knew her. Her name was Beverley King."

"Was she a nurse?" asked Jim.

"Yes," replied George. "She was a community nurse. She was widowed suddenly by what I've been told."

"I didn't know her personally," said Jim, "but I've heard of her. She was caught up in some scandal in Haleton. There was a child's death and she was involved. I can't remember all the details but my wife would probably know. Hang on, and I'll ask her."

George heard him calling, "Jean! Can you come here a sec?"

There was a pause and then he heard Jim asking his wife, "You know something about that nurse, Beverley King, who lived in Haleton didn't you?"

Jim put the phone on loud speaker so George could hear Jean speak, "There was a nurse called Beverley who was involved in a poor child's death. I don't think her name was King though it was something similar. Apparently, she didn't take the parents seriously when she was asked to visit the boy. They were worried but she dismissed their concerns and that night the child died of meningitis. The parents accused her of neglect, but it couldn't be proved, so it never went to court. She said she had advised them to take the child to hospital but the parents said she never said that. They said she told them it was just a cold, and to give their son Calpol. He was only six. They split up after the child died and both moved away."

"Did you hear that, George?" asked Jim.

"Yes, I did," replied George. "It probably explains why Beverley moved away from the village. Was she widowed at the time?"

"No, but her husband couldn't cope with fingers pointing at them both and he killed himself," said Jean.

"Wow," said George. "How did he die?"

"Overdose of tablets," replied Jean. "His father found him when he couldn't get an answer when he called at the house. He had arranged to go around so he thought it strange he wasn't answering the door. He had a key to their house and found him dead in the bedroom. He was distraught, obviously. Beverley was out at work at the time, and came home to the police at the house. Her father-in-law blamed Beverley for her husband's death and I suppose he was right."

George thanked them for the information telling Jim they needed to meet up sometime for a beer.

He then told Anne what he had learned from Jim and his wife.

Not long after the steak pie and vegetables had been eaten along with apple crumble and custard for pudding, Simon called around. He shrugged off his jacket and accepted a cup of tea from Anne.

George filled him in on what he had learned from Jim.

"That's a lot to take in, but it might explain some things that we weren't aware of before talking to Jim and his wife," said Simon.

"Do you think someone from her previous village was out for revenge?" suggested George.

"I don't know. No one's ever asked or told me about Beverley's previous life before coming to Merrydale," said George.

"Me neither," replied Simon and Anne together.

"Let's all have a think. Who would have it in for Beverley if her death is linked to her previous village?" asked Simon.

George got up and got a notepad and pen from a drawer in the kitchen.

"One, her father-in-law, but we don't know his name. Two, the parents of the child who died, but again we don't have names, but I'm sure it should be quite easy to find out." wrote George.

"There could be other people who could blame Beverley. The parents may have relatives," said Anne.

"Shall we Google it?" asked Simon.

George took out his mobile phone. He asked Google for "Death of a child in Haleton 2019"

Nothing came up on the Google search.

"What do we do now? Do we tell the police what we have found out?" asked Simon.

"I'm sure if we can find this out then the police can, too," replied George. "They are going to be speaking with everyone who was at Mary's house anyway so let's see what they say."

Simon got up saying he would be off and to keep in touch. He thanked Anne for the tea.

*It had been so easy. She had had no idea she was being watched. When she moved into the village a year ago, she thought it was all behind her. Silly woman! She really thought she had got away with it but no way! She deserved to die. Seeing her lying dead on the kitchen floor had been worth all the planning, watching and waiting. It has taken longer than planned for the right time to arrive, but during an event, where there lots of people around, was brilliant. No one saw the sandwich and adrenaline pen being removed from that silly little red handbag. Who on earth has a red bag nowadays? A woman who deserved to die, that's who!*

# Chapter Seventeen

Julie arrived at school the next day to the teachers gathering around her asking about Saturday night's events. A couple of them had bought tickets for the Safari Supper but had been at Celia's house for coffee, so had not been at Mary's to witness Beverley's demise.

Julie told them what she knew. "The police will want to interview everyone who was there. Beverley was severely allergic to prawns, and it appears someone put a prawn in Beverley's cheese and pickle sandwich, and also removed her adrenaline pen from her handbag."

"How absolutely dreadful!" exclaimed the headmaster. "Surely, that amounts to murder!"

"Yes," replied Julie. "Someone murdered her knowing about her allergy to prawns."

There was silence in the staff room.

The teachers made their way to their classrooms before assembly at nine.

The assembly began with the hymn, "Morning has broken."

He then chatted about the upcoming parents evening next week and reminded the children to take their letters home to their parents reminding them of the evening when they received them later today.

Freddie stuck his hand up.

"Yes, Freddie?" asked the headmaster.

"Is it true there's a murderer about and who will be murdered next?"

The children giggled but were quickly hushed by the headmaster holding up his hand.

"You are all quite safe. All of you just remember what I talked about last week in assembly. Never talk to strangers. Stay close to your family when out."

"So it's true about the murder then?" asked Freddie. "We need to know whether we need to carry something to protect ourselves when we see the murderer."

"That's quite enough, Freddie. You do not need to carry anything."

The children sitting either side of Freddie nudged him and he grinned at them. "I want to be a policeman when I grow up and catching a murderer will be good practise," he whispered.

His friends laughed behind their hands. The headmaster glared at them.

Assembly concluded with another hymn and then the children and teachers returned to their classrooms to begin the school day.

During break in the staff room, Julie was speaking with her classroom assistant, Sally. "I know the children do not really understand, but it's very worrying knowing there might be a murderer about."

Sally replied that it appeared Beverley was the intended victim so others should be safe enough.

"But what if someone saw something and was seen by the murderer? They could then be targeted, too," replied Julie.

Sally said she hoped that was not the case.

School finished at three forty-five. As was the policy, two teachers took the children out to the gates and relinquished them to their waiting parents.

Julie was tidying up in her classroom with Sally. They had handed letters to the children reminding them of the parents' evening next week, but also reminding them to keep their children close at all times.

"Not that they should need reminding to keep their children safe, but the likes of Freddie may try investigating, so should be watched very carefully," said Julie.

At home, she later repeated to Julian what Freddie had said in assembly.

"It's true then that there is someone about who murdered Beverley?" asked Julian.

"Yes," agreed Julie sadly.

Celia was also talking to her husband Luke about the murder. She had been to the village shop that morning and said everyone was talking about it. She had also seen police presence at some houses.

"Make sure the girls are with either one of us at all times," said Luke.

"Of course, it goes without saying," replied Celia. She called the girls saying tea was almost ready. They were in the lounge watching television.

"Oh, Mum, we need to see the end of this programme," yelled the eldest.

"Five minutes and then you come in," said Celia.

Luke went off to his shed. He and Celia ate later than the girls. They liked to bathe them, read the younger ones a story and get them settled into bed and then have some time to themselves.

They settled down later, snuggled up on the settee and watched the news. Mostly politics and what was happening in America. Celia yawned and said she was going up to bed.

"Just stay and watch the local news. There may be something on about Beverley."

The local news started and sure enough, the death of Beverley in Merrydale was the top story. A policeman was being interviewed by a reporter asking anyone who may have information to come forward.

The second report was an update on the still missing bail jumper. The reporter said he was still missing and if anyone saw him, was not to approach him but to call the police immediately.

It still didn't name him or the crime for which he had been bailed for. It was thought he was still in the area as a local man walking his dog about a mile outside Merrydale, thought he recognised him from a description the police had given in an earlier report. He had been spotted in a wooded area quite a way from the dog walker but had been wearing a green camouflage jacket and a cap. The man had rung the police but the missing man had not been found.

"I can't believe we are in the news twice, normally nothing ever happens here!" said Celia.

They finished watching the news, checked the children and then went to bed.

*So, you made the news tonight! Well done! Your claim to fame! Shame, you can't hear them talking about you, but you are much better off where you are now. Are you having a nice time? Have they cut you open yet? What a shame you can't feel it. You deserve to suffer, even in death.*

*The police have been talking to people in the village today. Did anyone see anything before you met your maker? I did. I saw your sandwich!*

*You hated being the centre of attention but now you are well and truly in the headlines! Well done!*

# Chapter Eighteen

Roger rang Simon on Tuesday morning.

"The buggers been in one of my sheds!" he told him.

"Who and how do you know?" asked Simon.

"That bloody bail jumper, it has to have been him. I found cigarette stubs and beer cans in my barn, I stupidly forgot to lock it up last night."

Simon asked if anything had been stolen.

"Not as far as I can see, there not much in the barn to steal. Only a few old sacks, some bird food and grass seed," Roger replied. "I have rung the police and they're on their way but there's no sign of him."

"Well make sure you lock everything up in future!" said Simon.

"Don't you worry I will. I'll also keep a lookout when it's dark and show him my shotgun if I see him."

"Don't do anything rash if you do see him. I don't want to see you up on a charge," said Simon.

He put the phone down and told Marie. "It must be the same person who was in our barn if he found cigarette ends and beer cans," she said. "I hope he doesn't come back here again."

"He must be lying low somewhere near the village. Perhaps once he sees the police in the village, he'll move away somewhere else," Simon said. "I wonder why he's in this area. There must be something that is keeping him here."

Later on, while Simon was out on his tractor in one of his fields, there was a knock on the farmhouse door. A policeman and a female officer stood there. They identified themselves and showed Marie their warrant cards.

"Can we step inside and ask you some questions about Beverley King, please?" the male officer asked.

Marie let them in and they followed her into the kitchen. It was a large homely kitchen which boasted an Aga.

"I would love to have one of those," said the female officer pointing to it, "but it wouldn't fit in my small kitchen."

"I wouldn't be without mine. Please, sit down. Can I make you a coffee or tea?" offered Marie.

They accepted the offer of coffee and their eyes lit up when they saw a large, homemade fruit cake being taken out of a tin. Marie asked if they would like a slice.

"Yes please!" they both replied.

She collected plates and cut a large slice for each of them.

Marie made their coffee plus a tea for herself.

"We are asking everyone who was involved with the Safari Super on Saturday night if they can tell us anything that they may have seen leading up to Beverley King's death," said the female officer.

"Well, I was hosting a course here. I admitted thirty people for a starter dish. I knew who to expect as every diner had been allocated a house for each course."

"So you had access to prawns then," said the male officer making notes.

"I did, but I certainly never put one in Beverley's sandwich!" Marie replied. She looked flushed as she was telling them this.

"I suppose someone could have taken a prawn off their plate and hidden it?" asked the male officer.

"Yes, I suppose they could have," admitted Marie.

She suddenly had a thought.

"The diners here went on to Heather's house once they had finished. All the diners knew which house to go to next. If I remember right, they then went to Kerry's house for the pudding course. Surely, you should be asking the people who ended up at Mary's house for the coffee course."

"We are asking everybody who had bought a ticket," the male officer replied. "All the diners would have had access to the prawns as all of them had a starter course at one of the three houses."

"Did you see anything suspicious amongst your group of diners?" asked the female officer.

"No, I didn't," replied Marie. "I saw nothing odd at all. They were cheerful and chatty and enjoying themselves. Not everyone had prawns though, some had soup."

"But someone having soup could have taken a prawn off someone else's plate."

"I think that would have looked a bit odd if they had," said Marie, "but no, I saw nothing suspicious at all with any of the group."

"Do you know how many people would know she had a prawn allergy?" asked the female officer.

"I really don't know. I knew because Simon told me she said it at one of the committee meetings," replied Marie.

The officers got up and thanked her for the coffee and cake.

"If you do remember anything else or if your husband knows anything please let us know on this number," they said to her as they handed her a card.

Marie said, "While you are here, have you found the missing man who has jumped bail, yet? We think it was must have been him in one of our barns last week. Our neighbour, Roger has also had him on his property twice. This morning he found cigarette stubs and beer cans in his barn just like we did in our barn last week."

"Another police team is looking into that," Marie was told.

She let them out the front door.

She hadn't really been able to tell them anything. She wished she could have told them that she had seen something odd on Saturday night so the whole affair could be over. She would have a good think.

# Chapter Nineteen

Lorna was having an afternoon cup of tea at Mary's house. They had been over and over the events of Saturday night. Mary said she was coming to terms with what had occurred in her kitchen now.

"I have thoroughly cleaned everywhere and also rearranged the kitchen a bit so it looks a bit different. I do keep seeing Beverley sliding slowly from the sink to the floor, though, holding her throat."

Lorna patted her arm.

The doorbell rang. Mary looked out of the window and saw a police car. "It's the police," she told Lorna.

Mary opened the front door. A male and a female officer were standing there. They identified themselves and showed Mary their warrants.

"May we come in, please? We should like to ask you a few questions about Beverley King's death."

"I have my friend Lorna here, but do come in," she said. She led them into the lounge and asked them to sit down. She introduced Lorna. Lorna had not been at the Supper as she had babysat for her son and wife so they could attend the evening.

"The grandchildren are fourteen and fifteen, but someone still needs to be there for them," she explained.

Mary asked them if she could make them a drink. They declined saying they had just had one at the previous house.

"We are talking to everybody who was involved with the Safari Supper last Saturday night," the female officer said. "We know that Beverley unfortunately died here. We are so sorry."

Mary got a tissue out of her pocket and wiped a tear away. "It was awful. One minute, she was alright and the next she was gone."

"Can you tell us what happened?" asked the male officer.

"I have been to Olehampton police station on Sunday to tell them all about it," replied Mary.

"Yes, we know but would like to hear from you again what happened. You may have remembered something now it's a couple of days later."

Mary recounted everything she could remember of Saturday night.

"So, you knew she had a sandwich in her red handbag?" asked the female officer.

"Yes. Beverley told me she made herself a sandwich to eat as she hadn't eaten all evening. I expect she was too busy serving the pudding course at her house."

"Where was the handbag?"

"I think she put it on a chair when she went into the kitchen. She had come into the kitchen with me but then asked if she could use the bathroom. I told her where it was. Second left door on the landing I told her."

Mary wiped another tear away with her tissue. Lorna got up and pulled another one from the box on the sideboard and handed it to Mary.

"So, the bag remained in the kitchen while she was upstairs," asked the female officer, "and it was in full view of everybody in the kitchen?"

"Yes, I suppose it was," replied Mary.

"Was the sandwich on show?"

"It was poking out of the bag. The bag was small and the sandwich didn't quite fit in it," said Mary.

"So, someone could have taken it out of the bag and put the prawn in the sandwich?" asked the police woman.

"But why would anyone do that?" interrupted Lorna.

"We do not know yet but it had to be someone who knew she was allergic to prawns and what may happen when she ate it. Her adrenaline pen was also taken out of the bag," said the male officer.

"It's so awful. Poor, poor Beverley. How could anyone do this? They must be a wicked monster!" said Lorna as she wiped a tear away.

"Who would have known she had a prawn allergy?" asked the female officer.

"Quite a few people, I should think. I've heard her say it myself and she also wore an allergy alert bracelet on her wrist saying "prawn allergy,"" said Mary.

The officers stood up and thanked them. One handed her a card and asked to ring if she recalled anything else. Mary got up from her chair and showed them out. Mary looked out of the side window by the door and saw them consulting a list and then the female officer pointed at a house a little further down the road. Mary knew Sheila lived there and had been friendly with Beverley so she presumed they would be talking to her next.

"Dreadful, dreadful business," repeated Lorna as Mary entered the lounge. "Yes, awful," agreed Mary with a shudder.

Mary went into the kitchen to make a cup of tea. She *wouldn't look at the floor by the sink*, she told herself.

She managed to avoid doing so and took the tea into the lounge.

Lorna suggested they have a day out the next day. "Let's have lunch at that new garden centre just outside Olehampton. We have been saying we ought to visit it."

"Okay, you're a good friend Lorna," said Mary.

"As you are to me," Lorna smiled. "I'll pick you up at eleven o clock tomorrow."

They finished their tea and then Lorna left.

# Chapter Twenty

Sheila was upstairs sorting out a bag of charity clothes for the schools table top and jumble sale being held next month before the summer term ended. She was expecting someone to come and collect it. When she heard her doorbell, she presumed it was the collector.

She brought the bag downstairs and opened the door to hand it over.

"Oh!" she exclaimed when she saw the two police officers standing there. "I thought it was someone coming for the bag of charity clothes," she said holding it up.

"No, we've not come for them," smiled the female officer. They identified themselves and asked if they come in and ask her some questions about Beverley.

Sheila's face dropped. "Of course, please come in."

She closed the door behind them, leaving the bag of clothes in the hall and showed them into her lounge and asked them to sit down.

The male officer offered their condolences as they had heard Sheila had been Beverley's friend.

"I was her friend, but she was quite a closed book. I didn't know her very well. I didn't know much about where she lived before, she moved to Merrydale."

The female officer asked her about Saturday night.

"Beverley told me about the Safari Supper fundraising event. I thought it was a great idea. I love cooking, so offered to host a mains course."

"Did you come across Beverley, at all, in the evening?" asked the male officer.

"I popped in her house once all my diners had finished to ask if she needed any help with her puddings. She told me she was fine and coping well. There were still a few people there when I arrived, but they were getting ready to move on to their coffee course house. She was enjoying it, which was good to see as she was quite a shy sort of person. I was very surprised she was on the fundraising committee."

"Why was that?" asked the male officer.

"Well, she wasn't a big talker. She was a person who stayed in the background of anything."

"We heard that it was Beverley's idea of holding a Safari Supper," said the female officer.

"Yes, it was," replied Sheila. "Beverley told me she had been to one in the village where she used to live and suggested it to this committee who really liked the idea. She told me she was pleased that they agreed with her idea."

"So how much did you know about her?"

"Not a lot, like I said. We met at a Christmas school function late last year. We got talking, I can't remember what about now, it might have been cooking, but we seemed to hit it off. We used to go round to each other's houses for a meal every couple of weeks. I love cooking and did a mains course here or took one to hers, if the meal was being held there. Beverley always did a pudding, both at her house, or brought one here. We both live alone and enjoyed each other's company."

"So did you know about her prawn allergy?" asked the male officer.

"I certainly did. She told me when we first decided to dine at each other's houses. I never made any fish dishes because of it. She wore an allergy alert bracelet and always carried an adrenaline pen in her bag."

"There was no adrenaline pen found in her bag at Mary's on Saturday night."

"She would *never* have gone anywhere without checking it was in her bag," said Sheila vehemently. "I also saw her check it was in there before she left her house to go to Marys."

"Have you any idea who may have wanted to harm her?" asked the female officer.

"No, but like I said, I didn't know much about her before she moved to Merrydale so I don't know if there was anyone there who she perhaps didn't get on with but even so, surely no one would deliberately kill her? Who in Merrydale would do such a thing?"

"That's what we are trying to find out. Someone obviously had it in for her. Did you know, she made a sandwich to take with her to Mary's house?"

"I did, actually. I was there when she made it. Cheese and pickle on brown bread which she wrapped in cling film. We laughed as it wouldn't fit in her small handbag. I told her to eat it before she went, but she said she wanted to get to Mary's quickly to help, now all her diners had left. She was a kind person. I also definitely saw her adrenaline pen, she checked she had it in her bag."

"Did you not want to go with her to Mary's house?" asked the male officer.

"No, but I wish I had now, I wanted to clear everything up here. My kitchen was a mess and I didn't want to leave it till the morning," said Sheila on the verge of tears.

"Well, if you think of anything else, please get in touch on this number," said the female officer handing her a card. "You've been very helpful thank you and we are very sorry you have lost your friend."

Sheila saw them out of the door. A van pulled up and a lad got out. "I've come for the charity clothes," he called to her as he leapt out of the driver's seat. Sheila retrieved the bag from where she had left it in the hall and handed it to him.

"Cheers, love," he said and threw it in the back of his van. He then drove off with a roar of his engine.

Sheila closed the door. She felt very sad and went into the kitchen and had a good cry. She would really miss Beverley and their friendship.

# Chapter Twenty-One

The next day, Lorna called round to Mary's house at eleven o'clock. She would do the driving today to the Garden Centre. Mary was ready and waiting and seeing Lorna's car pull up at the arranged time she put on her summer cream jacket and collected her handbag. She locked the front door and went out to the car. She got in the passenger seat and fastened her seat belt.

"How are you today?" asked Lorna with a concerned look.

"I didn't sleep too well thinking about everything," said Mary.

"Me, too," replied Lorna looking in her rear-view mirror, indicated, and drove off down the road.

The Garden Centre was about twelve miles away, just this side of Olehampton. Lorna was a keen gardener like Mary and they enjoyed their many trips out to horticultural events, fetes and garden centres.

Lorna had also worked in an accounts firm before retiring so she and Mary had lots in common.

It was a fine sunny day and the drive passed pleasantly.

Mary commented on people's front gardens. She frowned at some where the owners obviously didn't have green fingers.

"You'd think people would make an effort, especially if their next door neighbours have a nice frontage? The ones who bother must get frustrated living next door to a mess."

"Not everyone likes gardening," replied Lorna, "but I agree with you. Even a bit of nicely mowed lawn would be better than not bothering at all."

Lorna pulled up at the Garden Centre. The car park was quite full.

She parked up and they got out. Lorna locked the car.

They walked towards the entrance. Large window posters welcomed customers to the new garden centre. "20% off all plants today only."

Mary read aloud to Lorna.

"We've chosen the right day to come."

Another poster proclaimed that lunch in the cafe also had 20% off the price of a meal today.

Large automatic doors opened as they went up to them. Trolleys were available for the customers. Lorna grabbed one.

"I could do with some compost and fertilizer," said Mary.

There were nicely laid, waist-high tables full of colourful plants. They wandered over to one table and Mary picked up a mauve and white geranium flower in a pot.

"How pretty!" she exclaimed reading the label. "It's called 'Anne Folkard'. I wonder who she was! I think I'll get half a dozen of these."

She chose six and put them in the trolley.

"I would like some delphiniums, if we see any. A couple of mine haven't survived. I cut them down in autumn as you are supposed to do but they didn't grow like the others did."

They both bought some pots of dahlias and begonias and put them in the trolley.

They wandered through the centre admiring the extensive stock of plants and flowers.

Mary collected a bag of compost and fertilizer and put them in the trolley making sure the pots of plants weren't squashed.

"Look, there's George's sister, Frances."

Mary pointed out to Lorna. Frances was bending over a large tank of fish. Mary and Lorna went up to her and Mary called out, "Hello, Frances."

Frances turned around. "Hello, fancy seeing you both here! Obviously great minds think alike!" she grinned.

Mary looked at Frances's trolley which was quite full of potted plants.

"They have a good assortment of plants here, don't they?" she said.

"Yes, they do. I haven't been here before but someone recommended it to me. I was just admiring these colourful fish. Its 20% off everything as well today!"

"We're planning to have lunch here, why don't you join us?" Lorna asked Frances.

Frances said she would love to.

They wandered further into the centre. There were a couple of clothes shops and a book store as well. Mary picked up a pale blue buttoned sleeveless jacket and said she would try it on. She shrugged off her cream jacket and donned the blue one. It fitted well.

"I'll have this," she told the others. "I have lost a button on my blue jacket. I put it in my pocket when I caught it on a door handle the other day, but it must have fallen out because I can't find it now. I'll have to just use the jacket for gardening now as I can't wear it out with a button missing."

She paid for it at the cash desk assigned to the clothes shop. She had her own carrier bag and put the jacket inside. She then put the bag in the trolley making sure it didn't touch the plants so she didn't damage them.

"Let's pay for our plants and put them in the car and then find the café." suggested Lorna.

They took the trolleys to the cash desk and paid.

They went out to their cars. Mary and Lorna packed the plants, fertilizer and compost in the boot and Frances did the same with hers.

They met up again and walked back to the entrance doors and then made their way to the cafe.

They found an empty table. There were quite a lot of people sitting down at tables. Some had a drink in front of them but Frances noticed more people were having something to eat.

"Everyone likes a bargain," she grinned at Mary and Lorna.

They looked at the menu. All decided on fish and chips. Frances went up to the desk to order their meals.

"I've left the tab open in case we want puddings and coffee," she said on her return.

Mary's face fell on hearing the word "Coffee".

"I shudder every time I hear that word," she said.

"I'm so sorry, I didn't mean to upset you," said Frances laying her hand on Mary's.

"It's not your fault. Obviously, I can't avoid hearing the word but it's very raw at the moment after Saturday night," said Mary looking sad.

"It's such a terrible thing that's happened," said Lorna. "But the police will find out who did such an awful thing."

"Do you think so? The police don't always catch the culprit." asked Mary.

"They're bound to. They have ways and means of finding things out that we, the Joe public, have no idea about. That's their job."

"They *will* find out what happened," Lorna reassured Mary.

Mary got a tissue out of her handbag and wiped a tear from her eye.

"Three fish and chips lunches!" announced a waitress arriving at the table. She placed two plates down and went to the counter to collect the third. "Here are your knives and forks. Sauces and condiments on the table. Are you alright dear?" she asked looking at Mary as she wiped another tear away.

"She's upset, well actually, we all are, because we lost a friend at the weekend," explained Frances.

"Oh, I'm sorry to hear that," said the waitress. "Was it cancer?" she asked in a hushed voice.

"No, actually she was murdered," said Lorna.

"What???" said the waitress in a shocked voice. "How?"

"She died after eating a prawn to which she was allergic to. She went into anaphylactic shock and died."

"How come she ate a prawn if she was allergic to them?" asked the waitress.

"She obviously didn't eat it deliberately. Someone put it in a cheese and pickle sandwich, and she didn't realise she was eating a prawn with it," said Lorna.

"How dreadful! What sort of person would do that? She must have *really* upset someone. Murdered!"

"It is dreadful. Obviously, the police are investigating and the culprit will be found," said Frances.

"Don't be too sure about that," replied the waitress. "They don't always solve crimes. A friend of mine had a friend who was stabbed nine months ago and the police still haven't arrested anybody."

"Well. I'm sure the police will do their very best to bring someone to justice. This person is dangerous and must be caught," said Frances.

"I'll let you all eat your lunch. I really hope they find out who did this to your friend," said the waitress laying a comforting hand on Mary's shoulder. Mary said she hoped so, too.

The three ladies ate their fish and chips, with a little chatter but were all thinking about Beverley. They decided against puddings and coffee.

They left the Garden Centre after lunch. They said goodbye to Frances. Lorna drove back to Merrydale and dropped Mary off at her house. Mary said she had a headache and was going to have a lie down after unloading the plants that she had bought. Lorna drove off home saying she would see Mary soon.

"I know it's easy for me to say but try not to dwell on it too much. The police *will* find out who did this dreadful thing."

Mary, with her cat beside her, lay on her bed unable to stop thinking about last Saturday night.

# Chapter Twenty-Two

Roger was on a stakeout. He had deliberately left the barn door open tonight. He would "get the bugger, if he dares come back tonight," he told Fay. Fay told him to be careful.

"If it is this person that's been on the news, he could be dangerous," she said.

Roger held up his shotgun telling her he was ready for him should he appear.

He went outside. It was eleven thirty and very dark and he could see many stars twinkling in the inky sky. Everywhere was still and silent. He suddenly heard a noise which made his heart race but then saw a fox slinking round the back of the barn.

His heartbeat slowed down. He walked silently over to the barn and gingerly opened the door. Nothing leapt out at him. It was dark inside but heard and saw nothing untoward in the barn. He closed and locked the doors.

He had another wander round outside but then went back into the house.

"Anything or anybody out there?" asked Fay who was waiting in the kitchen, drinking a mug of Horlicks.

"Nothing but a fox," Roger replied. He returned his gun to the cabinet and locked it.

They locked up, turned off the downstairs lights and went upstairs and prepared for bed. Fay used the bathroom first and Roger changed into his pyjamas and waited in the bedroom.

He drew back the curtain and looked out of the window. He could see some sort of light over one of the roads in the village. He opened the window and then saw orange lights shooting up into the sky.

"What the hell was that?" he said to himself.

Fay walked into the bedroom, "Bathrooms free," she told him. "What are you looking at?" she asked, wandering over to the window.

"I think there's a fire in the village," cried Roger. He quickly started getting dressed.

"Stay here, don't go out. Call 999," he shouted at Fay.

She was looking out of the window with her hands to her face. He raced downstairs and grabbed his keys. He heard Fay speaking on the phone.

He unlocked the front door and raced out of his driveway towards the fire.

He ran down the road leading to the village. It wasn't far. He could see the flames. It was a house on fire in Main Street. He saw other people coming out of their houses and go towards the flaming house. The sky was lit up. A siren was heard in the distance. *Good, the fire brigade was on the way* he thought.

He came to within a couple of houses from the one on fire. He could feel the heat on his face. People were rushing around and screaming that Sheila was in there. An upstairs window shattered with a large bang and glass sprayed down onto the path. People stepped back. Someone came out of their garden with a ladder but the fire engine pulled up and said they would take over.

"Stand well back," shouted a fire officer. "Leave it to us."

Everyone stood back but shouted at the firemen that Sheila was in there and to hurry up and rescue her. Another fire engine arrived, sirens blaring. It came to a screeching halt and firemen spilled out.

A fireman erected a ladder up to the shattered upstairs window. Others were projecting water hoses on the house. A second upstairs window shattered.

The fireman went through the first shattered upstairs window. Everyone was holding their breath and then cheered as the fireman came back through the window with Sheila over his shoulder.

He descended the ladder and laid Sheila on the ground. She wasn't moving. He started chest compressions. The on lookers watched with horror. Another fireman took over. There was still no movement from Sheila. The flames were now being dampened down and were much less intense.

An ambulance arrived with its screaming siren. Paramedics leapt out and went over to where the fireman was working on Sheila. One bent down and took over the resuscitation process. Another took over after five minutes.

After a further tense five minutes, the paramedic stood up and shook his head.

"Noooo," cried the onlookers who had been watching with fingers crossed. *Surely, she wasn't dead?* She was. Sheila had not survived. People started crying and holding on to each other. It was a nightmare scene with Sheila lying dead on the path in her nightclothes. Her neighbours and friends were distraught.

Simon and Marie arrived and stood with Roger and a couple of other men. Simon looked up and saw Mary standing a bit further down the road with a couple of women. They were in their dressing gowns and gazing at the house, hands to their mouth in shock. Mary looked up and raised a hand in greeting when she saw Simon. He heard a voice calling his name from behind him. He turned around and saw it was George and Anne.

"What the hell's happened? Whose house is it?" George shouted at Simon.

"It's Beverley's friend, Sheila. Her house is on fire. She's died."

"My God, how awful," George replied. He put his arm around Anne who started crying.

He felt a tap on his shoulder and turned round to see his sister Frances. Julie's husband Julian and Celia's friends Sarah and Heather were with her. He hugged Frances.

"Terrible, awful," cried Sarah holding a tissue to her nose. Celia's husband Luke arrived in his dressing gown and slippers.

The police arrived and dispersed the onlookers telling them to go home. The flames were now out but there were plumes of black smoke drifting up into the night. The smell was awful. People left in silence, many with arms around each other. Sheila was carefully lifted onto a trolley by two paramedics and taken into the ambulance. The firemen remained behind to make sure the fire was out.

Roger returned home and told a waiting Fay what had happened. She was shocked to hear the awful news.

"They will find out what caused the fire and why Sheila died," he told her as he put his arms around her. They went to bed but found it hard to sleep.

Next day, the villagers were talking about the fire and Sheila's death. They knew there would be a full investigation into the fire but it didn't make it any easier as Sheila had been a popular person and well known in the village.

George rang Simon and said how shocked he was. He shared his disbelief with him. "It's terrible," he said. "That's two deaths in Merrydale in less than a week."

Simon said he was sure that the culprit would be found where Beverley was concerned but surely Sheila's death was an accident?

"She didn't smoke so it couldn't have been started by a cigarette," said George. "It must have been an electrical fault so that should be easy to establish by the fire brigade."

Simon agreed. He asked George if he knew if Sheila had any close family.

"I've heard talk of a sister who lives in Olehampton. I don't think they were very close though."

"Still, she'll need to come and sort the house out when the investigators have finished," said Simon.

He then reminded George that they hadn't drawn the raffle from Saturday night. "I've had some people ask me about it so I suppose we need to do it."

"Shall we do it tomorrow night? Do you want to come to my house at seven? I can go around people's houses later today and collect the tickets that were sold. The prizes are here."

George agreed and said he would see him tomorrow at seven o'clock.

*I'm sorry you had to die but I couldn't take the risk that you knew something. I had to ensure your silence. Please don't take it personally. I actually liked you. I hope you didn't suffer.*

*When the fireman brought you out of the upstairs window and down the ladder, I thought I saw you move and my heart stopped for a moment. Thankfully, it was your heart that stopped and mine is still beating.*

*Rest in peace Sheila.*

# Chapter Twenty-Three

The next day friends and neighbours gathered outside Sheila's house. The bricks were blackened. The upstairs windows were smashed. They could see blackened strips of what remained of curtains half hanging out of the shattered windows.

Some people laid flowers against the small fence which stood in front of the house.

"I can't believe it," said the lady who lived next door to Sheila. "I was only speaking to her yesterday morning," she sniffed into a tissue.

A lady standing next to her put an arm around her. "She will be much missed, she was a very nice person," she agreed. "I wonder what caused the fire?"

"The fire people will investigate so we should know what caused it," her friend replied.

"Sheila was quite friendly with Beverley who died last week. That's two deaths in Merrydale in less than a week. Who would have imagined that?" said Sheila's neighbour.

They saw Mary walking down the path towards them. She was carrying a bunch of flowers.

"Hello, Mary," said the neighbour. "Isn't it just awful?"

"Unbelievable," replied Mary. "I wonder what caused the fire?"

"The fire brigade will find out. They have an investigative team for this sort of thing."

Mary laid the bunch of flowers against the fence and bowed her head.

A man who lived a couple of houses away turned to the women and said, "I hope our houses are safe. It could be an electrical fault. These houses could probably do with a re-wire. They were built in the sixties; I think I'll find an electrician to come and check mine out."

"Me, too," said Sheila's neighbour. "I'm just relieved my house wasn't damaged from the fire. Let me know if you find an electrician and I'll get him to check mine too."

"Will do, I'll get on to it straight away," he replied.

"My house should hopefully be alright. It's only fifteen years old," said Mary.

Bystanders were starting to drift away, after they had laid flowers and paid their respects.

Mary said goodbye to the two women, offering a comforting pat on their arms. She turned to go back to her house.

A police car drove up and parked outside Sheila's house. As the two officers got out, Mary turned back as she recognised one of them from yesterday when they had visited her house asking about Beverley.

"Hello, again," she said to him.

"Hello," he replied recognising her from yesterday. He looked at Sheila's house and shook his head.

"Did you know the lady who lived here?" he asked.

"Yes, I did. Not very well but she was one of the people hosting a course for the Safari Supper last Saturday."

"I understand she was a friend of the lady who died in your house at the Supper?" he asked.

"Yes, she was a friend of Beverley's. That's how Sheila became involved with the Safari Supper."

"We know that, because we spoke with her yesterday afternoon after leaving your house," he said.

The second officer went up to the fence and looked at the flowers.

"She was obviously popular judging by the amount of flowers being laid here," he commented.

"She has neighbours who speak well of her. She was well liked," said Mary. "They are very upset."

"Bound to be, living in a village, people generally know their neighbours, more so than when they live in a town."

Mary asked what would happen now.

"The fire brigade will send a team in to see if they can find the cause of the fire. We're meeting them and they should be here in a minute," he replied looking at his watch.

As he spoke a small fire and rescue vehicle drew up and parked. A couple of large men got out. They were in fire brigade officer uniforms.

They greeted the police officers and then said hello to Mary.

"Are you a neighbour?" one asked.

"I live at the end of this road," said Mary pointing her house out. "I came to pay my respects and lay some flowers."

The two fire officers nodded and went through the small gate leading up to the front door. One took a key from his pocket and inserted it in the door.

The door opened and they went into the house. Mary stood with the police officers looking at the open front door. The police turned and said goodbye to Mary, dismissing her, and went to the door but didn't go in.

Mary turned away and went home.

Inside the house the fire officers looked around the hallway. It was sooty and smelt.

The first man bent to look at something on the floor. "Look at this, Jim," he said to the second officer. He took some vinyl gloves out of his pocket and put them on.

The first man held up some rags. He couldn't identify what they were as they were badly burnt.

"Arson?" asked the second officer.

The policemen waiting outside heard what he said and one called out "Was it started deliberately?"

They didn't go in through the door.

"Possibly," said the first fireman turning to the policemen. "This bundle of rags was just inside the door. It could have been lit and put through the letter box."

"Blimey," said the second policeman.

"Let's have a look around," said the first fireman. He called to the policemen to enter the house. "Be careful, put gloves on and don't touch anything," he said.

They all looked around very carefully. The stairs were intact so the firemen went up them to look in the bedrooms.

The policemen looked around downstairs without touching anything.

The policeman that had been in the house yesterday, looked at the lounge chair that Sheila had sat on while talking to him only yesterday. *How sad*, he thought. You never knew what was round the corner.

The lounge wasn't too badly damaged. Smoke damage was evident and the smell was horrible.

The firemen came downstairs and had a look in the kitchen and lounge.

"It looks like a case of arson. From what I can see it wasn't anything electrical but I'll get an expert to check it out."

They locked up and left. A couple more bunches of flowers had been added to the front of the wall since they had been inside.

The police attached "Do not cross" tape across the gate.

They got in their vehicles and left to go back to their respective stations to make their reports.

# Chapter Twenty-Four

George was calling at the houses that had hosted a course on the safari Supper evening. He collected the raffle tickets that had been sold on the night. No one's heart was in drawing the raffle but a lot of tickets had been sold so it needed to be drawn.

He called first at Kerry's house. She had just come in from work and expressed her shock at the deaths.

"I couldn't concentrate at work so they sent me home. I still can't believe it. Poor Beverley and poor Sheila."

She looked close to tears as she handed over the money and raffle tickets that she had sold on Saturday night. George put the tickets in his bag and said he would see her soon.

He then called next door to Sarah's house. She had just arrived home. He didn't go in so she handed him the raffle tickets and money saying how awful it all was and how she couldn't stop thinking about it.

He went out of Sarah's house and saw Celia was just coming back from collecting her eldest daughter from school. She had the youngest in a pushchair and the middle child was clutching the handle.

"Hello, George," she said. "Let me open the door and get the children in." She unlocked her front door going into the hallway and released the youngest one from the pushchair who promptly ran off into a room with her sisters. She folded the pushchair up and leant it against a wall. He told her he was collecting the raffle tickets from Saturday night.

"What an awful business," Celia said. "Everyone's talking about it outside the school."

"Mum, can we have a drink please?" one of the girls called.

"In a minute," she replied.

She gave George the raffle tickets and the money. "I sold quite a lot as I had a lot of people here for coffee," she told him. "I was grateful to you and Simon coming to help."

Her eyes welled up. "Poor Mary, she was hosting the coffee course as well. Beverley could have been helping me instead of Mary, and then it could have happened here which I don't think I would have been able to handle."

George patted her on the back. "It was good of you to take Mary back with you for the night. That was kind."

"It was the least I could do after what she had been through. Seeing Beverley collapse and die in front of her must have been dreadful. She was in a right state. And now, poor Sheila's dead too. It's too awful for words," she said tearfully.

"Muuuuum!" cried a young voice "We are thirsty!"

"You're obviously needed so I'll be off now. You take care," said George.

He left the house after putting the tickets and money in his bag.

He next went to Mary's house. She answered his knock at the door. "Come in, George," she beckoned letting him in. "I've not long come in. Do you want a cup of tea?"

"Best not. I'm going round houses collecting the raffle tickets and money which were sold on Saturday night. We've had people asking when it's going to be drawn," he replied. She led him into the lounge and asked him to sit down while she went to fetch them. She left the room. George looked round the lounge. It looked out onto the garden through French windows. It was looking lovely and colourful. Anne would like to have a larger garden he thought. Perhaps I'll do something to make ours bigger. I could move the fence at the far end of the garden back a couple of feet. The field wouldn't miss it.

Mary came in with the tickets and money. "Here you are, George," she said as she handed them over. He put them in his bag.

"Lorna and I went to a garden centre today for lunch. She thought going out would help me. We saw Frances there so we all had lunch in the café," she told him.

"That's nice. I hope it took your mind off things even for a short while," said George.

"It did a bit but then I keep remembering. Horrible business about Sheila, isn't it?" said Mary. "The fire officers and police arrived today and went into the house. I was outside laying flowers when they came."

"I wonder what caused the fire?" asked George.

"I don't know but I'm sure they will find out in due course," replied Mary. She sat down on the sofa.

She looked at him asking if he had any theories on what caused it.

"I have no idea but the experts will find out," he said. "Well, I'd best get off. I have a few more houses to get to. Simon's coming around this evening and we'll draw the raffle. You look a bit better today, Mary. Going out with Lorna today must have helped. You have a bit more colour in your cheeks. You looked awful on Saturday night after Beverley…"

He stumbled over the next word.

"Died," said Mary. She wiped a tear away. "I will never forget seeing her collapse onto the floor."

George got up and said he would see himself out. "You take care of yourself, Mary," he said, patting her on her shoulder.

He left and carried on to Julie's house.

She opened the door and invited him in.

He declined the offer of a cup of tea and explained why he had called by.

"I'll just fetch them. Mum sold most of them, she did really well. They're in the kitchen, come through."

He followed her into the kitchen and put the tickets and money in his bag.

"Isn't it dreadful about Sheila?" asked Julie. "Everyone at school is talking about it. Monday morning Beverley's death was being discussed and two days later it's Sheila!"

"It is awful, but I'm sure the experts will find out what caused the fire and also how Beverley came to eat the prawn in the sandwich," he said.

Julie shuddered and said she hoped that answers would be found out soon, as everyone was very nervous. "Do you think they were connected?"

"I can't see how, as both deaths were totally different. I know they were friends but surely that's just a horrible coincidence," he replied.

He left saying he would see her soon.

He continued calling at the other houses collecting the raffle tickets and money. He was delayed at all of them as they wanted to talk about Sheila and Beverley.

He arrived home just after six o' clock. Anne was in the kitchen ready to serve their evening meal.

"Go and wash up and then it'll be on the table," she told him.

George went upstairs and on returning to the kitchen found a roast chicken dinner being served. He rubbed his hands together saying she knew how to look after her man!

"Go on with you! Now eat up as Simon's coming around at seven," she laughed.

As they ate, he told her about his busy afternoon. "It took longer than it should have because everyone wanted to talk about Beverley and Sheila."

"That's understandable," Anne replied.

They ate their chicken dinner and had apple pie and custard for pudding.

George patted his full stomach and thanked Anne for the delicious meal.

Anne collected their plates, cleared the table and washed up. George took the raffle tickets out of his bag and put them on the table. "There were a lot sold. We've made quite a lot of money," he told Anne.

Simon arrived at seven o'clock. He took his jacket off and put it on the back of a kitchen chair and sat down. Anne made a cup of coffee for all of them.

George had a list of all the available prizes to be awarded. They put the individual tickets in a large bowl and asked Anne to do the picking. Each pulled ticket was awarded a prize. The first ticket pulled out won the most expensive prize with the last ticket winning the least expensive prize.

It took a while but it was eventually done. The buyer's names had been written on the back of the tickets so George knew who to distribute the prizes to. He wrote the winners names down on his list. There had been a heart stopping moment when Sheila's raffle ticket had been picked out of the bowl. Anne put it to one side in silence.

George told Simon about his busy afternoon.

"Mary said the fire people and police were at Sheila's house today but she doesn't know any more than that."

"They will find out what caused the fire," said Simon. "They will have experts investigating."

"It's most likely to be an electrical fault, surely?" said Anne. "There can't be any other cause."

"I wonder when we will hear any more about Beverley's death. Also, I wonder if they've traced any relatives?" said George.

"I suppose we will find out some time," said Simon. "But if there's no relatives found then who would pay for the funeral?"

"I'm sure the village will contribute if there's no family found," said Anne.

"I think she rented her house so there's no money coming in from a sale," said Simon.

George agreed he had heard she had rented her house rather than owning it.

"I wonder when Sheila's sister will appear. Of course she might have come over already and we haven't heard or seen her," said Simon.

Simon left at eight o'clock after helping count the money raised from selling the raffle tickets.

"I'll put the money safely away," said George to Anne.

He went upstairs.

He returned downstairs telling her he would distribute the prizes around to the winners over the next couple of days. Being the boss of his haulage business, he didn't need to go in every day. He had a good team and trusted them to carry on without him going in all the time. He usually went in a couple of days a week just to catch up.

# Chapter Twenty-Five

Next morning, Julie was talking to Derek Grant, the headmaster, in the staff room before the school day began. She put the kettle on intending to make them a cup of tea.

"The children are all talking about recent events. We need to calm them down and reassure them. They need to settle down and get back to talking about normal things again which doesn't involve death and dying," she said.

He agreed and said he would speak with them in assembly. They had their cup of tea and then went to their classrooms. The headmaster had his own group of children to teach. He much preferred teaching to sitting in his office looking at budgets and sorting out problems. He sighed. Perhaps he wasn't cut out to be head of a school but when the previous head had left, he was the one that the governors had approached with a view to taking over the headship. He would continue for another year and then weigh up his options. He had a wife and young family to think of so needed a good salary so perhaps he would have to carry on regardless.

He went into the school hall to open the assembly.

The teachers and children sang, "All things bright and beautiful."

Everyone sat down except for the headmaster who stood in front of them.

"I need to talk to you all," he began.

The room was silent waiting for him to speak.

"I know you are all worried about what has occurred recently but we need the police to get on with the job of finding out what happened. You are all safe and should continue your lives as normal. No talking to strangers and no playing out on your own."

Freddie stuck his hand up to the delight of his friends.

"Yes Freddie?" said the headmaster with a hidden sigh.

"When we *think* we have seen the murderer, what shall we do?" Freddie asked. "But we also might not know it's the murderer when we talk to them."

"You will not be speaking to any strangers," replied the headmaster.

"But what if it's someone we know?" Freddie insisted.

"It will not be anybody that you know," reassured the headmaster.

"In the book that I'm reading, the murderer was someone that people knew."

"I don't know what book you are reading, but perhaps you can bring it in and let me have a look at it. It doesn't sound as if it's suitable material for a ten-year-old," was the reply.

Children sniggered, held their breath, and looked at Freddie to see what he would say next.

"It's about wizards and witches. The witch put a spell on a boy and he died. *He* knew the witch before he died."

"It's a fairy tale story and that would not happen in real life," said the headmaster. "I may need to have a word with your parents about finding more suitable books for you to read."

Freddie didn't reply. He didn't want his parents to take the book away. It was a good story. The headmaster closed the assembly and everyone went to their classrooms.

Julie was Freddie's form teacher. He was a favourite of hers, a real cheeky chappie. He was an intelligent child and would go far. She knew she should not have favourites, but she treated all children the same so it didn't show.

Freddie sat down at his desk. His friend, Charlie, sitting by him, nudged him and whispered if he could borrow the book when Freddie finished it.

"Alright," agreed Freddie in a low voice, "as long as I don't have it taken away first."

Julie clapped her hands and asked the children to settle down.

"We now have a maths test," she told them. There was a collective groan from the children.

Maths! Who needed to know about maths!

# Chapter Twenty-Six

George collected the winning raffle prizes to start distributing them around the village. He had the list of winners.

He had enjoyed a good egg and bacon breakfast and two large cups of tea. Anne said she was going to do some more gardening. George had spoken of his idea of taking a bit of the far field to make the garden bigger.

"I can move the fence back a couple of feet," he told her. "I'll think about it." Anne replied.

George put on his jacket and cap and collected his keys. "See you later," he called to Anne.

He drove to the far end of Merrydale first. He pulled up outside a very nice red brick detached house.

The lady was delighted to hear she had won first prize. "A meal for two at the pub! Lovely, thank you, I never usually win anything!" she said with a huge smile.

He handed her the voucher and said to present it to the landlord who would provide the free meal.

He got in his car and drove a bit further down the road.

He delivered two more prizes to the winning recipients.

He then called at Celia's house. She was sitting in her kitchen drinking a cup of coffee after having a busy morning. Bed sheets were blowing on the clothes line. She looked at her watch and saw she had an hour before collecting her two youngest daughters from nursery school. Next term they would be attending school all day like her eldest. She might consider a part time job but it may not be practicable because of school holidays. She would like to do more than just being a housewife and mother. Luke always came home talking about his day at the medical centre, whom he had seen and spoken with and what he had been doing.

She got up to answer the doorbell. "Hello, George," she said with a smile. "What can I do for you?"

She asked him in. He handed her a raffle prize which was a big box of chocolates.

"How nice, thank you!" she exclaimed. "Have you time for a coffee?"

"Yes, please, but just a quick one," he replied. They went into the kitchen and she switched the kettle on.

She made George and herself a coffee and offered him a biscuit which he accepted.

"How are you?" he asked.

"I suppose I'm alright. I try and keep busy here but then I suddenly remember about Beverley and Sheila," Celia replied. "And everyone keeps talking about it outside the school when we collect our children."

She smiled and said she was speaking earlier to young Freddie Carter's mum when they dropped their children off. "She told me Freddie's obsessed with the deaths and because he says he wants to be a policeman when he grows up. He's going to find out who the murderer is. She's quite worried about him because it's all he's talking about."

"I suppose it's natural; everyone's talking about it because it has affected us all in the village, but the children should be speaking of other things, whatever it is that children talk about!" said George.

"I agree," replied Celia. "My eldest daughter, Freya, is very friendly with Freddie and tells me what he's been saying at school. Apparently, he keeps asking the headmaster questions about it in assembly."

"I can just imagine!" said George. "He's not slow in coming forward from what I know about him."

"No, he's not!" said Celia, "but he does need to quieten down a bit as it is causing the other children to egg him on about how he's going to investigate, from what Freya tells me."

"Oh dear," replied George. "Let's hope something happens to take his mind of it before too long."

"Do you mean if they find the person who killed Beverley?" asked Celia.

"I suppose I do mean that. Once someone's under lock and key, then Freddie will calm down," replied George.

"Is there any update about the fire yet?" asked Celia.

"I haven't heard anything other than its obviously being investigated," said George.

Celia sighed and said she hoped they would find the cause of the fire soon.

George got up from the table and thanked her for the coffee. Celia walked him to the front door.

She grabbed the pushchair from the hall and made her way out of the house. She arrived at the nursery. Parents had to wait outside and each child was personally escorted to them by a teacher.

Celia walked home with Freddie's mum Sarah and her youngest son Max. Sarah had hosted a main course for the Safari Supper and had enjoyed it. They spoke about Sheila's house fire.

"I hope it turns out that it was an electrical fault," said Sarah.

"Surely no one's really suggesting it was anything else?" replied Celia.

"I've heard the word arson being bandied about."

"God, I hope not," said Celia.

She turned towards her driveway saying goodbye and said she would see her later when they collected Freya and Freddie from school. Freddie's mum lived a couple of houses down next door to Kerry.

Celia unlocked her door and went inside with the girls. She prepared their lunches and afterwards the girls had an hour's nap while she brought in the dry washing from the line.

George was still delivering the raffle prizes. He kept getting delayed as everyone wanted to chat.

He had dropped most of them off. Some people weren't at home, presumably they were out at work. He would have to call around in an evening to catch them in.

His last raffle prize drop was at Mary's house. He wasn't really sure if he wanted to deliver the bottle of red wine which she had won. It might remind her of the fateful evening. He pulled up outside her house, thought about it and then decided not to drop it off and was just about to drive off when her front door opened.

Mary raised her hand in greeting. George turned his engine off, got out of the car, and went to the door. He admitted what he was doing outside her house and said he had decided to drive off without delivering it as he believed it might upset her.

"I wondered why you were sitting outside in your car," she said looking at the bottle. "I like a bit of red wine."

George handed it over.

"Do you want to come in for a cup of tea?" she asked.

George looked at his watch. It was three o'clock. He could do with a cup of tea. He had nipped home between deliveries for a quick sandwich but that was a couple of hours ago.

He accepted the invitation. Mary showed him into the lounge and went to switch the kettle on in the kitchen. She put the wine on the kitchen table.

George sat down on the sofa, took his cap off and put it by his side.

"A bit of cake, George?" she called to him from the kitchen.

"Yes, please," he replied.

Mary came into the lounge holding a tray which held two mugs of tea and a large slice of fruit cake.

She placed it on the table in front of him.

"Thank you," he said as she told him to take the slice of cake.

"Not having any yourself?" he asked.

"No, I've not been so hungry over the past few days."

"I can understand that, but you need to keep your strength up." he replied as he took a bite of cake.

Mary took a sip of her tea.

"I keep thinking about Sheila and the fire. I hope she didn't suffer," said Mary looking at George.

He replied that from what he understood about people and fires, they are rendered unconscious quite quickly by the smoke so, no, he didn't believe she would have suffered.

"That's a good thing then," replied Mary sipping her tea. "I wonder when the investigation into it will be made public?"

"These things take some time," replied George. "It could be ages before we hear anything. There will be a post mortem and then an inquest."

Mary asked if the police had been in touch with him this week about Beverley's death and if there was any update.

"No one's been in touch with me," he replied. "I see the police are still calling at houses in the village. Not sure if they would tell me anything anyway. I'm not a relative or anything. I know some of the police chiefs as I'm on the council but even so, I can't see them telling me anything. Again, like with Sheila there will be a post mortem and inquest."

"I wonder if they have traced any of Beverley's family yet?" asked Mary.

"I really don't know. We need young Freddie Carter on the case!" he grinned.

"Freddie Carter? What on earth's he got to do with it?" asked Mary in surprise.

"According to Celia, who was speaking to his mum at the school, Freddie told his friends he's going to investigate and catch the murderer. He says he wants to be a policeman when he grows up!" chuckled George.

Mary laughed saying she didn't believe a ten-year-old could catch a murderer.

George finished his tea and stood up with his cap in his hand. "Thanks for the tea and cake, Mary," he said as she showed him out the front door.

Mary closed the door and went into the kitchen. She saw the bottle of red wine on the kitchen table and decided to have a glass with her supper.

# Chapter Twenty-Seven

According to the local news that evening the bail absconder was still on the loose.

The presenter said there had been no further reported sightings but if anyone believed they saw him they must inform the police immediately.

Simon watched the news with Marie.

"I wonder what he has done wrong," said Simon. "You would think they would give us a clue?"

"Yes, they ought to tell us something," agreed Marie. "Just because there's been no sightings around here for a few days we must still be careful about locking up at night. Hopefully he's left the area."

Simon said he would have a last look outside before bed. He yawned as he stood up.

"Don't be long," Marie said. She turned the television off and went upstairs to prepare for bed.

Simon took a torch and went outside. It was a dark. He looked up at the night stars.

He walked around the barns. He didn't see anything untoward. He suddenly heard a slight noise behind him and the next moment he was hit on the head and knocked to the ground. He heard footsteps running off.

He put a hand to the back of his head and felt blood. He swore and got up. He looked around but saw nothing. He retrieved his torch as he had dropped it and it had rolled away when he fell. It was still working so he found it easily.

He went back into the house and yelled for Marie. She came flying downstairs in her nightie.

"I've been clobbered by someone," he told her holding the back of his head. "I'm bleeding."

"Sit down. Let me have a look," said Marie.

Simon bent his head and Marie saw a small cut. Being a scalp wound, it bled easily. She wet some kitchen roll and held it on the cut. Simon winced. It didn't look deep enough to need stitching she told him.

"What happened?" she asked Simon.

"I was looking around the yard but didn't see anything. Then I heard a noise behind me and next thing I was hit on the head and on the bloody ground."

"We need to call the police," said Marie. Simon said not to bother, the attacker would be long gone by now.

"Even so, they need to know. Now hold the pad on the cut to stem the bleeding while I ring."

She rang 999 as she didn't know the number of their local police station.

It was answered at once and Marie explained what had happened to Simon.

The police controller listened and said they didn't think an ambulance was required but they should report it to their local police station in the morning. They didn't have any police available to come out now as they agreed the intruder would be long gone. In the meantime, should Simon feel faint or collapse she should call for an ambulance immediately.

Marie wrote down the local police station number and thanked the controller.

She looked beneath the damp, now red, kitchen roll pressed on the wound. "It's stopped bleeding now. Thankfully it's only a small cut," she told Simon.

"It stings a lot even if it is only small!" he groaned.

Marie found a bandage and applied it to his head. "I don't want you bleeding all over the pillow case," she told him.

She locked the door and they went upstairs to bed.

"I'd love to get my hands on whoever did this," Simon told Marie. He looked in the mirror and grinned. "I do look stupid wrapped up like a mummy, good job no one can see me."

"Come on, undress and get into bed. You must wake me if you feel funny in the night. Promise?"

"Promise," agreed Simon.

They lay in bed talking.

"Do you think it's the bail jumper who hit you?" asked Marie.

"Bound to be, who else could it be?"

"We will tell the police tomorrow," said Marie.

"I'll let Roger know as well," said Simon.

Marie fell asleep quickly but it took a while before Simon could relax and drop off. He was very annoyed as he had to lie on his side as it hurt lying on his back like he normally did.

# Chapter Twenty-Eight

George's sister, Frances, was having a cup of morning coffee with her neighbour Belinda. They were in their early sixties and both were retired. Frances used to work at George's firm in the accounts department. Belinda was widowed and had taken early retirement, a year ago, from the local council where she used to work in the Environmental Health department.

They had become friendly since retirement with both being at home in the day and often meeting up at each other's houses for a coffee and chat.

They were talking about the night of the fire when Sheila died. "I can't believe I never heard a thing!" exclaimed Belinda. "I take a sleeping tablet and was out for the count."

"It was horrible," said Frances. "Seeing her lying on the pavement in her night clothes was just dreadful. I didn't know her well but from what I have heard she was a really nice person."

"Were there many people there?" asked Belinda.

"Loads of them," replied Frances. "They heard the sirens and dashed out of their houses to find out what was going on."

"I wonder what caused the fire?" said Belinda.

"No one knows yet, but obviously the fire brigade and police are investigating. Some folk are saying it was electrical but some are saying it was deliberate," said Frances.

"Coming so soon after the other death is dreadful."

"Yes, two deaths with only a few days apart. Did you know Beverley?" asked Frances.

"Not really. I had seen her about in the village but only knew her to say hello. Its dreadful thinking someone slipped a prawn into her sandwich deliberately. I hope the culprit is found as soon as possible."

"She came to the village about a year ago, George says," said Frances. "She used to be a nurse in her previous village he told me. She was quite a shy person.

Apparently, Beverley and Sheila were friends here in Merrydale. They used to have meals at each other's houses quite often."

"And to think they died a few days apart!" said Belinda with a shudder.

"Have you heard about the bail jumper?" asked Frances.

"Only what I have heard on the news."

"He had a night in a couple of farm barns apparently," relayed Frances. "He has also been spotted just outside the village too. You be careful when walking Jonas."

Jonas was Belinda's dog. He was a cockapoo and enjoyed two long walks a day. Belinda said she would be careful. "I carry a whistle with me, not that I've ever used it but it may come in handy if anyone tried to attack me. Jonas would probably jump up and lick them!" she grinned.

Frances repeated her advice to be careful.

They finished their coffee and Frances got up to go.

"I've got to go shopping," she told Belinda. "I need some serious stocking up."

"And I've got a dog to walk," said Belinda, patting Jonas who was rubbing his face against Belinda's leg. "Fetch your lead!" she told him.

Jonas ran off and quickly reappeared with his lead dangling from his mouth. Frances laughed, saying what a clever dog he was and patted his neck.

She thanked Belinda for the coffee and saw herself out the front door.

Belinda took the lead from Jonas and went to fetch her jacket. She made sure she had her mobile phone and whistle in her pocket. She attached the lead to the dog's collar, locked up, and went outside.

She walked down the road and at the end turned left towards the park. It was a lovely warm sunny day and she breathed in the fresh air. Small fluffy white clouds were making their way slowly across blue sky.

She entered the park through the open black gates which were closed at night. Her late husband had worked for the council where he had been in charge of the park gardens. Walking through the park brought back happy memories of him. He had worked hard and was proud to have the many compliments from people walking and enjoying the gardens. There was a bench in his memory overlooking a flower garden. Belinda often sat on it alone with her memories.

There were not many people about as probably most were at school or work. She nodded hello to a couple of dog walkers.

She and Jonas reached the end of the park and entered a wooded area. She was able to let Jonas off his lead here and he went sniffing in the undergrowth. He barked loudly at something and Belinda could have sworn he was saying squirrel!

She called for him to come back as he had run off ahead of her. She heard him bark again and followed him. He was busy sniffing and barking at something in the scrub at the bottom of a large tree. She saw something out of the corner of her eye and with a start, saw a man suddenly appear. He was wearing a green camouflage jacket, jeans and had a cap on. He looked straight at her as he picked up speed and ran off ahead.

She remembered hearing on the local news that the bail jumper had last been spotted in a green jacket. She called Jonas who still didn't come back to her. There was no one else about. Her heart was beating fast.

"Jonas!" she called very loudly.

She felt for the whistle in her pocket and held it tightly in her hand.

"Jonas!" she called again.

The man had run ahead and disappeared into a more densely wooded area. Jonas returned reluctantly with his tail wagging. She attached his lead and turned back quickly to the way from where she had entered the wooded area. She started to run.

She re-entered the park from the wooded area breathing heavily. Her heart was racing nineteen to the dozen.

She went back through the park towards the gates.

"Are you alright?" a concerned lady asked her, seeing Belinda was flushed and out of breath.

"I think I've just seen the man who the police are looking for," she replied looking behind her.

"Really? Where?" she asked.

"Back in that wooded area at the end of the park. I need to ring the police."

"Calm down. Come and sit down on this bench and ring the police. I'll stay with you."

She and the lady sat on the nearest bench. It just so happened to be her late husband's memorial bench. She didn't tell the lady. Belinda told Jonas to sit and for once he obeyed first time.

Belinda rang 999 on her mobile and asked for the police. A voice answered immediately and she told them where she was and what had happened.

"Please stay where you are and someone will come to you," she was told.

The lady offered Belinda a fruit sweet. "Sugar, for shock," she told her.

She had one as well. They unwrapped their sweets and put them in their mouths.

Jonas pushed his nose against Belinda's knee. "No, you can't have one!" Belinda told him with pat on his head.

"He's a lovely dog," said the lady. "Is he a cockapoo?" She patted him and Jonas turned and licked her hand.

"Yes, he's five now but still thinks he's a puppy!"

"I used to have a collie dog called Colin. He lived to a good age. He was twelve when he died last year. I still miss him. I like to walk and it's so much nicer with a dog," said the lady. "I'm thinking of getting another one but I like to go on holidays abroad a couple of times a year, so I need to use kennels when I'm away. Colin never liked going to them. He'd see me pack my suitcase and he knew where he was destined for! It took a good week for him to forgive me after I got back."

Belinda smiled. She was calmer now. Her heart beat was back to normal.

She saw a police car pull up at the entrance to the park. Two policemen got out and went through the park gates.

She got up from the bench. The lady asked if she'd be alright now.

"Thank you so much. I really appreciate you waiting with me." Belinda told her.

"No problem at all. Let's hope they catch him and then we can all rest easier in our beds at night." she replied and went off.

The two policemen came over to the bench when they saw Belinda raise her hand.

"Can we have your name please?" asked the taller officer. He was about thirty and his colleague probably a few years younger.

*It's true*, thought Belinda, *the police are getting younger all the time or perhaps it's because I'm getting older!*

"Belinda Tebbutt," she replied.

"And who is this lovely fellow?" asked the second officer.

"Jonas," replied Belinda patting her dog.

"Can you tell us what happened and show us where you saw the suspect, please?"

Belinda explained where she had seen the man. She couldn't tell them much, only that he had suddenly appeared and then ran off. "I recognised what he was wearing. It was on the news."

"Did you see his face?" asked the tall officer.

"Yes, for a fleeting moment. He looked right at me."

She accompanied them to the wooded area where she had seen the man. "Jonas had run ahead and was sniffing around the bottom of a tree. I called him but he was too interested in whatever he could smell in the undergrowth."

The policemen looked around. There weren't any people about.

"Which direction did he run off to?" asked the tall policeman.

"Over there," said Belinda pointing.

They walked over towards the densely wooded area. There was nothing and no one to be seen. It was all very quiet. The younger policeman asked Belinda to point out which tree Jonas had been interested in.

She showed him. Jonas was straining at the lead to investigate the tree again.

The younger policeman bent down, then took some vinyl gloves from his pocket and picked something up. "A cigarette stub and an empty crisp packet," he showed his colleague.

"Bag them up," he was told. The policeman took a plastic bag from his pocket and dropped the stub and crisp packet in it.

Jonas started barking and was shushed by Belinda.

"I will call for more officers to search the area," said the tall policeman.

He then asked if Belinda would go to Olehampton police station and make a statement. "I will call the station now for more officers to come out and also tell them your name so they are expecting you when you arrive."

He turned away and spoke into a radio attached to his jacket.

She said she would take Jonas home first and then go to the station.

"Thank you for reporting this. You have been very helpful," she was told. "Let's hope we find him or at least have something to go on that will eventually lead to his arrest."

Belinda left the park to take her dog home. She left him happily chewing a dog chew and then drove to the police station in Olehampton.

# Chapter Twenty-Nine

That morning, Simon had been around to Rogers and told him about being hit on the head by the intruder. They had a cup of coffee together in the kitchen. Roger was very concerned. "I wonder why he is still hanging about. I don't understand it. Surely, he would realise people are on the lookout for him."

"You'd think so, but perhaps he's not seen the news. He's obviously lying low somewhere and I wouldn't think he's got access to a television to see it."

"It still stings even though Marie says it's only a small cut," said Simon laying his finger on the small dressing on the back of his head.

"Good job it wasn't any worse. You hear of people having problems after a head injury and are never right again," said Roger.

"Thanks very much," replied Simon with a grin. "It might have knocked some sense into me, Gary told me, when I rang to tell him earlier."

"What are we going to do about all this? We've got our barns locked up which he must know by now. He probably tried yours again last night wanting to kip down for the night," said Roger.

"I might put up a couple of sensor lights in the yard, I've thought about this before but never got around to doing it," said Simon. "I've already got some lights out there but they need to be switched on and off manually."

"Good idea," agreed Roger.

"I will ask around to find if anyone knows a good electrician to come and sort it," said Simon.

"Let me know if you find an electrician and I'll have some installed as well," said Roger.

"Is there any update on Beverley's or Sheila's deaths yet?" asked Roger. "Fay is really upset about it and she only knew them a bit. It must be terrible for the people who knew them well."

"The police are still questioning people about Beverley. I know they asked you and Fay about it," replied Simon.

"We didn't see or hear anything at all," said Roger. "We told them we went to Celia's house for coffee so weren't at Marys at all. We had our starters at Julies, mains at Heathers and puddings at your sister's house."

"The fire brigade and police must still be investigating the fire at Sheila's and I haven't heard any update," said Simon.

"It's very odd, I think. Two deaths, two friends and one village. There has to be a connection somewhere surely," commented Roger.

"The police will find out, I'm sure," replied Simon.

"Do you think the intruder has anything to do with it?" asked Roger. "Let's face it, nothing much goes on in Merrydale and now in the space of a week or so all this happens."

"It is very strange when you put it like that," said Simon.

"We must keep our ears and eyes open. I will let you know if I find an electrician," said Simon as he stood up to leave.

Roger walked out with him into his yard. The day was overcast and there was a threat of showers later.

"We could do with a bit of rain," said Roger looking up at the sky.

Simon agreed and went home.

# Chapter Thirty

Villagers were sorting out their unwanted clothes and various items for the table top and jumble sale being held at the school in a couple of weeks. It was a well-supported annual event. Coffee and tea would be served to raise profits.

The children who were in their last but one school year and the leavers at the primary school before going to secondary school always enjoyed the event as they were allowed to stand with a teacher behind the different stalls and help sell the clothes, toys and knick-knacks that had been donated by the villagers. They felt like shopkeepers.

Bags of clothes that had been delivered or collected were being stacked up in a mostly unused back room at the school. Boxes of other items for sale were also in there.

All the teachers and teaching assistants who had free periods from teaching were sorting them out when they had time.

"Look at this!" was a comment often heard whilst they were sorting things out. "Fancy giving us that to sell or fancy getting rid of this!"

The villagers were always happy to donate. It was a good way of clearing out their unwanted items, and all the profits went to the school.

Julie was sorting items out this morning as she had a free hour from teaching. She had Sally helping her.

Clothes in the best condition went into one pile. Some clothes would never sell, so these went into another pile for disposal. It did annoy Julie that some people sent things that were tatty and unsellable. Obviously, they were making space in their wardrobes and getting the school to dispose of them instead of taking them to a tip!

There were a lot of books donated which always sold well. Toys, jigsaws, and ornaments also sold very well. The children poured over the toys when they were displayed on the tables for sale on the day. They all brought in some money on the day for their bargains!

Julie and Sally were chatting as they were sorting the items out. Sally did not live in Merrydale but travelled from Olehampton each day. "Any news on the two deaths yet?" she asked Julie.

"I haven't heard any more," replied Julie. "The police are still investigating."

"It's awful isn't it," said Sally. "Two people dead within a few days of each other and both suspicious deaths."

"It is horrible but the police will find out what happened. It's not yet known if the fire was caused by an electrical fault," replied Julie examining a floral blouse.

They put some more clothes in the unsellable and sellable pile. Sally picked up a red jumper. "Look at this. Fancy someone sending in a jumper to sell with a massive hole in the elbow!" commented Sally tossing it in the unsellable pile. "That's not on, whoever sent it must have known about the hole."

"Oh well, at least the unsellable items are a smaller pile than the sellable pile!"

Julie picked up an ugly ornament of a dog. "I'm sure I've seen this in someone's house but can't remember whose," she grinned. "It should fetch about twenty pence!" she told Sally.

There were quite a few donated boxed toys. Some of the boxes were a bit battered but looking inside, the toys were in a reasonable condition for selling.

They heard a knock on the door before it was opened. The young lad Stuart, who was collecting things from people's houses, came through. He was the student son of one of the teachers and had volunteered to collect items in his van. He had finished university early for the summer break.

"Hello," he said. "More things for you."

He deposited five bags on the floor.

"Thanks!" said Julie. "Have you many more collections organised?" she asked him.

"Not many more now." he replied.

"Have you been very busy collecting things?" said Sally.

"Yes, I've collected from a lot of houses over the last few days. Did you know, I collected some stuff from the lady who died in the fire?" Stuart asked. "It's awful. I saw her the very afternoon on the day she died."

"It was terrible," said Sally. "It can play on your mind remembering things like that."

"Yes," he said. "I keep trying to remember what I said to her which wasn't much. Poor lady," he said shaking his head.

He left the room and Julie and Sally started tidying up as they needed to return to their classroom for the next lesson. They left the room after stacking the boxes and bags in the corner and alongside one wall so no one could trip over them if they came into the room.

# Chapter Thirty-One

The next day at three fifteen, Mary decided to walk down the road towards the park. It was a lovely sunny day and she wanted to get out of the house for a bit of fresh air. There had been a couple of rain showers last evening but the sun had soon dried any puddles up.

She had spent a busy morning cleaning her windows and afterwards had eaten a snack lunch and then had a half hour doze.

She was nearing Sheila's house and saw a red car parked outside. A lady was coming out of Sheila's front door. The police tape had now been removed.

Mary stopped and said, "Hello." She wondered who she was.

The lady was in her late forties and was dressed in a bright, blue cardigan over a lighter blue dress.

She acknowledged Mary's greeting.

"I'm Jane, Sheila's sister," the lady said. "I've just been in the house looking at the damage. I can't get my head around what's happened to her."

"It's awful. We can scarcely believe it either. Sheila was well known around here and people liked her."

"That's nice to hear," replied Jane wiping a tear away with her finger. "We weren't that close and didn't see each other very often, but even so, she was still my sister."

"Are there any other relatives?" Mary asked.

"Just my husband and two daughters. Our parents died a while ago."

"Have you been told what caused the fire?" asked Mary.

"The fire brigade officer in charge of the investigation believes it was arson. The electricity wiring was checked out and they don't think that was the cause."

"That's dreadful."

"Yes, it is because it means someone deliberately caused the fire and she was meant to die in it. Who on earth would do something like that and what had she done to deserve it?" said Jane tearfully.

"I have no idea. Is there much damage in the house?" asked Mary.

"There's lots of smoke damage inside. The upstairs windows obviously need replacing and the front of the house will need cleaning. It will all need re decorating inside once I get the go ahead from the investigators and insurers. I think that should be soon. The fire people told me I could come in it today so I think they've finished looking for evidence. It will then be for the police to try and find out who set it alight and killed her. I have met with them a couple of times now and they tell me they have eliminated me from their enquiries," she said with a wry smile.

"I suppose they have to suspect family first and make sure it wasn't carried out for monetary gain," said Mary.

"Yes," said Jane. "I understand that."

"I suppose you will sell it then when it's all done up?" said Mary.

"Yes, if people want to buy a house where someone died. I don't know whether I would want to," Jane replied with a shudder.

Mary commiserated with her saying, "It's a nice house in a nice village. Once it's completely redecorated and restored it will be a good buy to potential purchasers."

"I'm really glad to have met someone who knew Sheila. It gives me some comfort knowing she had friends here," said Jane.

Mary smiled and said she was glad she could offer some comfort at such a sad time.

Jane turned back and locked the front door and made her way to her car.

"I'm sure we will meet again as I will be coming over a lot to oversee the redecoration when I get permission to start," said Jane.

Mary said she would look forward to seeing her again and repeated how sorry she was about Sheila.

She watched Jane drive off.

She continued her walk down the road and saw Celia and Sarah walking along towards her returning home after collecting their children from school. Celia was pushing her youngest daughter in a pushchair and the other two girls were chatting with Sarah's two sons Freddie and Max.

"Hello, Mary," greeted Celia. "Who was that lady?"

"Sheila's sister Jane. She was given permission to go inside the house."

"That must mean that they have finished sifting through it. Did she say what the police think?" asked Sarah.

"They don't think it was an electrical fault so they are looking at arson."

"What's arson?" asked Freddie who had been listening to them talking.

"It's when someone deliberately starts a fire and so it wasn't an accident," said Freya.

"Wow!" said Freddie. "Did they know she was inside when they set it alight?"

"I really don't know," replied Sarah. "You mustn't worry about it as the police will find out."

"But that person could do it to someone else's house as well," he replied. "It could be our house next."

"Stop it, Freddie. No one's going to burn our house down," said Sarah.

"You're going to be a policeman when you grow up, Freddie. You can find out who did it," said Freya. "You might even get a police medal for finding out who did it."

"Now stop it, children," intervened Celia. "Leave it for the grown-up police to find out."

Freddie whispered something to Freya who grinned.

"What was that you whispered?" asked Celia.

"Nothing," said Freddie.

"Freya?" asked Sarah.

Freya shrugged, staying silent but looking at Freddie.

"Come on, let's all get home now and talk about something else, like what to have for tea," said Celia.

Sarah and Celia shooed the children ahead to continue walking home. "See you soon, Mary," said Celia.

"Bye," said Sarah.

They carried on up the road to their houses and Mary continued walking to the park.

# Chapter Thirty-Two

Simon had asked around to know if anyone knew a good electrician. George said he knew one who lived in Olehampton and had carried out some work for him about five years ago.

"He did a good job, arrived when he said he would and charged a reasonable price, too."

He told Simon he couldn't recall his name but would find out his number when he found the receipt given to him for the work carried out.

"I keep all my receipts. Anne tells me to sort the receipt file out as some of them are over twenty years old but I tell her you never know when you may need to look for one!" he told Simon with a grin.

He told Roger who asked to pass the electrician's name and number to him when George found it out and gave it to Simon.

"I'm getting fed up patrolling my barns every evening. Having a sensor light will make it much easier and also, hopefully, scare any intruders off," he said.

Simon agreed with this. "Same here."

That evening George looked in his overflowing receipt file that he kept in the lounge cabinet. Anne asked him what he was doing.

"Having a good clear out, I hope. It's ridiculous keeping ones that are years old. Probably half of the contractors are no longer in business!" she told him.

George grinned and said you never know when you may need to find one even from years ago.

He sifted through the most recent receipts and eventually found the one from the electrician.

"Bingo!" he told Anne holding the receipt up.

He made a note of the name and telephone number to give to Simon.

He rang him up and gave him the details.

"Hi name's Jerry Field and the number is 0776743221. Hopefully, he still has the same mobile phone number."

"Thanks a lot. I'll give him a ring later," said Simon. "Roger wants his number as well. Having sensor lights fitted should make it harder for intruders to hang around our farms. I've even thought about having CCTV but I'll start with the lights first." He rang off thanking him again.

Simon rang the number that evening. It rang for a bit before being answered.

"Hello?" said a voice.

"Hello, is that Jerry?" asked Simon.

"Yes," was the answer.

"My name is Simon Godfrey. I've got your number from a friend of mine who you did some work for about five years ago. I'm a farmer and need some sensor lights fitting in my yard near some barns. I've recently had an intruder and need to make it a bit safer outside."

"No problem," replied Jerry. "I've fitted a lot of sensor lights. Where do you live?"

"I live in Merrydale," said Simon.

"I've recently been over in Merrydale. I was asked by the fire brigade to go and look at a house which had caught fire to establish whether it was an electrical fault or something more sinister."

"I know the house you mean," replied Simon. "What did you find out?"

"There was nothing wrong with the wiring from what I could see," said Jerry.

"So, the house must have been set alight deliberately?" said Simon.

"That's for the brigade investigators to say. All I can say, is that I couldn't see any wiring problems which may have caused the fire so that's what my report said."

Simon told him the work that he was wanting done in his yard. He told him that his neighbour also wanted sensor lights installed.

Jerry said it was no problem but he was committed to someone else's job for the rest of the week but he could come over to have a look at both his and his neighbour's yards.

"That's fine," replied Simon. "When could you come?"

"I could come about six tomorrow evening to look at both yards," said Jerry.

"That's fine. I have to help with milking from four but six o'clock should be ok."

It was agreed that Jerry would come over at six tomorrow.

Simon rang Roger who said that was fine. He wouldn't need to phone him himself then. He would be ready to see Jerry and show him where he wanted the lights fitted after he had been to Simon's.

Simon also told him that Jerry had told him that he had been asked by the fire brigade to see if Sheila's house fire had been started by an electrical fault but according to Jerry it hadn't.

"So, it was definitely started deliberately then?" replied Roger.

"It appears so," said Simon. "Who on earth would do such a thing though?"

"I can't imagine. It had to be someone with a grudge against her."

"But she was well liked by all accounts," said Roger. "Everyone I've spoken to said how nice she was."

"Let's hope the police find out quickly," replied Simon.

He rang off saying he would bring Jerry around the next evening.

# Chapter Thirty-Three

The police were coming to the end of their initial enquiries into Beverley's death on the night of the Safari Supper. They had sent several officers into the village to interview the diners who had bought tickets for the event. It took a while as there were many people to interview.

The officer in charge was Detective Inspector Ron Bailey. He was aged around forty and was a popular member of the constabulary.

He held a meeting at the police station with his officers and asked for their findings. He stood in front of a board on which was a photograph of Beverley and one of Sheila. It was one of Beverley that they had found at her house. It appeared to be one from a few years ago but they hadn't been able to find a more recent one. Sheila's sister had provided the most recent one of Sheila that she had but again it was a few years old.

Inspector Bailey said the post mortem on Beverley had confirmed that the cause of death was due to her allergy.

"I'm told she would have died within about ten minutes of eating the prawn," he told them.

One officer raised his hand. "It appears no one really knew her well. She had come to live at Merrydale about a year ago and was reluctant to talk about her past, except to say, she used to be a community nurse. We have interviewed all the diners who bought tickets and attended the supper."

"It appears she was a quite reserved person and was quite shy," said a second officer.

"We need to find out about her life before living in Merrydale. It must have some bearing on her death," said Inspector Bailey. "I will be contacting the force in the village where she came from. It's called Haleton, about fifty miles away near Burford."

"Do you need any of us to go over there and speak with them?" said the first officer.

"I will let you know once I have spoken to their Inspector," said Inspector Bailey.

They discussed the interviews which had been held with the villagers.

"It appears her best friend was Sheila Davies, who was the lady who died in the house fire a few days later," said one officer.

"There has to be some connection surely. Two suspicious deaths in one village a few days apart is not just a coincidence," said an officer at the back of the room.

"I agree with you," replied the Inspector. "We need to know whether they knew each other before meeting up in Merrydale?"

"I don't think they did, by all accounts," said an officer raising his hand. "According to some people, Beverley was quite a loner in the village and then she met Sheila at some school function a few months later and became friends. They had not been seen together in the village up until then."

"Unless they deliberately kept apart until it suited them?" said another officer.

"This is what we need to find out," said Inspector Bailey. "Keep talking to the villager's; make sure police presence is seen out and about. Someone knows something, I'm sure."

He then went on to talk about Sheila's death. The post mortem showed she died of smoke inhalation. "At least we have a relative, her sister Jane, to talk to, but they weren't close and she can't throw any light on why someone would want her out of the way. She has been questioned but we have now eliminated her from our enquiries."

He said they would meet up again in a couple of days, hopefully with some updates. "I will report back after speaking to the police in Burford."

"Any news on the bail jumper?" asked an officer.

"Unfortunately, not yet," the Inspector replied. "He was seen in the park yesterday but disappeared. The lady who saw him has made a statement but it hasn't helped us other than confirming he was still in the area yesterday. We have to assume it was him because her description of what he was wearing was identical to what he was wearing when he was seen at the police station the last time, he reported in. We don't know why he scarpered."

"How dangerous is he?" asked an officer.

"He was on bail for possession of a knife," Inspector Bailey replied. "He was due in court a week ago, but didn't report in and has since been on the run."

"Where was he living when he was arrested?"

"No address known. He was picked up in a street about ten miles away from Merrydale. He was bailed to a hostel for the homeless but disappeared."

"Name?" asked an officer.

"Mickey Mouse, he told the arresting officer. He refused to give his real name," the Inspector said with a smile.

The police officers laughed.

"We have no idea why he ended up in Merrydale, but there must be a reason why he's still hanging around. We think it was him that hit a farmer on the head when he surprised him in his yard the other night. We need to catch him as soon as possible," said the Inspector.

"Any more questions?" he asked looking around the room.

No one had any.

"Keep asking around the village and I'll get onto the Burford police."

He left the room and the officers dispersed to return to their various duties.

# Chapter Thirty-Four

The next evening at six o'clock the electrician arrived in his van at Simon's farm. He had just finished the milking and James had left for the day. Jerry was a small man of around forty. He said he remembered doing some electrical work for George about five years ago. He was a cheerful person and liked a good chat. He shook hands with Simon and they wandered into the yard together.

They started chatting about the recent house fire in Merrydale.

Jerry was telling Simon that he was often called in by the fire brigade to assess electrical wiring of any house fire to see if that was the cause.

"Nine times out of ten it is."

"It's been awful here thinking that Sheila's house fire was started deliberately," replied Simon. "The whole village is in shock."

"I bet they are. It certainly looks like it was a deliberate act. Arson's a terrible business and even worse when someone's died because of it," agreed Jerry.

He then related several fires over the years to which he had been called in by the fire brigade to make a report on. "Sometimes, there's so much damage it's almost impossible to find the cause."

Simon pointed out where he thought the sensor lights would be most effective in the yard. "I've got these two barns here and I would be able to see the lights from the house if they came on."

"Don't forget that an animal like a fox would trigger them," said Jerry.

"Yes, I realise that, but I would hopefully spot a person who would not be expecting a sudden light. A fox is quick and would probably run off a lot faster than a person when a light came on," said Simon.

He told him about disturbing an intruder a couple of nights ago and how he was hit on the head before he ran off.

"It was only a small cut to the back of my head but it shook me up a bit."

"You were lucky he didn't do more damage. You read of some awful cases on the news about people being attacked and being left with a lasting injury," said Jerry.

"Yes, I've been told that by someone else!"

Jerry looked at the most appropriate places in the yard for the lights.

"I could easily fix you some up," said Jerry making notes. "I can't come till next week as I've got a big job on at the moment. I'm working on a house having a total rewire which is a bit of a nightmare as it's not proving an easy job, but I hope it should be finished by the end of this week."

"My neighbour, Roger, wants to have some put up in his yard as well," said Simon. "When we've finished here, I'll take you over to his farm. We've both had an intruder lately. It's most likely the chap that's jumped bail who is hanging around the village for some reason."

"Yes, I've heard about him on the news," replied Jerry. "There's a lot going on in your village at the moment!"

"You could say that!" said Simon.

He then told him about Beverley and her untimely death.

"Crikey!" said Jerry. "And I thought nothing much happened in these small villages!"

"Nothing normally does," agreed Simon with a grin.

He then took him over to Roger's farm.

Roger answered the door and shook hands with Jerry. The three of them wandered into the yard.

"Simon's been telling me about recent events in your village," said Jerry.

"Yes, terrible times at the moment." agreed Roger.

Roger pointed out to Jerry where he thought the sensor lights should be installed in the yard.

"No problem. I've explained to Simon that I can't do it till next week though," said Jerry taking notes.

"That's fine. I'm grateful you can do it as soon as that. I know how busy you people are," replied Roger.

Simon told Roger that Jerry had been called in by the fire brigade to assess what caused Sheila's house fire.

"Rum business, that," said Jerry. "It was definitely not down to the wiring so it had to have been deliberately started. Apparently, the lady wasn't a smoker so it wasn't caused by a cigarette either."

He said cheerio to Roger and said he would be in touch with a date and time.

Simon and Jerry walked back to Simon's farm and Jerry went over to his van.

"I'll give you a ring to let you know when I'm coming. I will order the lights for both of you."

He drove off with a toot on the horn and a wave.

Simon went into the house and told Marie what Jerry had said and that he would install the sensor lights next week.

"Good. It will make us feel a bit safer," she replied as she served up their meal. "Now come and eat your dinner, you must be starving."

*I see the police are still about in the village asking questions. I wonder who is saying what? I need to find out who is opening their big mouth. It would be a shame if someone else has to die. I don't want to cause any more harm, but I might have to. I need to be careful though.*

# Chapter Thirty-Five

George decided to call a fundraising committee meeting. He thought they needed to get together and talk over the events that had happened since the fatal Safari Supper.

He rang the four remaining members and invited them around to his house on Wednesday evening at seven thirty next week. They all agreed to the invitation.

It was a fine evening and Celia and Mary walked together to George's house. Simon arrived just after them and Julie a few minutes later.

"Everyone settle down, make yourselves comfortable," he said showing them into his lounge.

"Anne has baked a cake!" he showed them. A large fruit cake sat splendidly on a plate surrounded by five mugs of tea.

He sliced the cake and handed each person a plate and napkin.

"I thought we should all meet up and have a chat," he said passing each person a slice of cake.

"It's a good idea," agreed Mary sipping her tea.

Celia thought they ought to start with a thought about Beverley. "It's a dreadful time for everybody. She will be missed by all of us. She came up with such a good idea of holding the Safari Supper. It's awful thinking about that evening now and how it ended," she said sadly.

All five members held up their mugs of tea. "To Beverley." They were silent for a few minutes with their own thoughts of Beverley.

George coughed and said the Safari Supper had been an excellent idea and hoped she would have been pleased with how much the event had raised.

"£2035 was raised," said George. "It was the most amount we have ever raised since we have been a fundraising committee. Well done, Beverley!"

He said they would have another meeting to decide where the money would be spent. "All have a think about it," he told them.

Simon asked if anyone had heard how the investigation was going.

Celia said she knew the police were still making enquiries. "There's a police car in the village most days. I asked an officer the other day how things were going but all he said was the investigation was still ongoing. I don't suppose he would have told me even if they are getting closer to finding out anything."

Mary asked if they had found any family members yet.

"We just don't know," replied Simon. "If anyone knew it would most likely to have been Sheila. They were quite close and must have talked about relatives."

Julie said, "Do people think the two deaths were connected?"

"I can't think how. One dies from an allergy and another in a fire. Two completely different ways to die," replied Celia with a shudder. She took a sip of her tea.

"The only connection between them is that they were friends," said Mary.

"But even though that's true it's still very strange they both died like they did," said Simon.

"Has anyone met Sheila's sister yet?" asked George.

"Yes, I have," replied Mary. "I saw her coming out of Sheila's house after the fire brigade investigators told her she could go in."

"Did she say what she's been told?" asked Julie.

"Only that they had eliminated her from their enquiries, apparently, its normal to interview family, and that an electrician had been in and reported that he didn't think it was an electrical fault that caused the fire, so they think it was deliberately started."

Simon said he was having some electrical work done on his farm and it was by the electrician who was asked to go in by the fire brigade and report on the wiring and whether it was the cause of the fire. "The electrician said in his view there was nothing wrong with the wiring and did not cause the fire," he said.

"So, if it was started deliberately, then that person is still at large," said George.

"Do you think the bail jumper is involved?" asked Julie.

"Perhaps, it may be just a co incidence that he's about as well. Surely, the police will be looking into whether he had known Sheila," said Simon.

"Going back to Beverley's death," said Julie, "it must be someone who attended the Safari Supper. That's the most awful thought. We might have spoken to them on the evening without knowing their evil intentions. Did we all know the people who bought tickets? Were there any strangers? We all sold the tickets. Do we have any suspicions about anyone who bought a ticket and ended up at Mary's house?"

"I knew all the people who I sold tickets to," replied Celia. "I might not have known them all very well but I had seen them about the village."

"Me, too," said Mary. "I knew nearly all the people who I sold my tickets to."

The others all agreed that no tickets had been sold to complete strangers but all were sold to a villager.

"So it has to be someone we know," said Julie. "It might make it a bit easier if it had been done by a stranger but to think we might be actually seeing or talking to someone who committed murder is terrible."

"It's the same thing with the fire. On the night, loads of villagers were there watching. The arsonist must have been one of the crowd by the look of it if we are ruling strangers out," said George.

Anne entered the room and asked if anyone wanted another cup of tea. They all replied in the affirmative. She collected their mugs and took them out on the tray.

She came back with five fresh mugs of tea and cut some more cake for them.

"Good cake, love," said George taking a large bite.

They all agreed and thanked her for baking it. She smiled and said they were welcome. George asked her to stay but she left the room saying she was trying to get through a load of ironing.

"What happens now then?" asked Celia.

"I suppose we have to leave it to the police but we ought to be kept informed of their enquiries," said George. "But keep your ears and eyes wide open. If it is someone we know, they are bound to slip up sometime."

They all agreed.

Julie reminded them about the table top and jumble sale being held at the school next week. "Any donations are very welcome," she said. "We have had quite a lot given to us so far. The children are really looking forward to it."

"It makes a nice change from English or Maths lessons," said George with a grin. "Anything different on a school day was welcome when I was at school."

"Can you remember that far back?" joked Simon.

"Ha-Ha," replied George with a grin. The others laughed.

The tea and cake were finished and Simon got to his feet. "Must go," he said. "Early morning milking calls. Cows wait for no man!" he grinned.

The others got up as well. They called cheerio to Anne who was ironing in the kitchen, thanking her again for the tea and cake.

George went into the kitchen after seeing his guests out.

"It's so frustrating," he said to Anne. "Everyone wants to know why Sheila and Beverley died and the police aren't telling us anything. I have a good mind to go to where Beverley used to live before coming to Merrydale and asking around myself."

"You just leave it to the police. They won't thank you for interfering in their enquiries," said Anne.

She unplugged the iron and asked him if he wanted a Horlicks before bed. "I'll just put the ironing away and then make us one."

Celia and Mary walked home together. "I just hope they catch whoever has done these awful things soon," said Celia.

"So do I," agreed Mary.

She said goodbye to Celia and walked a bit further down the road to her house.

Simon told Marie about what was discussed at George's. "It has to be someone we know," he said.

Marie agreed and said everyone must be very careful.

Julie also told Julian what was discussed this evening.

"Keep your ears and eyes open and be careful," he told her.

"Don't worry, I will," she promised him.

He hugged her and said he wanted nothing to happen to her as he couldn't bear to be without her.

# Chapter Thirty-Six

Simon had been contacted by Jerry saying he would arrive on Friday morning at nine to install the sensor lights in the yard. He apologised for not coming sooner but the re-wiring job had taken longer than he had anticipated. He asked if he could contact Roger and tell him he could carry out the work for him after installing Simon's lights. Roger had told Simon that would be fine.

Jerry arrived on time. Simon introduced him to Marie who offered him a cup of tea or coffee.

"Always tea for me, thanks. Good and strong with two sugars!" he answered with a grin.

He drank his tea and then went out to his van which he had driven into the yard.

"Do you need any help?" asked Simon.

"No, I'm fine thanks but I'll give you a shout if I do!" Jerry replied. He confirmed with Simon where the lights would be going.

He whistled as he got his equipment and ladder out of his van.

Simon left him to it and went off to find Stan who was mending some fencing in one of the fields.

He'd told Stan about the lights going up so he could be alerted if anyone came into the yard when it was dark. "Good idea," he replied. "I wish they could catch this man who's on the run."

"So do I. I haven't heard any more news reports about him so I assume he's still on the loose," said Simon.

They worked well together and soon made the fence secure. Some of the cows had wandered over to them to see what they were doing. Cows are inquisitive creatures at the best of times and anything different going on in their daily routine was cause for investigation!

It took a couple of hours before Jerry was finished. He accepted another cup of tea from Marie who came out to see him after an hour. He told her he would be working at Sheila's house the following week.

"It's just so dreadful. The village is still in shock," she told him. She left him to his work.

An hour later, Simon arrived back from his field to find Jerry just finishing the job.

Jerry showed Simon the lights and said he hoped they did the job. Simon said he hoped so, too.

"Any more news on the village happenings?" asked Jerry.

"I haven't heard any more this week. The police are not in the village as much now so it's assumed they've finished speaking with the villagers," said Simon.

"I've been contracted to repair the damaged wiring in the lady's house that died. Although the wiring wasn't to blame there's still damage that needs fixing. I start there on Monday," said Jerry putting his ladder and equipment inside his van.

He told Simon he would send him an invoice in the next few days.

Jerry said cheerio, thanks for the work and drove off to Roger's farm.

Roger greeted him and Jerry confirmed with him where the lights would be going to be installed in his farm yard.

He declined Roger's offer of help and spent the next couple of hours installing the sensor lights.

Jerry completed the job to Roger's satisfaction and said he would send the invoice in the next few days.

He whistled as he stacked his work tools and ladder in his van. He drove off with a wave.

Roger looked up at the newly installed lights. *That'll put you buggers off dossing down in my barn,* he thought to himself with a grin. He went and told Fay the lights were installed.

"Good," she replied. "I expect you'll be looking out when it's dark hoping to see something so you can run them off!"

"Actually I don't really want to see anything!" he replied with a grin.

"Waste of money then," she replied.

"Not if I catch an intruder," he replied laughing.

He rang Simon to thank him for sorting an electrician out and they agreed Jerry had done a good job for a good price.

"Let me know if you spot anything," said Simon. "And I'll do the same!"

# Chapter Thirty-Seven

The following Tuesday morning saw the tables being set up for the table top and jumble sale in the school hall. The bags of donated items were being sorted onto the appropriate tables.

Some lessons were still being delivered for the first part of the morning but the eldest children were being allowed to set up their stalls.

There were six clothes tables and five white elephant stalls.

"Why is it called a white elephant stall?" asked Freddie putting things from a box onto the table. Julie was overseeing things on a nearby table and answered Freddie.

She replied, "The phrase originated from Thailand where the King gave rare albino elephants to people who had displeased the King. The cost of keeping these elephants were very high and the people who had been given the white elephants might be ruined financially."

"But why do selling toys here be called white elephants?" he insisted.

"I will find out and let you know," sighed Julie.

Freddie and his friends continued laying their stalls out. There was a lot to sell. Each toy was examined by the children and some items were put under the table so they could be taken home without being offered for sale.

Freddie spotted a magnifying glass. He showed it to Freya who was helping him lay his table out.

"I need this for my police investigations," he told her.

He put it underneath the table, so he couldn't show it for someone else to buy, and he would be able to take it home later.

"I'll put ten pence in the pot," he told her.

Teachers who were allocated to certain stalls were also busy laying out their wares. All the clothes had been examined beforehand and were in a sellable condition.

The sale started at ten o'clock. Coffee and tea were going to be sold and tables and chairs had been set up in the hall. The water boiler was switched on and cups and saucers ready for filling.

It was a slow start but by eleven o'clock there were plenty of customers. Mothers arrived with their younger children who made a bee line for the toy stalls. Items were being sold for a small price and children were soon clutching their bargains. Mary and Lorna arrived together and started browsing.

Quite a few retired villagers were happily looking at items for sale on the tables.

The clothes stalls were doing well. A lot of children's clothes were in good condition but no longer fitted the original offspring. Adult clothes were also selling well.

Celia arrived at the school towards the end of the morning after picking up her two younger daughters from nursery. She waved at Freya and Freddie behind their stall. She saw Julie behind her stall talking to her sister Heather and went over to speak with them. Sarah arrived at the same time. She waved at Freddie. Max ran over to Freddie's stall.

"How are you doing?" Celia asked Julie as she started sorting through what was left on the table.

"Very well indeed. It's amazing how much is being sold," replied Julie.

Celia spotted a pink sparkly jumper that she thought would fit Freya. She held it up catching Freya's eye.

Freya made a grimace with two fingers in her mouth so Celia put it back down on the table. Sarah rummaged through some clothes and bought a couple of T-shirts.

Celia and her two daughters went over to Freddie and Freya's stall.

"How are you doing, are you selling much?" she asked them.

The girls started rummaging through the items for sale.

"Good," Freya replied. "We've made a lot of money," and showed her the money pot.

Celia congratulated them and said well done. She handed some coins to the younger girls. One chose the ugly dog ornament and the other chose a jigsaw. They dropped the money into Freya's hand.

Freddie ducked under the table and retrieved the magnifying glass.

"Look, I've got this for my police investigations into Beverley and Sheila," he told Celia.

Sarah wandered over with her younger son Max and heard what Freddie was saying.

"Freddie, what have I told you. Leave the investigation to the police. You are only ten years old!"

"But I want to find out who did it to them," he replied.

"Now I have a magnifying glass I can look for clues." He looked up at his mum peering at her through the magnifying glass.

Freya giggled as did Max and the girls. Max asked his mum for some money as he wanted to buy something from his brother's stall. He took a soft toy off the table and gave Freddie ten pence which went into the money pot.

Simon and Marie arrived at the school hall and saw Frances. She was talking to George and Anne who had just had a coffee and were now looking at the various stalls.

"A good crowd as usual," said Simon to the headmaster who was standing behind a clothes stall.

"Yes, we've had a really good turnout," he replied. He received some money from Julie's sister, Heather, who had purchased a blouse.

Mary and Lorna were going over to the refreshment tables but stopped to say hello to Celia and Sarah standing at Freddie and Frey's stall. Mary had a carrier bag with her, and showed Sarah a blue jumper she had bought from one of the stalls. Lorna bought a colourful paperweight from Freya for twenty pence. Freddie was peering around the room through his magnifying glass. Lorna laughed and asked what he was doing.

"I'm looking for clues," he grinned.

"He's practising being a policeman," laughed Freya.

"I'm looking to see who looks like a murderer," said Freddie.

"Stop it!" reprimanded Sarah. "I shall take it away from you if you carry on saying things like that."

Freddie quickly put the magnifying glass under the table. Freya grinned at him.

Mary and Lorna went over to the refreshments and ordered two teas.

"Freddie's a real little character, isn't he?" said Lorna as they took their teas over to an empty table and sat down.

"He certainly is!" replied Mary.

Frances and Anne came over and asked if they could sit with them. They pulled up two chairs and Anne sat down. Frances went to collect tea for them both.

"How are you, Mary?" Anne asked when Frances returned with their drinks.

"Well, just like the rest of us, I'm finding it difficult to comprehend what's happened. Also I keep seeing the image of Beverley on my kitchen floor," Mary replied with a shudder.

"George is frustrated at how little we are being told. He thinks something should have been found out by now. The village doesn't feel a very safe place to be living in at the moment," said Anne. "He's even talking of going to where Beverley used to live to start making his own enquiries."

"Really?" said Lorna. "I should think the police have already been looking there to find out if Beverley had any family."

"They probably have, but we're still no closer to finding anything out," replied Anne. "I've told him to leave it to the police."

Lorna asked if any more had been found out about the house fire.

"Nothing as far as I know," said Anne sipping her tea. "Again, George wants to find out what really happened that night and if the two deaths are connected."

Simon and Marie wandered over to the table with cups of tea.

They pulled up two chairs and sat down placing their cups on the table.

"I don't suppose you've any updates on the deaths, have you?" Lorna asked them. "We're just talking about them."

"No, we've haven't heard anything," replied Simon.

George came over and told Anne he'd had a phone call and that he needed to go into work to sort something out.

"I'm just telling them that you want to go over to where Beverley used to live but I've said to leave it to the police," said Anne.

"Well, I think the police are being slow in finding things out. They haven't even caught the absconder yet. It might need us to try and solve things for them," replied George.

"We are not the police so we should keep out and let them do their job," said Lorna. "It might be dangerous if any of us interfere."

Mary and Marie agreed with Lorna and Anne.

"Be careful," he was warned.

They finished their drinks and got up. The hall was now emptying of people and the teachers and children were starting to pack up the unsold items.

"We'll drop them into a charity shop," said the headmaster when Anne asked what would happen to them.

"My brother Ned's partner, Wendy, works in a Heart Foundation charity shop in Olehampton. If the things can be delivered to my house I can take them to her," said Mary.

"Thank you that would be great," replied the headmaster. "I'll get Stuart to drop them in to you later this afternoon if that's ok?"

"I'll make sure I'm in," said Mary. "I'm glad to help. I will ring Ned up this evening and organise when I can take them over to the shop."

"That's good of you, Mary," said Lorna laying a hand on Marys.

"No problem at all, it will give me something to do," replied Mary. "Come with me if you want to. Wendy's really nice. I can introduce you to her."

"I will. Thank you," beamed Lorna.

They all left the school hall and went their separate ways. George told Anne he was nipping into work for a couple of hours. Mary said she had some shopping to do and Marie and Simon went home for lunch and then Marie went shopping at Tesco's as she always did on a Tuesday afternoon.

# Chapter Thirty-Eight

There had been no unusual activity in either Simon or Roger's yards since the sensor lights had been installed.

Marie laughed each evening when Simon stood behind the curtains and peered out of the window. "Are you actually wanting to see something or someone?" she asked, grinning.

"I'm not sure if I do or not! The only two times the lights have come on is when an animal must have passed by. Most likely a fox. No sign of a person lurking. Roger says the same!"

"Perhaps the police have caught that man and we've not yet been told," said Marie.

"I think it would have been on the news if he'd been caught," replied Simon.

They were watching the local news on Tuesday evening when the presenter mentioned the absconder for the first time for well over a week.

The reporter said that the police were now confident he would soon be caught as another sighting of him, informed them he was still in the area. He was bound to be found before too long as everyone was on the lookout for him.

He had now been named as Jarvis Shelby. He apparently had been living in Haleton near Burford town but had not been seen around for at least three months prior to his arrest and being bailed.

The public were again warned not to approach him as he could be dangerous.

"I can't believe they don't tell us what he was originally arrested for!" cried Simon.

"Well I just hope he doesn't come on our land again," said Marie.

The reporter then showed a photograph of the missing man. He was thirty with stubble and short dark hair. The photo was taken when he was arrested so it was up to date.

"At least we know what he looks like now," said Simon. He got up to make a drink, asking Marie if she wanted one.

"Tea, please," she answered. Simon went into the kitchen and switched the kettle on.

"Haleton," murmured Anne. "Simon!" she called to him. "They said he's from Haleton! That's where Beverley came from before coming to Merrydale!"

Simon hurried back into the room. "That can't be a coincidence surely!"

"There must be some connection between the two of them. Do you think he was responsible for her death?" said Marie.

The news report had finished. The weather forecaster was gesticulating over the map of the United Kingdom. Normally Simon was interested in the forecast but tonight he was distracted.

He went back into the kitchen and returned with their mugs of tea.

"He can't be responsible for Beverley's death as he was not at Marys or the Safari Supper so it had to have been someone there on the night," he said to Marie.

"You're right," she said. "He couldn't have done it but surely there must be a connection between the two of them."

"I'm sure the police will know that Haleton is where the connection between the two of them is."

Simon said. "I wonder whether George has watched the news this evening."

"It's too late to talk to him now but give him a ring in the morning," advised Marie as she finished her tea.

"I certainly will," said Simon. He took their cups into the kitchen.

"Come on, it's time for bed," he said switching off the television.

He peered behind the curtains but the yard remained in darkness. Marie grinned and told him to come away.

Earlier that evening, Mary had rung Ned up and asked him about dropping the unsold jumble sale items off at Wendy's charity shop when it was convenient. Wendy was there at Ned's so she spoke with Mary.

"I'm there tomorrow so any time is convenient," Wendy said. "That's great, we are always grateful for donations."

"The clothes are in a good condition because they all get sorted and examined prior to the school sale and the miscellaneous items are in a good condition and fine for selling," replied Mary.

Stuart had dropped them off at Marys late afternoon and had very kindly stacked them in her car. It was helpful because there were several boxes and bags and they only just fitted in on the back seat and boot of the car. Mary drove a blue Honda Civic so there wasn't a lot of room.

It was arranged that Mary would drop them off at the charity shop early tomorrow afternoon.

Ned asked her how much had been raised from the Safari Supper. "Just over £2000," Mary told him.

"That's great," he replied. He then asked her how she was coping in the aftermath of Beverley's death.

"It's getting easier," she told him. "I can now enter the kitchen and not look down at the floor as soon as I go in."

"It must have been awful for you and everyone who was there. Have the police found out who did it?"

"No, the investigation is still going on," she said.

"Is there any news on the fire?" he asked.

"Again, the police haven't told us anything yet," Mary replied.

They ran off with Mary saying she would see Wendy at two o'clock. Mary went into the kitchen and made herself a cup of tea. She kept her head up and did not look down at the floor.

She took the tea and phone with her into the lounge and sat on the settee.

Mary rang Lorna to tell her about going to the charity shop tomorrow.

"Shall we have lunch out?" asked Lorna.

"That will be nice, there some nice pubs in the town," said Mary. "I'll pick you up at eleven so we can have a look around a few shops first."

"Good. See you tomorrow then," said Lorna.

Ebony jumped up onto Mary's lap.

"Is it tea time?" asked Mary, stroking the cat who started purring loudly.

She got up with Ebony following her into the kitchen. Ebony was quite a fussy eater and Mary only bought her expensive meaty pouch food rather than cheaper tinned food. Ebony soon ate it with obvious enjoyment and then disappeared through the cat flap into the garden.

"Now, what shall I have for my tea?" she said to herself.

She opened her fridge and saw some ham, lettuce and tomatoes so prepared herself a nice salad. She boiled an egg and scraped a few new potatoes and put them in a pan to boil. She went into the lounge and switched the television on to watch while she waited for the potatoes to cook.

When it was ready, she took it into the lounge and ate it off a tray watching The Chase with Bradley Walsh.

She heard Ebony returning through the cat flap, who then strolled into the lounge and jumped up onto the settee by Mary. Mary stroked him.

"It's just me and you, isn't it?"

She smiled at her cat who soon settled down for a sleep beside her.

# Chapter Thirty-Nine

The next morning Simon rang George to see whether he had seen last night's news.

"I certainly did," replied George. "Both Anne and I immediately recognised Haleton as being the possible connection between Beverley and the bail jumper. At least they've named him now and shown his mug shot."

"It's got to be a connection. It's too much of a coincidence not to be linked," said Simon.

"I agree," said George. "The police must know and surely are linking the two."

"They would be daft not to," replied Simon.

"I would really like to go there and ask around the village about both of them," said George.

"If you do go, I'm happy to come along with you."

"That would be good. When's a good day for you? I can do any day," said George.

"Let's say Friday, shall we? I've got another couple of fences to repair with Stan today and tomorrow. Daft cows keep butting against them."

It was arranged that George would pick Simon up at ten o'clock on Friday morning.

Simon told Marie what the plan was.

"You be careful," she warned him. "Don't go getting yourselves into any trouble."

"What sort of trouble can we get into?" enquired Simon.

"I don't know, but just be careful, that's all I'm saying," she replied.

Anne was also having the same conversation with George.

"Don't get yourselves into trouble. The police are investigating and won't want you two amateur detectives butting in."

"We'll be very careful and discreet in our enquiries!" grinned George.

"A couple of PC Plods more like," she retorted.

Freddie was having a whale of a time with his magnifying glass. "I feel like a real detective," he told Freya on their way to school.

"How come?" she asked.

"Well, Mum dropped a needle when she was sewing up a hole in my school jumper last evening. She dropped it on the carpet and couldn't find it. She told me and Max not to go without our slippers in case we trod on it. I got my magnifying glass out and found it!"

"Well done!" said Freya "I bet she was pleased you found it."

"Yes, she was very pleased that I found the needle, but still told me not to keep going on about finding anything out about Beverley and Sheila. She's worried that the murderer might get me!"

"I hope they don't get you. I would miss you if they murdered you, and I bet Max would be upset as well," said Freya with a worried look.

"Don't you worry! No one's going to murder me," replied Freddie laughing. "I am a great detective and will find out who the murderer is!"

"It would be really good if you can find out who the murderer is. You might even go to Buckingham Palace and get a medal from the Queen," said Freya. "Can I come with you if that happens?"

"I expect Mum and Dad and Max will want to come with me. But I'll tell you all about it and what the Queen says to me when she gives me the medal," replied Freddie.

They chatted some more and arrived at the school gates. They said goodbye to their mums and siblings and went into the school.

It was an assembly day and the headmaster was holding audience.

After the first hymn, he told them how pleased he was with how the table top and jumble sale went on Tuesday.

"We made just over £400. Thank you all very much for giving items to sell and buying things in return. The money will be invested in the school."

Freddie stuck his hand up to the amusement of the other children.

"Yes Freddie?" he asked.

"I didn't sell any white elephants on my stall so why was it called a white elephant stall?"

"We will organise a lesson on why we say things which do not make a lot of sense. There are many sayings and proverbs which originate from long ago which we use today," the head master replied.

He concluded assembly with a rousing hymn.

Julie shepherded her children into her classroom.

Freddie and Freya went to their seats. He started telling Charlie about finding his mums needle with his magnifying glass last night when Julie clapped her hands to shush the children.

"It's a geography lesson now. We are going to talk about Spain," she said.

The children groaned.

Freddie raised his hand.

"Why do we need to know about other countries when we live in England?" he asked.

"You might go on holiday to a foreign country like Spain and would want to know all about that country," she explained.

"I'd rather know about England and where we live, especially now we have a dangerous murderer about," replied Freddie.

The children sniggered. They could always rely on Freddie to make the lessons more interesting!

Julie held up her hand to shush the class and told Freddie to hush up and listen.

"I've been on holiday to Spain," said Charlie holding up his hand.

"I've been to Spain as well," said Gareth from the back of the class.

"Good. You can both tell us what you thought of Spain then."

The lesson continued without further comments from Freddie. He didn't want to know anything about Spain, so left it to Charlie and Gareth to contribute to the lesson.

He spent most of the lesson thinking about ways to catch the murderer. He needed to run a few ideas by Freya. He caught her eye and made a circle over his right eye with his fore finger and thumb. She did the same back with a grin.

# Chapter Forty

Wednesday morning, Mary pulled up outside Lorna's house at eleven o'clock. Lorna was ready and had been looking out of the window for Mary to arrive.

She locked the front door and made her way to the car.

"Morning!" she greeted Mary as she got into the front passenger seat.

"Goodness!" she exclaimed as she saw the back seat was full of boxes and bags.

"The boots full up as well," Mary told her.

Mary drove off after Lorna put her seat belt on. It was a lovely day again.

It was nice drive over to Olehampton, it took around thirty minutes. Mary enjoyed driving and was a safe and careful driver. They admired some of the gardens that they passed by.

Wendy had told Mary where the charity shop was situated in the town. She found a nearby car park and purchased a ticket that she placed on the dashboard. Lorna got out with a stretch.

"Let's have a wander around the shops and see where we can have lunch," suggested Mary locking the car.

The main street of the town held many interesting shops but they saw some were shut down and boarded up.

Lorna said it was a shame that some shops were closing down but she had heard the cost of renting them were too high for some businesses. "If the cost was lowered, and shops remained open, then surely, it would make more sense as it would bring more money into the town."

Mary agreed with her. They went into a card shop as Lorna needed a retirement card for a friend.

Mary browsed through the cards picking some up and then putting them back on the rack. She then picked up a birthday card and a couple of spare ones as she knew it was Marie's birthday in a couple of weeks. She liked to have some spare ones in as well. She found an appropriate card for Marie and paid for it and the others at the till. Lorna took a while choosing a card and went to the till.

"I'll wait outside for you," said Mary turning away from the counter.

Outside the shop they looked in the window of a nearby clothes shop. Lorna admired a light green summer jacket and so they went in to see if they had one in her size. The shop assistant said they had and collected it from a rail.

Mary sat on a chair while Lorna tried it on. She gave Mary a twirl which made her laugh.

"I'll take this," she said and went to pay for it.

She asked the assistant if she knew of a good pub to have lunch.

"The Feathers at the top of the High Street is good. I went there a couple of weeks ago with a friend and we had a really nice meal," she said as she gave Lorna her receipt.

She handed the jacket to her and Lorna put it in a carrier bag which she pulled out of her handbag.

Mary and Lorna left the shop and made their way up the High Street. They saw The Feathers pub and went inside. It looked clean and welcoming. There were a few people in there already.

They went up to the bar and Mary asked Lorna what she wanted to drink.

"Just a lemonade, please," Mary replied. There was a young lad who looked about twenty serving and he poured two lemonades. Lorna paid for them.

They collected a menu from the bar and found a table.

Mary decided on vegetable lasagne and chips and Lorna said she would have fish and chips. Mary went up to the bar to order the meals.

They only had to wait ten minutes for the meals to arrive. The young lad brought them over to the table. He gave them cutlery and napkins and a basket of condiments.

"Are you having a day out?" he asked them.

"Yes, we are," replied Mary. "We are delivering some items to a friend's charity shop and thought we'd make a day of it!"

"Which charity shop is that?" he asked.

"The Heart Foundation," replied Lorna.

"That's just a bit further up the street from here," he told them pointing over his shoulder.

"We had a school jumble sale yesterday and things were left over," said Mary.

"Which school was that?" he asked.

"Merrydale village school," said Lorna as she opened her napkin and laid cutlery on the table.

"I've heard of Merrydale. That's where that house fire was and someone died isn't it? I heard it on the news and saw something on my phone. Did you know the person who died?"

"Yes," said Mary. "We did know her. It was a tragedy."

She sprinkled salt on her chips.

"The police think it was deliberate, don't they?" the lad said.

"They're still looking into the cause," said Lorna eating a chip.

"You be careful if the fire was started deliberately and the person's still at large. I'll leave you to eat up. Hope you enjoy it," he said as he returned to the bar.

"We can't get away from it even fifteen miles away!" said Lorna.

"Well, I suppose it's fodder for gossip," replied Mary, eating a forkful of lasagne. "This is very good lasagne," she commented. "How's your fish?"

"It's tasty. Its real fish and not constituted," said Lorna with obvious enjoyment.

They finished their meals and ordered two teas. Mary said she would pay the bill and went up to the bar offering her debit card to the young lad. He brought the card machine over and Mary paid.

"You both be careful," he repeated as he gave Mary the receipt. "Until the police arrest someone no one's safe," he said with a shudder. "It must be awful to die in a fire. I hope she didn't know anything about it."

"We all hope so, too," replied Mary putting her card and receipt away in her purse. "Thanks for the meals, we really enjoyed them."

There were a few more customers arriving through the door and were wandering over to the bar so the lad started asking for their orders. Lorna came over and they both left the pub.

"We must remember that place," said Lorna.

"Yes," agreed Mary. "It was very good."

They went to the car park and got in the car. Wendy had told Mary that there was a small parking area at the rear of the charity shop. She drove out of the car park and turned down a road which would lead them around to the charity shop.

They parked up in the back of the shop. It was just gone two o'clock.

They got out and went around to the shop entrance. Mary saw Wendy behind the counter serving a lady. She looked up when she heard the door open and raised a hand in greeting.

Mary and Lorna went over to her and waited for her to be free.

Mary introduced Lorna to her and they shook hands.

"There a lad in the back room sorting stuff out who can come and collect the things from your car," she told Mary.

"Will!" she called through a door behind the counter.

A young lad came out of the door.

"Yes?" he asked.

He looked about seventeen and had a bad case of acne. He had his fair hair tied up in a top knot on top of his head.

"Can you unload a car out the back? These are friends of mine dropping donations off."

Mary said she would come around and open the car. Lorna said she would have a wander around the shop.

"Might find some bargains," she grinned.

Mary went through the door behind the counter and opened the car for Will. He said to leave it to him and he would unload everything. She said the boot was full as well as the back seat. She left the keys with him to lock up when everything was out.

Mary went back into the shop and had a wander around the shop herself. She picked up a small footstool. She showed it to Lorna.

"This is nice," as she looked at the tartan plaid velour material.

Lorna agreed it was nice and asked how much it was.

"Only five pounds," said Mary reading the ticket. "I'll have it."

Lorna found a white elephant ornament which was three pounds.

"Elephants are good luck as long as they face a doorway or window in the house. I know just the place in my lounge where I can put it," she told Mary.

They took their finds over to Wendy who rung up the sales.

"I'm always picking things up and taking them home or over to Ned's house!" she grinned.

Will came back through the back door and told them he'd unloaded everything. He handed Mary her car keys.

Wendy asked if they would like a cup of tea but Mary and Lorna declined. Mary told her about having lunch at the Feathers in the High Street.

"I must tell Ned and we'll try it out one evening," she replied.

Wendy asked if there were any updates on the deaths in Merrydale.

"Not yet," replied Mary. "The police are still investigating."

"It's really dreadful, it must be awful for you living there and perhaps even knowing the person who killed them. I hear the person who jumped bail is still on the run as well. Gosh, it's all happening in your village, isn't it? You must be very careful."

Mary and Lorna agreed and said people were indeed being very careful.

They said goodbye and went through the back door to the car park. Mary unlocked the car and they put their purchases on the back seat.

Mary manoeuvred the car out of the small car park.

"The car feels a bit lighter now!" she said to Lorna.

Half an hour later, Mary dropped Lorna off at her house.

"Thanks for a nice day. See you soon," said Lorna getting out of the car holding her bag containing the jacket, card and elephant. "Next time, lunch is on me."

Mary drove away with a wave.

# Chapter Forty-One

Celia, Sarah, and their children were walking home after school. They passed Sheila's house in silence glancing at the sprays of dead flowers.

Freya's sisters were chattering with Max. For once, Celia's youngest daughter, Susie, was walking and not sitting in the pushchair.

"She's got to learn to do without it. She can't be taken to primary school in it!" Celia was telling Sarah.

"Freddie was always eager to walk and not want to sit in his pushchair," Sarah said remembering with a smile. "The only time he's still is when he's asleep!"

Mary's car came up the road. She had just dropped Lorna off after taking the donated items to the charity shop. She pulled up on the side of the road and got out to say hello to Celia and Sarah. She told them that she'd been to Olehampton with Lorna, dropping the school's unsold jumble items to a charity shop and they had enjoyed a nice pub lunch. She bent down to the children and smiled at them saying hello. They said hello back but quite shyly.

Freddie and Freya were walking together behind their mothers. They stopped when they came to Sheila's house. Freddie rummaged through his small back pack and got out his magnifying glass.

The flowers placed against the wall of the house were now dead and wilted. "Someone should take them away," said Freya. "They look horrible."

She looked at Freddie.

"They're dead just like Sheila. She got taken away when she was dead," he told her. He went up to the gate.

"What are you doing?" she asked him after looking at a couple of cards attached to the flowers.

He was bending down just inside the gate, looking onto the small path that led to the front door peering at something through his magnifying glass. "Looking for clues," he told her.

"Have you found any?" she asked looking to where he was spying.

"Not yet, but I've only just started looking," he told her, edging up the path.

"Freya, come here!" shouted Sarah when she turned around and saw Freya and Freddie were not immediately behind them.

Celia and Mary both turned around when they heard Sarah shout for Freya.

"Freddie, you come here now as well," called Celia.

"Come on, Freddie, we've got to go," said Freya.

They ran up the path to where their families and Mary were waiting.

"What were you doing at Sheila's house?" asked Celia.

"Freddie was looking for clues with his magnifying glass. He's investigating how Sheila died," Freya replied.

"And did you find any clues?" asked Mary with a smile.

"Not yet, but I've only just started looking," he told her with a grin peering at her through the magnifying glass.

"Freddie, how many times have I told you! Please talk and think about something else!" cried Sarah.

She shrugged and looked at Celia and Mary.

"I shall be glad when the police find out who did it so Freddie can go back to doing normal things that ten-year-olds do!" she told them.

"We shall all be pleased to get back to normal," agreed Mary.

She said goodbye, got into her car and drove up to the end of the road to her house. Ebony met her as she got out of the car, taking the footstool and birthday card from the back seat, then locked it and walked to the front door. Mary picked her cat up and went inside.

# Chapter Forty-Two

Friday morning arrived. It was warm but a bit drizzly and there were showers forecast for later in the day.

Grey puffy clouds were moving slowly across the sky promising the showers.

George put his cap on. He was remembering Anne's words of advice. "You be very careful. Don't go opening a can of worms. It is the police force who do the investigating, not a business man and farmer!"

He kissed her goodbye and assured her they would be very careful. "See you, later."

He drove to Simon's farm. He got out of the car and saw Stan in the yard sweeping up. "Hello Stan, how are you doing?"

"Not so bad, thanks," he replied. He looked up at the sky. "Rain's forecast for later, so I'm getting the outside jobs done before it comes."

Simon came out of the farm house. He too had a cap on.

Marie was having some friends around for a coffee morning and the kitchen smelt of a cake baking in the oven.

She had been telling him to be careful as well. He assured her they would be very careful.

He greeted George and said cheerio to Stan. "If it rains, then go home early."

"Ok boss!" replied Stan with a salute and a grin.

"Don't know how I'll manage without Stan," he told George as the car pulled out of the yard.

"He's so reliable and can turn his hand to most things. It will be a very sad day when he tells me he's retiring."

"Let's hope it's not for a while yet," said George.

"Marie's been bending my ear about this trip!" Simon said.

"Anne has too!" replied George.

They drove out of the village. George wasn't keen on using the sat nav he told Simon.

"I follow my nose and instincts," he grinned. "It usually leads me to where I want to go!"

Haleton was about fifty miles away. There was a motorway which would take them there probably a bit more quickly than driving through the countryside but they both agreed that the country route was a nicer drive.

"So where do we start when we get there?" asked Simon.

"Let's start at the shop, if there is one in Haleton. There's normally a village shopkeeper ready to gossip and then we can go to the pub if there's one. You know what villages are like now, half the shops and pubs are closing," said George.

"Yes, it's a real shame. I'm glad ours are still going strong," replied Simon.

They were driving along pretty countryside. George drove well and Simon was enjoying being driven as he could see more rather than concentrating on the road ahead. He was interested in seeing the livestock in the fields and spotting farms. It was still drizzling a bit and George needed his intermittent wipers on to clear the windscreen.

He came to a sign post advertising that Burford was five miles away. "We need to avoid Burford town if we can. Can you see a sign for Haleton?"

"There's not one on this sign post. Carry on this road a bit further and see if there's one further down," replied Simon.

George drove further down the country road. They came to another junction. This time a sign pointed to Haleton.

"Bingo!" said George as he turned left.

The sign welcomed them to Haleton asking them to drive carefully through the village.

George pulled up in what he thought was the main street.

He turned off the engine and looked around. Most of the houses were set back from the road with garages and driveways. The houses and gardens looked well kept. He saw a couple of women pushing pushchairs and an elderly man walking a dog. It had stopped drizzling now.

"I can't see a shop, can you?" he asked Simon.

Simon couldn't either and suggested they ask one of the people they had seen.

George started the car and slowly drove ahead. He pulled up towards the end of the road alongside the man with his dog.

Simon wound down his window. The man stopped walking and looked at him with a questioning look on his face.

"Excuse me," said Simon. "Is there a shop here?"

"Yes," the man replied. He wound the lead around his hand to shorten the dogs lead a bit as the dog was pulling and wanted to carry on walking ahead. "It's left around the corner from here," pointing to the end of the road. "It's not a big shop, it's not a supermarket, but it sells quite a bit of stuff."

Simon thanked him and wound the window up. The man lengthened the lead again so the dog could carry on with their walk.

George turned left at the end of the road and they saw the shop. It was a Co-op store.

The two women with pushchairs were about to enter through the automatic opening doors.

George parked up and they got out of the car. He locked it and looked at his watch. It was twelve fifteen.

"Let's go in and buy something and see who we can chat to," George suggested.

They went through the doors and Simon grabbed a basket. "What shall we buy?" murmured Simon.

"I don't know, just grab anything!" George replied with a grin.

It was a small shop but appeared to be well stocked. Simon took a washing up brush off a shelf and put it in the basket. George raised his eyebrows when he saw what Simon had put in the basket.

"Marie was only saying the other day she needed a new one of these!" he said grinning.

"You sure know how to please a lady," said George laughing.

They wandered around the shop. George put a loaf of bread in the basket and a packet of chocolate digestive biscuits. Simon added a bottle of orange squash.

"I think that's enough," said George.

The two women were pushing their offspring around the store. Their baskets were much fuller than the men's.

They went to the counter where a lady of about forty was stacking some sweets in a rack by the till.

She looked up at them as they took their items out of the basket. She returned to behind the counter and scanned their shopping.

"That's four pounds fifty-five pence please. Do you want to buy a carrier bag?"

"Yes, please," answered Simon as he handed the money over.

The assistant put their items in a carrier bag. "There's an extra twenty pence for the bag please."

Simon handed another twenty pence over. George asked the assistant if she lived in Haleton.

"No. I live in Burford," she replied. "Why?" she asked.

"We are trying to find out if an ex-colleague still lives here. We have lost touch over the years and as we are passing through, we thought it would be nice to see her," explained Simon.

"What's her name?" asked the assistant.

"Beverley King," said George.

"Never heard of her," the assistant replied. "I've only worked here for three months so I don't know everybody."

"I have heard of a Beverley but her name was Kingston not King," said a voice behind the men.

They turned around and saw one of the women with a pushchair.

"Does she still live here?" asked George innocently.

"Not likely, after what she did," said the woman shushing her child who was whimpering.

"Sharon!" she called to the other lady with a pushchair who was making her way to the counter to pay for her basket of shopping.

"These people want to know if that nurse Beverley Kingston still lives here," she told her.

"She doesn't live here anymore, thank goodness. She was more or less run out of the village after what she did," replied the second woman.

"Why, what did she do?" asked George.

"She killed a young boy, that's what she did!"

"What?" said Simon.

Simon had heard the story from George after he had spoken with the fellow councillor a few weeks ago but he wasn't going to let the women know this.

"But what happened? How did she kill him?" asked George.

"She was a community nurse here and misdiagnosed meningitis. She told the parents it was just a cold and not to bother seeing a doctor. That night the poor little kid died. The parents were distraught and they split up not long afterwards," said the first lady.

"And that's not all! She was married and her husband killed himself as he couldn't stand the shame," said the second lady.

"And don't forget it was the husband's dad that found him dead and he went mad with grief," the first lady said.

Her child was trying to climb out of his pushchair and started crying as the safety belt wouldn't let him out. She stroked his head and said she would get him home soon for his dinner.

"Wow," said George. "That's a lot to take in."

"Did she have any other relatives?" asked Simon.

"I think she had a cousin but he doesn't live here in the village. I'm not sure where he lives."

"What about her husband's family. Do they live here in the village?" asked George.

"No, they don't live here. I think her husband had a sister and a brother but I'm not sure where they lived," was the reply.

The assistant scanned the two women's shopping. They each paid and went towards the door to leave.

The first lady turned around and told Simon and George not to bother to try and find Beverley as she didn't deserve any friends after what she did. "I hope she's not a nurse anymore."

Simon and George left the shop and got in the car. They put the shopping on the back seat.

"So, we got some answers," said George.

"Yes, but we knew most of the story anyway. We need to try and find out where any family lives," said Simon.

"Let's find the pub, if there is one. Someone there might know where the family lives," replied George.

He started the car up and drove along the road.

"There's a pub!" Simon pointed out.

On the right-hand side of the road, The Crown stood amongst a row of cottages. George pulled into the car park. There were only another couple of cars in there.

"It doesn't look very busy. Let's hope there's a chatty landlord," commented Simon.

They entered the pub.

# Chapter Forty-Three

Marie had invited a few friends around for morning coffee and cake. She liked entertaining and enjoyed making cakes. She had baked a large coffee cake and had decorated it with walnuts on top.

She placed it on a cake stand in the middle of her kitchen table.

She had invited nine friends around this morning. She held it in a morning so friends with school children could attend.

The first guests to arrive at ten thirty were Celia and Sarah. Their youngest children were at nursery until twelve o'clock so they had an hour or so free before collecting them.

Frances, Lorna and Anne arrived just after them and then Mary arrived. Julie's sister Heather arrived five minutes later with Kerry. Kerry had a couple of days off work and so had been able to accept Marie's invitation.

Fay arrived at eleven apologising for being a bit late.

"No problem, come in," said Marie.

She made them all coffee or tea after asking their preferences. She was hosting the morning in her kitchen as the large kitchen table could accommodate them all comfortably.

The cake had been sliced and plates and napkins were handed out.

Everyone knew each other so there was lots of chat going on.

"Has Simon had any late-night lights coming on?" Fay asked Marie.

Marie laughed and said, "No, there have been only a couple of times the lights were triggered and he thinks it was a fox or another animal."

Marie explained to the group about Simon and Roger having sensor lights installed in their farm yards. She told them how he stood peering out of the side of the curtains each evening.

"Roger has been doing that as well," Fay laughed.

Heather said Julie had told her how well the school table top and jumble sale had gone. It had raised a good amount for the school.

Mary then told them that she and Lorna had delivered the unsold items over to Ned's lady friend Wendy's charity shop yesterday.

"I ended up buying a footstool in the charity shop and Lorna bought an elephant ornament," she grinned. "I defy anyone going into a charity shop and not to buy anything." She said they had also had a pub lunch. "It was very good and I would certainly recommend it."

She sipped her tea and took a mouthful of cake.

"This is a lovely cake, Marie, the walnuts on top really compliment the coffee flavour. Are there any walnuts in the cake mixture as well?" she asked her.

"No, I thought it might disguise some of the coffee flavour if I added them into the cake mixture as well. One flavour can overtake another."

"Yes, I agree. Some flavours can be very strong. You think you're eating one thing but the dominant flavour takes over." Mary smiled taking another mouthful of cake. "It's perfect as it is."

"Thank you. Heavens, I forgot to ask if anyone is allergic to nuts!" Marie exclaimed.

No one was, thank goodness, but that set them all thinking about Beverley.

"Is there any news yet?" asked Kerry.

"Not that we've been told by the police," replied Marie. "I might know a bit more later on though."

"Why is that?" asked Lorna.

"Simon and George have gone over to Haleton today to ask around and see if they can find anyone who knew Beverley," replied Marie. "I told Simon to leave it to the police but would he listen," she said looking at Anne who replied, "Yes, I said exactly the same thing to George."

"George never would listen if he's got his mind set on something," said Frances. "He was a bit of a nightmare brother! They need to be careful though."

"What do they think they're going to find out?" asked Mary.

"They are trying to find out if there is any family of Beverley's who may throw some light on her death."

"They should have taken Freddie with them!" said Sarah. "He's obsessed with finding out the reason Beverley and Sheila both died and the people responsible. I don't know how many times I've told him to forget it, but will he listen to me?"

"It's the same with Freya. She's just as obsessed as Freddie is!" agreed Celia.

"He's worse since having that wretched magnifying glass," said Sarah smiling. "He and Freya keep whispering together and then Freddie gets the glass out and looks for clues. He was looking at Sheila's path to her front door yesterday. Goodness only knows what he thinks they will find out. Mind you, the magnifying glass came in useful the other evening. I dropped a needle whilst sewing and Freddie found it for me by using the glass!"

Everyone laughed.

Marie got up to make her guests more coffee and tea. The whole cake had been eaten and thoroughly enjoyed by all of them. "None left for Simon!" grinned Marie as she collected the empty plate stand to take into the kitchen.

"Has anyone heard any more about the bail jumper?" asked Mary.

"No, nothing at all. I saw on the news they've now named him and shown his photograph but we've still not told what he was arrested and bailed for," said Kerry.

"I wonder why he's still hanging around the village?" said Fay.

"There must be a reason. There have been a few sightings of him apparently," said Marie. "I hope he doesn't come back to the farm; there's no saying what Simon would do to him. Being bashed on the head made him furious."

"I don't blame him. Being attacked in your own farm yard is just awful," agreed Frances.

The coffee morning finished at just before twelve o'clock. Celia and Sarah left first as they needed to collect their children from nursery.

Marie was thanked for her hospitality and told again how nice the cake had been.

She closed the door on the last guest. She had enjoyed the morning but was glad to be on her own as she had a few things to think about.

Lorna went home feeling a bit troubled but not actually sure why. Had someone said something that wasn't quite right? Had she seen something on someone's face that didn't ring true? She needed to think.

Celia and Sarah collected their children from nursery. They came running out with their teacher who made sure they were delivered safely into the care of their parents. They all walked home together and said they would see each other later when they collected Freddie and Freya from school. Sarah said she needed to call in at the village shop before going to the school.

"Actually, I need something as well, so I'll come with you before school," replied Celia. She fed her children and settled them in front of the television in

160

the lounge. She went into the kitchen and made herself a coffee and sat at the table so she could be alone with her thoughts.

Sarah returned home but had a worried frown on her face. She would put Max down for a nap after lunch and then sit and go over the coffee morning conversations.

Frances returned home after calling in at the shop before returning home. She had needed some milk and bread. She had enjoyed the morning but she had sensed something wasn't as quite as it appeared. She needed to think carefully.

Mary was sitting in her lounge thinking the same. Something had been said this morning that needed thinking about. She would try and remember who had said what.

The same was being thought about by Kerry. She couldn't quite put her finger on what was wrong. She tried to recall the conversations from the coffee morning.

# Chapter Forty-Four

Simon and George went up to the bar in the Crown. A man around fifty was serving a customer with a pint of beer.

"Shan't be a moment," he called out to Simon and George. Simon asked George what he wanted to drink. "Better have a soft one as I'm driving, I'll have a coke," he replied.

The bar man turned to them after finishing serving the other customer.

"Gents," he said. "What can I get you?"

"A lemonade shandy and a coke please," said Simon.

"I've not seen you in here before, are you just passing through the village?" the barman asked them placing their drinks on the bar.

Simon got his wallet out and offered his debit card. The barman took the card machine from under the counter and passed it to Simon. Simon punched in his PIN and handed it back. He accepted the receipt and put it in his wallet.

"We are looking up an old acquaintance that used to live here in the village," replied George.

"Who's that then?" said the barman.

"A nurse called Beverley Kingston," said George.

"Oh, her!" said the barman. "I knew her when she lived here. She moved about a year ago. Bad business, that."

"What happened?" asked Simon with an innocent expression, taking a sip of his shandy.

"Bad business," he repeated. "A child died because of her incompetence," said the barman.

"It split the young lad's family up, they couldn't cope and both moved away. The nurse's husband killed himself because of the shame and his father went off the rails after he found his son dead in bed after taking an overdose."

He shook his head.

"That's awful," said George looking at Simon.

"Did the police investigate?" asked Simon.

"They did, but they couldn't bring any charges because she said one thing and the lad's family said another. It couldn't be proved either way. The coroner gave meningitis as the cause of the lad's death and said it was natural causes, but he did say it probably could have been avoided if he had gone to hospital as soon as he became poorly."

"Did Beverley's husband have any other relatives other than his father?"

"He had a sister and a brother but neither lived in the village. His mother had died several years before."

"Did Beverley have any other family?" asked George.

"I think she had a cousin, but not living here in the village," replied the barman.

"So Beverley left the village then?" asked Simon.

"She resigned from her job and left after the inquest but I'm not sure where she went to."

"What happened to her husband's father?" asked Simon.

"I'm not really sure. He didn't live here in the village. He came in here sometimes with his son for a pint. Talk is that he turned to drink with his grief. I hope his other children supported him."

"What a sad story," said George taking a sip of his coke.

"It is sad," agreed the barman. "Wherever she is now, I hope she can live with herself. Two deaths were down to her actions."

"Would anyone here know where her husband's father lives?" asked Simon.

"I'm not sure, Old Ben Yeoman might have known. He used to be quite chatty when Beverley's husband and father came in."

"Where would we find Ben?" asked George draining his glass.

"He's in a care home now. I think he's got dementia," said the barman collecting their empty glasses.

"He used to come in and start accusing other customers of trying to pinch his wallet. His daughter eventually put him in the home when he started wandering the streets at night looking for his wallet believing someone had got into his house and taken it. It was just his imagination but it was happening too often. The police were called out many times trying to find him when he went walk about."

"Which care home is he in?" asked Simon. "It might be worth visiting him."

"Why are so interested?" asked the barman.

"Beverley ended up living in our village. She's dead and foul play is suspected," explained George.

"Crikey!" said the barman "Do you think someone connected with her here is responsible?"

"Possibly. We don't know yet," replied Simon.

"The care home is a couple of miles away from here on the way to Burford. It's called Haleton House."

"It might be worth dropping in to see him," Simon said to George.

He agreed. They thanked the barman for the drinks and the chat and left the pub.

They went to the car park and got in the car.

George drove out of the car park and headed towards Burford.

It was a straight road and a couple of miles ahead they saw the sign for Haleton House Care Home. It was just off the main road.

George pulled up into the car park and switched off the engine.

It was a large old house. There was a block paved path leading up to the front door. There were large tubs of beautifully coloured begonias outside the entrance porch. The name Haleton House Care Home was advertised above the front door.

George rang the bell. They could both hear it sound within the house.

The door was opened quite quickly by a lady who judging by her uniform, appeared to be care worker. She asked how she could help them.

Simon said they had come to visit Ben Yeoman if it was convenient. She said it was.

"Come in," she said and led them inside. "I think he's sitting in the sun room," she said.

They followed her and she turned into a large well-lit airy conservatory. There were several residents in there chatting or reading. Some had a visitor sitting with them. It appeared to be a cheerful place. There was lots of seating and several large potted plants were on show. The conservatory looked out onto a very well-maintained garden.

"Ben!" called the care worker. "You have some visitors."

She went up to a heavily bearded gentleman sitting near the window. Some of the other residents looked at the visitors coming in with the care worker.

Ben looked up from his newspaper and smiled at them. "Hello," he said "Do I know you?"

"No," said Simon, "but we have some friends in common and thought we would drop in for a chat."

"Have you come to return my wallet?" asked Ben. "It's been taken."

"No, sorry, we haven't seen your wallet," said George.

The care worker pulled up a couple of chairs so they could sit down by Ben. She offered them a cup of tea which they accepted with thanks. "I'll have a cuppa, too, please," said Ben.

"Won't be long," she promised with a smile as she went out of the conservatory.

Simon introduced himself and George.

"We have been asking around Haleton about a woman called Beverley Kingston," said Simon to Ben. "We went into the Crown pub and understand you were quite friendly with her father-in-law. We're not sure what his name is."

"I remember going in the Crown. Good pub that. They serve a good pint there!" replied Ben.

"We know what happened in the village with Beverley and the child and also heard about her husband killing himself," said George.

"Awful business, that. I never saw the chap again after his son died. He went quite mad with grief, I heard," said Ben. "You sure you haven't got my wallet? It's got a fiver inside."

"No, we haven't got it," said Simon.

The care worker returned with three mugs of tea. She put them down on a nearby table.

Simon thanked her and handed one to Ben and George.

"What was the father's name?" asked George.

"I can hardly remember my own name nowadays, let alone anyone else's!" said Ben with a chuckle.

"Do you know where he lived?" asked George.

"I can't remember."

"He had another son and daughter, apparently," said Simon.

"He came in once with the son. He was a bit odd, I thought."

"Why?" asked George.

"If I recall rightly, he didn't say much at all. He left all the talking to his dad. He mumbled and muttered a lot. I think he was a bit simple in the head," replied Ben pointing to his own head and twirling his finger.

"So, you wouldn't know where he lived then?" asked George.

"I remember he wore one of those camouflage jackets like they wear in the army," said Ben remembering.

"So, you don't know his name either?"

"No. I don't."

"Do you remember anything about the daughter?" asked Simon.

"Nothing at all," replied Ben.

Simon looked at George with a shrug. They weren't really getting any answers from Ben.

They finished their tea and said how nice it was to meet him. They stood up and shook hands with him.

"If you find my wallet, can you let me have it back please?" asked Ben picking up his newspaper.

"If we find it, we will return it to you immediately," promised George.

They left the care home and went out to the car park and got in the car. George looked at his watch and saw it was just gone three o'clock.

"Best make our way home," he said to Simon. "We should be home in time for tea!"

"I've missed the milking, but hopefully James should have coped alright. I did tell him I was going out for the day. So, what have we found out today?" Simon asked George.

"Not a lot that we didn't know already, but the most interesting bit was that Beverley's brother-in-law wore a camouflage jacket and that's what our bail jumper has been spotted in. Apparently, he's quite simple," replied George.

"It could be a coincidence," said Simon.

"I bet it's not. I think we know who he is but why he's hanging around is something we don't know. If he was gunning for Beverley because of his brother's death he must have heard she's dead, so why hasn't he scarpered?"

George was unable to come up with an answer.

The drive home was uneventful and they reached Merrydale just after five. George dropped Simon off at his house and then went home to Anne.

# Chapter Forty-Five

Over their evening meal, Anne was listening to George who was telling her about his day out in Haleton with Simon.

He was tucking into steak pie, peas and mashed potatoes covered with gravy. He was hungry as he had missed a proper lunch.

Anne listened carefully to what he was telling her.

"So, we know Beverley was hounded out of the village after the child's death and then her husband's as well," she said.

"Yes," replied George taking a mouthful of potatoes.

"It sounds like the husband's brother may be the bail jumper," she said.

George agreed.

He told her all about their visit to the care home and talking to Ben Yeoman.

"It was a really nice place. The residents looked well cared for and seemed content. Ben seemed settled and comfortable," he said.

"That's nice to hear. You read in the paper about some care homes that are not so good," she commented.

"Unfortunately, Ben couldn't help much. He didn't know any names of Beverley's relatives. He has dementia and was more interested in finding his wallet which he thought had been taken."

"But you found out that Beverley was definitely involved in a child's death," said Anne.

"Yes, that's right, it's got to be the reason why she left Haleton. Having her husband take his own life must have been the final straw," replied George.

"It must have been awful for her, thinking she may be responsible for two deaths," said Anne.

"Well, she was responsible if you look at what happened," replied George.

He cleared his plate and sat back patting his stomach saying what a good meal it was.

"Jam sponge and custard?" Anne asked him.

"Do you need to ask?" he grinned.

"So, who do we think might the bail jumper be?" asked Anne as she got up to heat up the custard.

"If it's someone who's looking for Beverley, it's surely got to be a relative of the child or her husband," replied George.

"I suppose it must be," said Anne stirring the hot custard before pouring it over the jam sponge and serving into bowls.

She brought the pudding bowls over to the table and sat down.

George tucked into it.

"Lovely!" he complemented her after eating it.

She washed up and then made them both a cup of tea which they took into the lounge to drink while they relaxed and watched some television.

# Chapter Forty-Six

Simon had also been telling Marie about the day out with George.

The conversation was running along the same lines that George and Anne had been saying.

"It all got to be connected with Beverley's death. She was obviously not able to stay in the village after what happened to the child and her husband," said Marie.

"But we're not much further on finding out things, and where does Sheila fit in with all this?" asked Simon.

"And who is the chap that's still hanging around?" said Marie.

"Let's forget about it all this evening," said Simon. "Let's watch that gardening programme with Monty Don. I like him and he has some good ideas."

They spent a relaxing enjoyable evening together.

Tuesday morning, the post arrived at a house in Mereford. Amongst the post that dropped through the letter box with a leaflet for a pizza delivery and an estate agent flyer, was a stamped addressed envelope. The recipient was not interested in pizzas or estate agents so opened the stamped addressed envelope after looking intently at the writing on the envelope which was written in bold capital letters hand written print.

Once the envelope was opened, it was seen to be a white card with the words, "Just for You", on the front.

Written on the inside blank page were printed words, "I know what you did."

The recipient dropped the card in shock. Heart beating fast, it was picked up from the floor and read again.

Frowning, the recipient shoved it out of sight in the letter rack behind the latest electricity bill.

*"I know what you did!"*

*How is that possible? Careful is my middle name. I need to know who sent this, but I have a horrible feeling I know. This is dreadful.*

# Chapter Forty-Seven

Freddie was at Freya's house after school on Wednesday. He had been invited around to her house for tea. The two younger girls were being annoying and kept asking him silly questions so Freya said, "Let's go upstairs and get away from them."

Freddie looked around her bedroom. It was predominately pink. There were several soft toys on the bed and posters of fairy princesses on the walls. She had a small television on a chest of drawers.

There was a small chair in the room so Freddie sat on that while Freya moved the toys off the bed and lay down on the pastel pink duvet.

"So, how far have you got with your police work?" asked Freya.

"I can't investigate much as Mum won't let me out on my own," Freddie moaned. "I'm ten now, so should be able to go out of the house on my own."

"But the murderer might be about and she doesn't want you to get murdered," said Freya. "Nor do I."

"I don't want to get murdered either," replied Freddie, "but I can't solve the case being kept in the house all the while and I haven't got a lot of time in the day because of going to school."

"Can't you sneak out one evening?" suggested Freya.

"Max would know if I went missing and then ask Mum where I was because he hangs around me after tea," Freddie said. "He says he misses me in the day when I'm at school so Mum says I need to spend time playing games with him in the evening."

"What time does he go to bed?" asked Freya.

"He goes about seven o'clock. I go about eight, but sometimes it's half past eight," Freddie answered.

"So, there's a bit of time when he wouldn't miss you because he's in bed," said Freya thinking about ways Freddie could escape from Max.

"But Mum and Dad might miss me if I wasn't there," said Freddie.

"You could go to bed and put a pillow in there and pretend it's you in there fast asleep. I saw that in a programme once. The mum looked in, and really thought it was her son asleep in bed."

"I suppose I could do that but I would have to be very quiet if I sneaked out of the front door. It's got a bit of a squeak when you open it," said Freddie thinking about it.

"Where would you want to go anyway?"

"I need to finish looking for clues at Sheila's house. I had only looked at a bit of the path with my magnifying glass when we had to run back the other day," said Freddie.

"Did you notice when we walked past her house today after school that the dead flowers have gone now," said Freya.

"Yes, I did see they'd gone. I wonder who took them."

"It was probably Mary. I saw her looking at them yesterday afternoon when we passed by Sheila's house and frowning at them. I feel sorry for her as she's now got two dead friends. It must be horrible," Freya shuddered.

"I wonder where she put the dead flowers?" asked Freddie.

"It doesn't matter where she put them, does it?"

"I suppose not. It was probably in the brown dustbin. That's where Dad puts his gardening rubbish," said Freddie.

"So are you going to sneak out one evening?" asked Freya.

"I will think about it and plan it," replied Freddie.

"Freya! Freddie! Tea's ready," came a shout from downstairs.

Freya sighed and got off the bed. She smoothed the duvet and replaced the soft toys back onto the bed.

"Come on, let's go down and see what's for tea."

They went downstairs to the kitchen where the two youngsters were already sitting at the table.

"Sit by me, Freddie," cried Susie pointing to the chair by her. Celia was serving their tea up.

He took his place by Susie at the table. Celia served them chicken nuggets with beans and chips.

"Lovely, my favourite," said Freddie tucking in.

The meal was enjoyed by all the children and each had a strawberry mousse for pudding.

He was a polite child and thanked Celia for his tea. The front door opened and Luke arrived home from work saying hello to everybody.

"You're very welcome, Freddie," Celia smiled as she collected the children's empty plates. She and Luke would eat their own meal a bit later.

Freddie was taken back to his own home at half past six. It was only two doors away but Celia said he mustn't be out on his own even for such a short distance.

Sarah answered the door and let Freddie in after thanking Celia for having him.

Max ran up to Freddie and asked him to play cars with him. Freddie sighed and said he would. He would be glad when it was Max's bedtime so he could be on his own as he had a lot to think about.

He had a shower at seven thirty and told his mum he was tired and was going to bed afterwards.

He lay in bed thinking about his forthcoming investigations but soon fell asleep.

# Chapter Forty-Eight

The next day was overcast with a threat of showers due sometime in the afternoon. Lorna had been intending to do some washing. She wanted to wash her net curtains as they were looking a bit off white instead of sparkling white, but was now thinking she needed to postpone it until it was a better day. She lived in a very nice bungalow which she had shared with her late husband. She still missed him.

She decided to remove her collection of photographs off her lounge cabinet shelf and give it a really good dust. It had been quite some time since she had done this.

She looked at each photo as she removed it off the shelf. Happy memories with her family!

Her son and daughter had left home several years ago. She did see them occasionally but they had busy lives and so didn't have a lot of free time. Her grandchildren were growing up fast now and didn't have too much time to do anything with her. She babysat when needed but they didn't really need her there as they really look after themselves.

She picked up a photo of herself with Mary. She seemed to remember it had been taken a couple of years ago at some function. She scrutinised it but couldn't quite remember where it had been taken as she couldn't make out what the background was. *It will come back to me*, she thought to herself.

Mary and she had a lot in common and had enjoyed many outings to various places and sales together. She rubbed at the glass with her cleaning cloth.

She polished the shelf and replaced the photos.

She heard the postman arrive so went to collect the post when she heard it drop through the letter box. There was a sharp rap on her front door as she bent down to pick the post up from the mat. She opened the door and the postman pointed to a parcel sitting on the doorstep.

"This was here already. I haven't delivered it though. I thought if you didn't go out of your front door today you wouldn't know it was there."

Lorna thanked him for telling her, and picked the brown parcel up wondering what it contained.

It advertised, "Chilled meals for your convenience", on the printed white label along with her name and address. There was no stamp on it which was a bit odd she thought.

She went into the kitchen to open the seal on the back of the parcel.

It was from a food company obviously promoting chilled meals that could be delivered and heated at home. There was a printed delivery note inside.

"Have this free meal on us," the printed flyer said. "If you enjoy this meal of chilli chicken and rice, please see what else we can deliver to your home at very competitive prices."

Lorna opened the seal on the inner brown packet that contained the chilled food.

The food was in a foil container with a white cardboard lid similar to a takeaway meal. Lorna opened the lid. It looked and smelled very nice.

*That's my tea sorted*, Lorna thought with a smile as she put it in the fridge.

The phone rang later. It was Mary ringing for a chat. They spoke about what they had both been doing that morning. Mary said she had been ironing. Lorna described the photo of them both, but Mary couldn't remember where it had been taken either. Lorna said she had been going to wash her net curtains, but had postponed it for a sunny day instead as she liked to dry them on the outside line.

She then told her about the free chilled meal that had been delivered. "It looks really nice," Lorna said.

"I hope I get picked to receive one as well," said Mary. "I wonder how the company picked who to send one to. Let me know what it's like."

"It's a bit odd though," said Lorna. "There doesn't seem to be a stamp or postmark on the outer envelope."

Mary said she sometimes received post without a stamp or post mark.

They said goodbye and planned to meet up on Saturday to go to a fete which was being held in the next village.

"I'll pick you up at two o'clock," said Mary.

Lorna continued with her dusting. She liked her home to be neat, tidy and clean. She had a snack lunch while watching the news and then had a forty-minute nap. She woke up and did a bit of ironing. She watched Tenable with

Warwick Davies in the afternoon followed by Tipping Point. It was quite a lazy day for her, she liked to keep busy but looking at the showers outside, she didn't feel guilty about not doing any gardening.

At five o'clock, she decided to heat the meal up in the microwave. She went through into the kitchen and heard Bradley Chase speaking on the television making jokes with the Chaser. She waited in the kitchen preparing a tray and collecting cutlery.

The meal was ready in eight minutes so she took it through to the lounge on a tray. Bradley was still joking, but this time with the contestants.

Lorna thoroughly enjoyed the meal. It was really nice and tasty and she would consider ordering more meals from the company. She must have another look at the delivery note to see where she could order them from. She didn't really enjoy cooking for one, and this would give her nice meals without the effort!

She continued watching the Chase and then yawned. She took the tray into the kitchen and washed the plate and cutlery up. She was feeling really sleepy and could hardly keep her eyes open. She went back into the lounge and sat down. The Chaser had beaten the contestants. She yawned again and slept.

# Chapter Forty-Nine

Next day was fine and sunny. Simon had been up since before five helping James with the milking.

He ate a cooked breakfast of scrambled eggs and tomatoes on toast at eight o'clock and asked Marie what her plans were for the day.

"I'm not really sure yet," she answered drinking a cup of tea. "I might just go for a walk as it's a nice day."

"Well, be careful," he reminded her. "That man is still on the loose."

"I do wish the police would find him, it's horrible thinking he might still be hiding somewhere nearby," she said. "What are you up to today?"

He said he was going to a field with Stan to repair yet another hedge.

"You'd think the cows would concentrate on the grass instead of butting hedges and fences?" he grinned.

He got up after thanking her for his breakfast. He went upstairs and put his overalls on. He returned downstairs and took his cap off the shelf and said he would see her later reminding her again to be careful. He made a flask of coffee and said he would call in at lunchtime for a sandwich.

Marie cleared up the plates and washed up. She took some pork chops out of the freezer and put them in the fridge to defrost.

She looked out of the kitchen window onto the yard. There had been no further disturbances in the yard or barns since the sensor lights had gone up.

She was still thinking about her coffee morning the other day. She hadn't yet been able to remember what had troubled her.

At ten o'clock, she started off on her walk. She made sure she had her mobile phone in her jacket pocket.

She turned left at the end of the farm's driveway. This would take her to the end of the village. There were some nice bridleway walks on this route.

She got near to Sheila's house and saw a car outside. A lady had just got out and was reaching into the back seat and getting out some large bags. She straightened up and locked the car.

"Hello," said Marie. "Are you Sheila's sister?"

"Yes, I'm Jane," the lady replied looking up.

"I'm Marie. I knew Sheila. What a dreadful thing to happen. We are all still in shock."

"Yes, it was awful what happened. I've got the go ahead to clear the house now," Jane said.

"That can't be an easy job to do," replied Marie.

"No, I'm not looking forward to doing it. The insurers have said it needs to be done so the renovations and decorating can begin."

"Would you like some company?" asked Marie.

"That's really kind of you to offer. I would like someone here with me. My husband is at work, and coming over this weekend to help but I thought I'd make a start."

She walked up the path to the front door with Marie following. Jane unlocked the door and they went inside.

The house still smelt of smoke.

They looked around at the damage that had occurred.

"Have the investigators finished now then?" asked Marie.

"Yes. It was definitely deliberately set on fire. The fire investigation team have been in here a few times now but apart from some oily rags found near the front door they couldn't find anything else incriminating," replied Jane.

"Are you able to hold a funeral?"

"Yes. It's being held next Friday at eleven o'clock here in the village."

"There will be a lot of people wanting to go," said Marie.

They went into the kitchen. Jane said she would start with smaller items which would fit in the bags saying said she would take them to the local tip. "I shall get a house clearance firm in for the larger items. They are no good to anybody because most of them are smoke damaged."

She started putting things into the bags. Marie did the same.

There was a knock on the front door. Jane went to answer it while Marie continued to fill some bags.

Jane walked into the kitchen with Mary.

"I saw your car and wondered if I could help," she was saying to Jane. "Hello, Marie."

"Hello, Mary. I saw Jane and offered to help as well."

Jane explained they were collecting the smaller items and bagging them up for the tip.

She said she would go upstairs and start clearing Sheila's clothes.

"I need to find something to take to the funeral directors to dress Sheila in." She went out of the kitchen and went upstairs.

"How awful for her," said Marie. "It's a dreadful task she has to do."

Mary agreed and started to help Marie put some stuff in the bags.

"Have the investigations into the fire been concluded?" asked Mary packing away a kettle.

"Jane says they've finished here at the house. It was definitely deliberately set on fire so the police will be investigating until they catch who did it," said Marie.

"Sometimes, they never find out," replied Mary.

"There must be some way the person will be caught," replied Marie. "There must be some clues. Jane said there was an oily rag found inside the front door. I suppose it had been set on fire and pushed through the letter box," she said with a shudder.

"What sort of rag was it?" asked Mary.

"I have no idea; I don't suppose it was identifiable if it had been set on fire."

Jane came downstairs with a couple of bags and a bundle of clothes.

"I think these clothes should be alright for Sheila," showing them to Marie and Mary.

"I remember her wearing this blue dress and cardigan when I last saw her," said Jane sadly, wiping a tear away.

Six large bags had now been filled. Jane went out and unlocked the car. They took the bags out and put them in the boot.

"I think that's all I can cope with today. I'll come back tomorrow with my husband and do some more."

She returned to the house and locked the front door.

"Thanks for your help. I'm very grateful to you both," she said.

"If there's anything else we can do, please give me a ring," said Marie writing her telephone number on a bit of paper.

"Me, too," said Mary adding her number onto the paper.

"The funeral is next Friday at eleven," said Jane to Mary.

"I'm sure a lot of people will want to come and pay their respects," Mary said laying a comforting hand on Jane's arm. Jane got into her car and drove off with another thank you.

"How sad," said Marie. Mary agreed with her.

Marie said she had been going for a walk but had seen Jane and offered to help when she had seen her pull up at the house.

Mary told her to enjoy her walk. She said she had some shopping to do otherwise she would have joined her.

Mary left to return home to collect her shopping bag, and Marie carried on to the end of the road.

She turned left up the next road which would lead her to the end of the village. She saw a lady frantically knocking on the front door of a house.

"Is everything alright?" Marie asked going up to her. She recognised it as Lorna's house.

"I can't get any answer. I can see Lorna in the lounge, but she's not answering the door."

Marie went up to the window and peering through the net curtains could see Lorna on the settee.

Marie knocked on the window shouting Lorna's name. Lorna did not respond.

"I should have been having a coffee with her this morning. It was arranged that I go around at eleven o'clock. When I couldn't get an answer, I thought she must have forgotten, but then I saw her through the window," explained the neighbour.

"I think we need to call the police," said Marie taking her mobile phone out of her pocket.

She dialled 999 and explained that she and a neighbour were concerned about someone who was not responding to loud knocking on her door or window. "We can see her in her lounge through the window."

"Someone will be with you very shortly," she was told after Marie told her the address. "Keep knocking and calling her name to see if you get a response."

Marie and the neighbour, who said her name was Shirley, kept shouting Lorna's name and knocking loudly on the window but Lorna did not respond.

They heard a siren coming closer. Other neighbours were coming out of their houses after hearing knocking and raised voices.

"What's going on?" asked a lady whose hair was decorated with rollers.

"We can't get Lorna to answer. We can see her through the window but she's not responding," said Marie.

A police car pulled up outside the house.

Two male officers got out and went up to the people who had gathered outside the front door. Marie explained what was happening. One officer knocked very loudly calling Lorna's name. The other officer went to the window where the neighbour was still knocking and shouting Lorna's name.

"Has anyone got a key?" asked one officer looking at the crowd.

No one had. The officer looked underneath a couple of flower tubs that were standing either side of the front door, but there was no key to be found.

"We're going to have to break in," he told the second officer. "Stand back everyone."

He was a big man and shoved his body with force against the door. Nothing happened.

"We haven't tried the back door!" Marie said suddenly.

The two officers looked at each other. They went up the path by the side of the house and went to the back door which opened.

Marie and Shirley followed them through the door into the lounge.

They saw Lorna on the settee. She was sitting upright, but had her eyes and mouth open. She had vomited at some stage and her bowels had opened. The smell in the room was awful.

Looking on in horror, with hands over their mouths, Marie and Shirley looked at the policemen.

One officer bent down to Lorna with his hand over his mouth, feeling furtively for a pulse. He shook his head and stood up.

Shirley ran out of the room screaming. "She's dead! Lorna's dead!" and burst into tears.

The crowd of neighbours looked shocked as Shirley ran outside. "She's dead!" Shirley repeated. Some burst out crying and put their arms around each other.

Inside, the first officer rang for an ambulance. He told Marie nothing must be touched and she should leave the house and wait for them outside.

She went out to the stunned neighbours.

"I can't believe it," she said and burst into tears. A man put his arm around her patting her back.

One officer came out of the house. "Please, all go home except for you and you," pointing to Marie and Shirley.

The crowd dispersed with everyone talking and asking each other what could have happened.

Marie and Shirley stood together not talking.

The officer asked them to tell him what they knew. Shirley repeated that she had been invited around to Lorna's house for coffee at eleven, but she couldn't get an answer when she knocked. "I looked in the window and saw her on the settee. I thought she was asleep."

Marie said, "I was out for a walk and heard Shirley knocking and shouting Lorna's name, so I asked if anything was the matter. I looked in the window and saw Lorna on the settee but not responding so I rang the police."

He took their names and contact details and said they could go. "Someone will be in touch with you to take a statement. We now need to inform her family. I saw an address book in the hall by the phone."

"She has a son and a daughter," said Marie tearfully.

She went home. She wanted Simon and his reassuring presence. As soon as she got in the house, she rang his mobile and blurted out that something had happened and she needed him straight away.

He raced home and burst through the front door. Marie was sitting crying at the kitchen table. "Oh, My God! What's happened, are you alright?" as he put his arms around her.

She told him what had happened to Lorna. He sat down feeling stunned.

"But how?" he asked her.

"I don't know anything except she was dead on her settee," said Marie crying into a tissue.

Simon didn't know what to say.

"She was only here last week. She was fine then," Marie said.

"Perhaps it was a heart attack," he suggested.

"Oh God, will anyone have told Mary? They were best friends," said Marie standing up. "I need to ring her."

Simon asked if she wanted him to call her but Marie said she would do it.

She rang Mary's number which was answered quickly.

"Mary, its Marie. I've got some awful news. I'm really sorry to tell this you, but Lorna's dead."

"What?" she heard Mary ask "But how, when?"

"She was found dead in her lounge about an hour ago. Her neighbour Shirley couldn't get an answer when she knocked. I was passing by and went to see what was happening. We looked through the window and could see Lorna on her settee but not moving. It's awful. We called the police. Her back door was open."

"I can't believe it!" Mary said crying. "I only spoke with her yesterday. We were going to a fete tomorrow; I was picking her up at two."

"I'm so sorry," Marie said. "Do you want to come around or shall I come to you?"

"No, I need to take the news in on my own. Have her family been told?"

"The police are going to tell them," replied Marie. "If you need to call or need anything at all please pick up the phone anytime you want."

"Thank you," said Mary as she put the phone down. She burst into tears and put her head in her hands. Her best friend Lorna was dead.

It was the talk of the village. Another sudden death in Merrydale. Three deaths in three weeks.

"How dreadful," people were saying. "Poor Lorna, it must have been a heart attack, it was so sudden."

George was on the phone to Simon.

"It's unbelievable, what the hell's happening in the village?" he said. "Anne and Frances are in bits."

"Marie is too. Do you think Lorna's death has any connection to the others?" asked Simon.

"How can it be connected? There will be a post mortem so we should have some answers then. Surely, it must have been a heart attack to be so sudden?"

"I hope it was. The others were deliberate, but hopefully Lorna's was natural causes," said Simon.

"Have your yard lights been triggered yet?" asked George.

"Not a sausage!" replied Simon.

"Mine haven't either. Let's hope the absconder is far away," said George.

"Are you going to Sheila's funeral on Friday?" asked Simon.

"Yes, I expect there will be a good turnout. Beverley's hasn't been arranged yet."

"I don't know when they release a body after a suspicious death like Beverley's when there's no family coming forward to claim her. I suppose it's different with Sheila's because her sister is about," said Simon.

# Chapter Fifty

Lorna's post mortem was carried out on Monday morning. The pathologist established that she had died from acute arsenic poisoning.

The police immediately launched a murder investigation.

They rang Marie on Tuesday morning to ask her to go into Olehampton police station to make a statement. Shirley was also asked to go in.

The news soon got around the village.

"It was arsenic poisoning, so that's another murder in Merrydale," said Marie tearfully.

Simon agreed how terrible it was. He was driving Marie into the police station. She kept bursting into tears saying she would never forget the sight and smell in Lorna's lounge.

They arrived at the police station at eleven o'clock.

Marie was expected so was escorted through into a back room and told someone would be with her shortly. Simon was asked to wait in the foyer.

Marie sat waiting for someone to come in. A door opened and a police officer entered the room.

He went up to a table on which was a recording device and switched it on.

"Good morning. I'm Inspector Morris. Can you state your name and date of birth for the tape please?"

Marie did this. Her heart was beating fast. She had never been in a police station before.

"Now, can you tell me the exact events leading up to the discovery of the body, please," Inspector Morris asked.

Marie told him what had happened and how she came to be passing Lorna's house last Friday morning. He asked her to repeat things a couple of times. Marie was nervous and it showed. She must tell it as she remembered it.

"It's terrible," she told him. "She was a friend of mine. This is the third death in as many weeks in Merrydale. You must find out who is doing this. Surely, they must all be connected."

"We are looking at all possibilities," he told her. "I'm very sorry about your friend. It must have been awful for you."

"It was. It's a scene I will never forget. I hope she didn't suffer," she told him tearfully.

"Hopefully not," replied the Inspector.

She finished talking and signed her statement.

The Inspector escorted her out to where Simon was waiting for her. Marie saw Shirley with a man who was presumably her husband.

"How are you?" asked Marie.

"Terrible!" replied Shirley with tears in her eyes. "I can't stop thinking about it. Now we hear she was poisoned so it was murder."

Inspector Morris thanked Marie for coming in and then asked Shirley to come through and make her statement.

Marie and Simon left the police station and returned home.

# Chapter Fifty-One

Simon got changed and went out to look for Stan on the farm after checking Marie would be alright on her own. She told him she'd be fine on her own.

She rang Mary to tell her that she and Lorna's neighbour had been to the police station to make their statements. "It was horrible," she told her.

"I know, it was horrible when I went in with George after Beverley died. It makes you nervous, doesn't it?" said Mary.

"It makes you feel as if you've done something wrong, even when you haven't," replied Marie.

"Yes, that's exactly how I felt when I made my statement about Beverley," agreed Mary saying she couldn't get her head around what had happened to Lorna.

She ran off and made herself a cup of tea. She needed time to go over everything in her mind.

Marie also made herself a cup of tea. It had been a horrible experience going to the police station.

She now wished she had asked Simon to stay with her. She felt at a loose end.

She rang Fay and Frances for a chat. She needed to hear some friendly voices.

*Lorna, I am so sorry you had to die but I couldn't risk you saying anything. You guessed what I had done. Everyone's asking who has done these dreadful things, but have not connected it with me. Why should they? Careful is my middle name. I hope your death was quick and you did not suffer. I am so very sorry.*

# Chapter Fifty-Two

Julie was in the staff room talking to the headmaster about Lorna. "It's really unbelievable. I can't believe there's been another murder in the village!"

"It's beyond belief," he agreed. "I suppose I need to warn the children to be careful again."

"I think you need to. Just let them know they must never go out without an adult unless they know them."

In assembly after the first hymn the headmaster stood in front of the children holding up his hand to shush them.

"I am going to repeat what I have telling you over the last couple of weeks. You must never go out alone and you must always be with your parents or someone you know and trust."

Freddie shot his hand up.

"What if it's someone we know and trust?"

The children sniggered. They loved it when Freddie asked questions like this.

"I'm sure you don't know the person who is doing these terrible things," he replied.

"But they could look innocent and be really friendly, but really they are the murderer," Freddie answered.

"Just continue to stay close to your parents and then you'll be safe," the headmaster replied with exasperation. "Now, we will all sing the next hymn which is 'Morning has Broken'."

Freddie turned to Charlie and whispered, "That's another death I've got to look into. I'm so busy with my investigations I probably haven't got time to come to school!"

Charlie whispered back, "So what's your plan?"

"I'm not sure yet," Freddie replied holding his hand in front of his mouth. He saw Julie frown at him so he started to sing loudly. Charlie nudged him and grinned.

After assembly, the teachers and children went into their classrooms to start the day's lessons.

Sally started handing out books to the class.

"We are going to discuss historical events today," said Julie.

"Are we going to talk about grisly murders and people having their heads chopped off?" asked Freddie.

"No, we certainly are not," replied Julie. "We are going to talk about kings and queens from long ago."

"Boring," whispered Freddie to Charlie.

After school finished for the day, Freddie ran out to meet Celia who was waiting with Max. Sarah was there with her two younger daughters to meet Freya. They made their way home.

Freddie and Freya walked together trailing behind their mothers.

"Have you decided whether to sneak out one evening to get some more clues?" she asked him in a whisper.

"I'm still thinking about it, but I probably will," he told her hiding his mouth behind his hand.

Celia and Sarah were discussing the recent events in the village.

"It's just too awful for words," said Sarah. "Three deaths, all different ways so how can they be connected?"

Celia said she didn't know but it was too big a coincidence not to be connected somehow.

They said goodbye at Sarah's gate and she ushered Freddie and Max inside.

Celia shooed her children inside their own house and locked the door behind them. Freddie went straight to his bedroom and got his magnifying glass out of his bedside drawer.

He looked at his action man toys sitting on a shelf and looked through the glass. It was amazing how it made everything look so much bigger and could identify small flaws and things that were not obvious without the magnification.

He would definitely need the glass to find clues. He was planning to sneak out this evening after Max had gone to bed. He replaced the magnifying glass back in the drawer.

He went back downstairs. Max was waiting with a pack of cards wanting to play Snap.

They played on the lounge floor and Freddie let Max win.

Celia was preparing their tea of sausages, beans and mash which both her boys liked.

She was distracted as she grilled the sausages. She was thinking about Beverley, Sheila and Lorna. Hearing about tragic events on the television or radio about people who you didn't know was bad enough but when you actually knew the victims it was so much worse.

At seven o'clock, Max went to bed. Freddie was in his bedroom playing a game on his X-Box. He was planning to "go to bed early", he told his mum, but really, he was going to sneak out of the house when his mum and dad were watching television after they had eaten their evening meal. He wanted to return to Sheila's front garden to look for clues.

He had a shower at seven thirty and told his mum he was going to bed to read a book. Luke said goodnight. Celia went upstairs to say goodnight to him and told him to turn his light off at eight o'clock. She went back downstairs to sit in the lounge with Luke to watch *Eastenders*.

Freddie lay in bed and watched his bedside clock hands go around. They appeared to be going much slower than normal.

At ten past eight, he got up quietly and dressed. He placed a pillow in his bed. He stood back and looked at the bed. It looked like he was in there and hoped if his mum came up to check, she would think he was snuggled under the superman duvet.

He took the magnifying glass from his drawer and put it in his backpack. He had a plastic bag already in there. His school lunch had been in there and he usually threw the bag away but today he had saved it. He may need to put clues in it. He turned his bedside lamp off.

He opened his bedroom door, holding his breath. He could hear the television and his parents talking.

He slowly made his way downstairs towards the front door. He took a key from the key rack so he could let himself back in.

He very carefully opened the front door. There was a slight squeak, but he managed to edge out without opening the door too wide.

He shut it behind him.

He quickly walked down the road towards Sheila's house. He let himself in through the small gate and bent down. He took his magnifying glass out of his backpack. He peered down at the path and the small edges of garden both sides of the path leading up to the front door. He was so busy looking for clues he nearly fell forward onto his face. He put his hand out to protect himself and felt something sharp press into his left palm. He looked to see what it was. He picked it up and put it into the plastic bag.

"What, on earth, are you doing, Freddie?" said a voice making Freddie jump with fright. He shot up and hid the bag and magnifying glass behind his back.

It was Mr Watson walking his dog. He was in his late eighties. An ex-military man, he always dressed smartly living alone with Jack Russell dog, Bobby. He lived a few doors away from Freddie's house.

"Nothing," replied Freddie.

"It doesn't look like nothing," replied Mr Watson. "What were you doing crawling up the path and does your mum know you're out?"

"I was looking for clues," Freddie admitted ignoring the question about whether his mum knew he was out.

"Clues?" said Mr Watson. "What on earth for?"

"To find out who started the fire that killed Sheila," Freddie said. "I want to be a policeman when I grow up so thought I'd get some practise in and look for some clues."

Mr Watson shook his head. "Oh, Freddie. The police are investigating. They don't need a young lad like you to help."

Freddie put his magnifying glass and plastic bag in his back pack.

Freddie was about to tell him he had found a clue when another voice spoke.

"Freddie?" said Mary. "I was coming down the road and saw Mr Watson speaking to someone through the gate and wondered who on earth would be in Sheila's front garden."

"He's looking for clues into Sheila's death," Mr Watson told her with a grin.

"Have you found any clues and also does your mother know you are out?" Mary asked Freddie looking at his backpack.

Freddie couldn't think what to say except he would be off now. "I will walk back with you," said Mr Watson.

Mary and Mr Watson walked with Freddie until they reached her house. She said goodbye to them and went inside.

Mr Watson and his dog turned into his house. "You go straight home now, Freddie," he said.

"I will," Freddie replied. He went to his own front door, inserted the key and very carefully opened and then shut the door. He could hear the television. The kitchen light was off so he presumed his parents were still in the lounge. He returned the key to the key hook in the hall. He went upstairs as quietly as he could. He reached his bedroom and went in quietly shutting the door. His heart was racing. He put his back pack down.

He quickly undressed and pulled the pillow out of his bed and got in. His heartbeat was slowing down now. He was pleased to be safely back in his bed.

He reached over for his backpack and retrieved the plastic bag with the clue in it. He took the clue out and looked at it before shoving it back in the plastic bag which he then returned to the bottom of his back pack.

It took a while for Freddie to fall asleep. He had a lot to tell Freya tomorrow.

# Chapter Fifty-Three

Friday morning was sunny and warm. There was a light breeze but it promised to be fine all day. The church bells tolled and the two funeral cars made their way to Merrydale church for the eleven o'clock service. The vicar was waiting outside the church.

Jane, her husband and two children were in one car following Sheila who was in the first hearse.

The turnout was good. A lot of the villagers were already in the church awaiting Sheila and her family. They were talking quietly and looking at the order of service.

The coffin which was being carried by four pall bearers from the funeral home and entered the church to Beethoven's Fur Elise.

Jane and her family followed the coffin and then went to sit in the front pews.

The service opened with the hymn, "Abide with me".

The vicar, Reverend Geoffrey Taylor, who lived in the neighbouring parish, opened the service by thanking everyone for attending.

"Sheila's life should be celebrated, not mourned, even though she passed away too early," he said as he started the prayers.

The service went without a hitch and the congregation filed out silently after listening to The Wind beneath my Wings by Bette Midler. Sheila was going to be cremated in a private ceremony so her family continued to the Olehampton crematorium for a short service saying they would see everyone in the village pub a little later for the wake.

The village pub was ready to receive the mourners. There was a buffet arranged on two tables at the back of the room.

"It was a lovely service," Marie was saying to Frances as they sipped a fruit juice. "It's a very good turn-out, isn't it?" as she looked around at the many people in the room.

Simon and George joined them holding their pints of beer. "I wonder when they will find out who killed her," Frances was saying.

"Did you see the police at the back of the church?" George asked.

"No," said Anne joining them at their table. "Why would they be there?"

"I think they normally go funerals of suspicious deaths to see if they can pick up on anything," replied Simon "I think they look at the mourners to see if they spot anything or hear anything unusual."

Frances said, "Surely, whoever is responsible would be very careful in what they say or do so as not to bring attention to themselves. Also, would the person responsible, actually go to the funeral of their victim?"

"Yes, they probably would," replied Marie. "If it was someone the victim knew, then it would be strange not to go. That would alert people as to why they were not there."

"Well I should think most of the people who knew Sheila are here. I can't see anybody missing that should be here," said Frances looking around. "Doesn't it make you feel awful thinking the actual murderer may be here amongst us?"

"It certainly does," agreed Marie sipping her drink.

Mary came over to them. "It was a lovely service, wasn't it?"

She had a lemonade drink in her hand.

"We were just thinking how awful it is if the murderer is actually here amongst us," said Frances.

Mary shuddered and said indeed it would be dreadful.

"I wish I had gone around to Sheila's a bit more often," said Mary. "I mainly saw her in the street but we always stopped to have a chat."

"Same here," said Frances. "I perhaps should have called around after Beverley's death but I only rang. Looking back now I should have called around to see how she was."

"Does anyone know yet when Lorna's funeral is?" asked Mary. "I spoke to her son not long after she died but he didn't have any date arranged. He said the coroner would contact him when her body would be released and then he would let me know. I wonder if it's now been organised but he just hasn't let me know yet. I will ask the vicar as I expect he will be doing the service."

"I wonder when Beverley's funeral is?" asked Marie.

"I don't know if they've traced any family yet. Judging by what we found out when we went to Haleton, there may not be anyone who wants to organise it," said George.

"Surely, they must have traced someone by now," said Frances.

"It might be down to us as a village to organise her funeral," said Marie. "She needs to be buried or cremated with dignity and with friends who knew her."

"Let's wait a bit longer and see what happens," said Simon sipping his beer.

Celia came over to join them. "Sarah is collecting the girls from nursery," she said to Marie when she asked where Sarah was. "She didn't know Sheila as well as I did, so she offered to keep them for a bit so I could come along."

"That was nice of her," said Mary.

"Julie is coming along in her lunch break," said Julian who had taken the morning off work to attend the funeral. "There's a couple of teachers off sick, so she couldn't take the morning off to come to the service."

Roger and Fay arrived with their drinks. Two chairs were pulled up to make room for them.

Kerry came over and sat down. She had a glass of wine which she put down on the table.

"I took the day off work. I would only be thinking about the service if I was at work, so I used a day's holiday to come."

She shuddered and said she hoped Sheila's death would soon be solved and the murderer brought to justice.

"We all do," said Frances patting her arm.

She looked around to see if she could see the two policemen who had attended the funeral.

"I can't see the police here," she commented.

"I don't think they would actually come to the wake. It's just for friends and family," replied Julian.

"I would have liked to speak with them and ask for an update," she said.

"I don't suppose they would tell us anything though, even if we asked. We can ask Jane when she comes back from the crematorium. She's the one they would tell anything to," said George.

He got up to get another pint from the bar.

# Chapter Fifty-Four

The two policemen who had attended the service were sitting in their car in the church car park discussing the funeral.

"It was a good send-off," said Harry.

"Not bad, there were a lot of folk there," his colleague, John, replied. "Did you spot anything?"

"Yes, I think I did. I was watching the suspects face," said Harry. "But there's no evidence which is so frustrating."

"There's bound to be a slip up soon. Usually. when someone believes they've got away with their crime. then they start to relax," replied John.

"We must be careful, we don't want our suspicions getting out to who we think is responsible," said Harry.

John started the car and they returned to the station.

Jane and her family returned from the crematorium. They entered the pub and George got up and offered to buy them a drink.

"Thank you," said Jane wiping a tear from her eye.

"Come and sit with us," he said pointing to their table. Simon caught George's eye and nod of his head and collected more chairs to arrange around their table.

They sat down and Jane introduced her husband, Ken, and two daughters, Colette and Hayley.

The girls looked about fourteen and sixteen.

"I'm so sorry about your aunt," Mary said to them. "We are all devastated."

"Thanks. We didn't see much of her, but even so, it's very sad how she died," said Colette, the younger one.

"We are waiting for someone to be arrested," said Hayley. "The police are closing in they told us."

"Is that right?" asked Marie to Jane. Everyone around the table looked at Jane.

"Well, they don't tell us very much, but from what they have said is that they feel it might not be too long before someone is arrested," replied Jane.

"Crikey," said Simon. "That's good news. Hopefully, someone will be charged soon," he said to the group around the table.

They all agreed it was good news, wasn't it?

Marie was about to say something to Anne but then the barman called, "Buffet ready!"

He had taken the coverings off the food and set pots of tea and coffee on the table.

"Please, all help yourselves," said Ken.

The two girls got up first and went over to the buffet tables.

The others followed them and took a plate and napkin each. The buffet looked very appetising.

"Oh, God," said Marie as she spotted a plate of sandwiches at the back of the table.

"What's up?" asked Simon who was helping himself to a sausage roll.

"Prawn sandwiches!" she answered pointing to the plate. She shuddered. "I don't think I'll ever eat a prawn sandwich again. They will always remind me of Beverley."

"Yes, I think I'll give them a miss, too," he said plumping for an egg and cress sandwich instead.

Anne and George had heard the conversation, looked at each other and opted for cheese and onion.

They all returned to their table to eat their lunch. The vicar came over to their table and held Jane's hand in a comforting manner. She thanked him for his services today.

Julie arrived from the school and sat down by Julian. She asked how everything had gone and gave her condolences to Jane. He bought her a lemonade from the bar while she collected a couple of sandwiches from the buffet table.

Julian brought her up to date with what Jane had been told by the police.

Some of the mourners took their plates of food outside in the sunshine and sat on the outside benches. The bar was busy with the pub doing a good trade. Jane and Ken went outside to speak with different people and thanked them for attending the funeral. Her two girls were on a bench playing with their phones.

Celia was the first to leave saying she needed to collect her daughters from Sarah.

"She's probably had enough of them now," she grinned.

Ten minutes later, Julie and Julian left to go back to work. Roger and Fay left as Roger said he had an appointment.

Frances and Kerry then left leaving George, Anne, Marie, Simon and Mary at the table.

George offered to buy another round of drinks but no one wanted one. He would have liked another beer but decided to forgo it after catching Anne's frown.

"So, by what Jane said, the police are closing in then," said Simon. "Let's hope they also find out about Lorna and Beverley."

"We can then sleep easy in our beds at night," said Mary.

"Any news on the jail jumper?" asked Anne looking at them all.

"We haven't heard anything at all. There's been nothing on the news," replied Marie. She said to Simon they should be going now but wanted to say goodbye to Jane and Ken. They got up saying goodbye to George, Anne and Mary and went outside to Jane, Ken and the girls.

Mary said she was also leaving as she had to go to the shop as she needed milk and bread. She found Jane outside and said now the funeral was over she could move on a bit.

"I can't move on until they find out who killed her," said Jane. Mary patted her arm and said hopefully it would be soon.

George and Anne also went outside to find Jane to say goodbye. They then walked home.

*So, the police are closing in? I need to be very careful. It's a good job people can't read my thoughts.*

# Chapter Fifty-Five

The coroner released Lorna's body back to her family so they could plan the funeral. Her son, Jack, rung Mary on Friday evening, to tell her that the funeral was going to be the following Friday at one o'clock at Merrydale church. He said there would be a private cremation after the church service.

Mary said she had been to Sheila's funeral today.

"I'm so sorry for you," he said. "Two funerals in one week, that's not good," he replied.

Mary said she would let people know as she was sure many people would want to attend.

"Have the police found out anything?" Mary asked.

"Well, it was definitely the ready meal that contained the arsenic. The empty packet was in Mum's kitchen bin. The food firm denied all knowledge of sending it. They have customer's addresses on their records and Mum's wasn't on their list. The police found all the packaging, but there was no postage on the outer packet, which means it was hand delivered by someone. The firm said they didn't think it came from them as their envelopes have their details stamped on the actual container lid and Mum's was blank. Also, they said the flyer was different to theirs. They think someone must have bought the meal from somewhere else and packaged it up pretending it had come from the firm."

"That's terrible," Mary replied.

"I know. There were only Mum's fingerprints on the package. It's an absolute mystery who sent it and the reason why. Whoever did it must have bought it and that person put the arsenic in the meal and then resealed it and dropped it off at Mum's house. The police looked at all their customer's names and addresses but no one in the village had ordered one."

"What a mystery," replied Mary.

"The police are obviously trying to find out but as yet have no answers. We need to know who hated Mum to do such a thing," said Jack.

He then asked Mary if she would say a few words at the funeral as she had been a good friend to his mother.

"Alright, I will try and come up with something to say, but I can't think of anyone who would hate her, she was well liked in the village. I really miss her. At least, she can be laid to rest now. I will tell people the date and time of the funeral," said Mary as she thanked him for ringing her.

She rang Anne and Marie with the funeral date and time. They said they would tell other people as well.

"I can't believe we are going to another friend's funeral," said Marie. "And we've still got Beverley's sometime soon."

"I know," said Mary sadly. "Let's hope that's all then."

# Chapter Fifty-Six

Lorna's funeral was attended by a lot of people, mostly the same ones that had attended Sheila's the week before. After the first hymn and prayers, Mary stepped forward to say a few words. She spoke of how she and Lorna had enjoyed many outings together to various garden centres, car boot sales and fetes and how she would miss her.

"She was such a nice, friendly person and her passing has been far too early," she concluded.

She wiped a tear away and sat down. George, who was sitting in the pew behind her patted her on the back and whispered how well she did. Mary wiped away another tear.

After the funeral the mourners gathered around a table at the pub.

"One week later, here we are again," said Marie sipping lemonade. George returned from the buffet with a plate of sandwiches. He heard Mary telling Marie that Lorna's son Jack had told her the police were no nearer finding out what happened.

Simon and Roger were at the bar buying a drink.

"Any night sightings in your yard?" asked Roger sipping a pint of shandy.

"Nothing at all! I think it might have been a waste of money!" Simon grinned.

"No, I think it's a good thing we've had them installed."

"I suppose so," Simon replied taking his beer over the table where the others were sitting.

Fay and Anne were talking with Mary and telling her how well she did with her eulogy in church.

"It's not easy standing up talking in front of people," said Marie.

Mary said it had been difficult but she was glad she had done it.

Anne asked Marie how her daughter in law was.

"Good," she smiled, "the baby is due in a couple of weeks. I've been invited to stay with them for a few days after the birth so I'm busy cooking dishes for Simon to heat up while I'm away. He won't eat ready meals from a supermarket."

George went up to the bar to buy another pint. The barman was busy so he turned to chat with Julian who had just arrived. Julie hadn't come to the service but he had taken the afternoon off to come and pay his respects.

"Rum business, this," he said to him.

"I know," replied Julian. "Two funerals in one week," he shook his head.

"Lorna's son Jack told Mary that the police are no closer to finding out who sent the food to her," said George. "Surely, they must find out soon if there's a connection between all the deaths."

"It's must be difficult because the three deaths were all so different," said Julian.

"But surely, there can't be three murderers strolling around Merrydale!" replied George.

"It would make a film if there was!" said Simon. "A real whodunit."

"Well, I wish the police would pull their finger out and solve them," said Julian. "It's got Julie looking closely at everyone she meets when she's in the village and those outside the school, wondering if she's speaking to a killer."

"It's the same with Anne and most people I should think," agreed George. "Even I look at people I know and think, *Is it you?*"

"Well it's not me so you're quite safe standing here," said Julian with a laugh.

"What can I get you?" asked the barman coming over to them.

George and Julian asked for two pints of beer.

"Sorry to keep you waiting, it's really busy. All these funerals are good for business, though!" the barman grinned as he drew their pints.

Julian and George took their drinks over to the table and sat down.

Lorna's son and daughter and their children arrived back from the crematorium.

They came over to sit down with them when George beckoned them over to join them. He pulled up some chairs.

"Everything go, ok?" Simon asked.

"Yes, as well as these things can go," said Lorna's son Jack.

"It's all so sad," said Lorna's daughter tearfully. "It's like a nightmare."

"Do the police know any more about what happened?" asked Anne.

"No, they have no real leads yet. The food company deny all knowledge of sending the meal out to her," Jack answered.

"I'm sure they will find out who was responsible," said George.

"Well, I hope it's soon as it's really awful not knowing who disliked her enough to murder her, and in such a horrible way," said Jack sadly. His wife agreed nodding her head sadly.

"Perhaps she witnessed something and had to be silenced," suggested George.

"We're not on *Midsomer's Murders* George!" cried Anne. "This is Merrydale, a small village. What on earth could she have witnessed here?"

"Obviously, I don't know yet," replied George.

Mary also asked what sort of thing she could have witnessed.

"I've no idea, but perhaps we ought to try and find out," he said looking around the table.

"How could you do that?" asked Mary.

"I'm not sure, but I will give it some thought," he replied. "We need to find out about her last few days. Something must have happened to have some bearing on her death."

"I spoke with her on the day she died and she was fine then," said Mary. "She didn't appear to be worried about anything. We talked about what we had been doing that morning and then arranged to go to a fete the next day."

Jack said he had spoken to her the night before her death and nothing had been different as far as he could tell. She had been her own normal cheerful self.

"Well, I will see if I can find out anything. I will ask around," said George.

"Inspector George will solve the case. Forget about leaving it to the experts!" said Anne smiling.

Everyone laughed.

"Don't forget that it could be someone we know," said Mary. "You must be very careful. How do you know you are not going to be speaking to the person who did all this? You don't want to be the next one to be killed off. I should leave well alone if I were you."

Anne, suddenly feeling alarmed said, "George, listen to Mary. I agree with her. You could be in danger if you start asking around in the village. Please leave it to the police."

Marie said she also agreed with Mary and Anne. Simon nodded his agreement as well.

"I'll be very discreet, careful is my middle name," he reassured them as he finished the last few drops of his pint.

He got up from the table saying he needed to leave as he was going to pop into work a bit later. A very worried looking Anne collected her handbag from by her chair and left with him after saying goodbye to everyone.

# Chapter Fifty-Seven

There was a bulletin on the local evening news. The bail jumper had finally been caught. He had been found sleeping rough about ten miles outside of Merrydale. A man had come across him whilst walking his dog in some woods. He had seen recent news reports and recognised the absconder by his green camouflage jacket and immediately phoned the police before he could wake up.

The police were there within ten minutes and promptly woke him up and then arrested him. He was dirty and dishevelled and didn't put up any resistance.

He was taken to Olehampton police station where he was put in a cell. He needed to be cleaned up before being interviewed. He also needed his social worker present as Jarvis appeared to be mumbling and not making a lot of sense. It turned out he had not been taking his prescribed medication. He was hungry so had a meal provided by the station canteen.

The news reporter said that it was indeed Jarvis Shelby. He had been on the run for almost five weeks and was going to be interviewed the following day.

Nothing else was said about him in the bulletin.

Simon was watching the news with Marie.

"That's good news at last. Now, they need to find out why he was hanging around Merrydale," Simon said to Marie.

George was saying the same to Anne. "I hope we find out why he was here."

They did indeed find out.

The following evening at half past six the local news reader reported that the arrested man had been interviewed at length and it was discovered he had been searching for a person in Merrydale. The person he had been looking for was Beverley Kingston who had recently been murdered said the reporter. "More details would be released in the next couple of days," said the news reporter.

Merrydale villagers watched with great interest. "Was Beverley's murder going to be solved at last?" was the question on everyone's lips.

George said to Anne, "But he wasn't at the Safari Supper so how could he have murdered Beverley?"

Marie was saying the same thing to Simon.

"Let's hear for the update when we get one," he said.

Three nights later, the news reporter stated that after being interviewed over the last couple of days the suspect had been absolved of her murder. Apparently, he hadn't actually caught up with her in the village. It turned out that he was the younger brother of Beverley's husband, and he said he had been looking for her to get his revenge for his brother's death once he had finally found out where she was now living. He was going by the name Shelby, as it had been his mother's maiden name so people didn't associate him with the name Kingston.

Upon hearing she had been murdered, he had left the area as he didn't need to take his revenge anymore. He said hadn't heard the news of her murder before which is why he had hung around Merrydale.

He was being charged with jumping bail and also attacking Simon in his farm yard, and the news report finally explained that he had been in possession of a knife when originally arrested and bailed.

"Well, at least we have an answer as to why he was here in the village," said George to Simon on the phone after the latest news report.

"But we're no closer as to knowing who killed Beverley," replied Simon. "At least he admitted to hitting me on the head."

"Yes, I'm glad about that but we're not any closer as to who killed Beverley. So, surely, it's got to be someone living here in Merrydale then," replied George.

Anne said it was horrible looking at people in the village and wondering who it might be. "Someone must be responsible, someone who we have probably been speaking to. It doesn't bear thinking about," she said with a shudder.

"You must be very careful when out and about," he told her. "Keep your ears and eyes well open and tell me immediately if you suspect anyone or hear anything you are worried about."

"I will but you must be careful too and stop all this nonsense about trying to investigate. Leave it to the police," she replied.

He said he would be careful.

# Chapter Fifty-Eight

Freddie had come to a halt in his investigations. He didn't know what to do next. He had showed Freya the clue he had found in Sheila's garden, but he said still didn't know if it was a real clue or not. He told her again it could be something important or something completely unconnected with the murder.

She had no new suggestions either. "Keep it anyway, it might be useful," she told him.

Freddie got it out of the plastic bag and showed her it again.

"Freddie, you've shown it to me it a million times. I have no idea what it means. It could be from the murderer or it could have been there a long time," she said.

"I really think it's a clue," he replied looking at it through his magnifying glass.

He replaced it in the plastic bag and put it back in his back pack.

*It would soon be the summer holidays. He would have more time to investigate further*, he thought.

At school in class, he told Charlie that he would be busy in the holidays investigating.

"Perhaps, I can help you," Charlie replied.

Julie overheard them as she was walking around the classroom and said, "Don't be silly, Freddie, the police are looking into everything that's happened. They don't need your help. Your mum told you this as well, and Charlie, you keep out of it, too."

"Yes, Miss," Freddie replied. Charlie nodded but with a sly look at Freddie. She walked back to the front of the class. Freddie then turned to Charlie with a wink and with a look of pure innocence concentrated on the maths lesson.

Julie looked at him and hoped he would heed her advice. She didn't want anything to happen to him.

He told Freya in the playground at break that Charlie had said he would help with his investigations. Freya was a bit put out. She was Freddie's best friend and should be the one helping him. "I may tell Mum about the clue you found," she told him with a huff.

"Don't do that," he said. "You are my assistant and Charlie is my next one. I will always tell you first if I find out anything more."

"Okay, but make sure you always do tell me first if you find anything else out."

Freddie promised he would.

# Chapter Fifty-Nine

It was Marie's birthday on the following Saturday. She had invited several friends around for a buffet over lunchtime. She prepared several platters of sandwiches, salad and quiche and Sarah had made a large birthday cake which she had delivered earlier that morning.

Simon had given her a lovely bracelet which she wore so she could show it off to her guests.

The party was going to start at one o'clock.

Simon was getting changed from his overalls into casual attire upstairs when the first guests arrived. Mary arrived with Celia, Luke, and their children and Sarah and her husband David and their children. Frances came just afterwards followed by Julie and Julian. Roger and Fay came, quickly followed by George and Anne. Stan and James arrived together.

Simon came downstairs to greet everyone. Around thirty people had been invited. They were mostly all congregated between the large farm kitchen and lounge. Everyone knew each other and the conversation flowed.

Everyone had come with a present and card for Marie. She happily accepted and opened them. Chocolates, wine, bath salts, plants and flowers were gratefully received. Stan started collecting up the discarded wrapping paper and put it all in a black bin bag which Marie handed to him. He tied the top with the drawstring.

"Thanks, Stan," Marie said. "That can go out in the recycling bin later."

Marie showed them her bracelet that Simon had bought her. Freddie and Freya were more interested in going outside to see the cows. Their parents said they were allowed to go as far as the fence of the nearest field next to the farmhouse and see them, but told not to wander any further. Freddie had his back pack with him and retrieved his magnifying glass from inside it. He peered at everyone through it.

"For finding my clues!" he told everyone with a big grin. He dropped his backpack in a corner of the kitchen.

The younger children remained inside with their parents.

Prosecco flowed and the buffet was enjoyed.

Predictably, the conversation came around to the recent events in the village.

"At least, the bail jumper has been arrested," said Celia. "That's one less thing to worry about."

Mary asked if anyone had heard any more about police investigations into the deaths.

"Nothing more that I know of," replied George. "But I see the police are still about the village asking questions."

Most people said they had seen them about.

Stan said he heard that they were getting closer to finding out more about Beverley's family but he wasn't sure who had told him. He was eating a cheese and pickle sandwich with enjoyment. He didn't mix much but he was very fond of Marie so had accepted her invitation.

Roger said he had heard that as well. "The police came around to ours again asking questions. I hope they don't suspect me because that's twice they've been around!"

Fay said it was because of him being almost first on the scene when Sheila's house caught fire. "They wanted to know if he saw or heard anything suspicious when other people arrived on the scene. They asked him to remember if anyone looked guilty."

"What does a guilty expression look like?" asked Sarah.

"I wouldn't really know!" said Simon.

"I told them that I didn't see anyone looking other than horrified," said Roger.

Freddie and Freya entered the room. They had come back inside after growing bored with watching the cows.

"They don't do anything but eat grass!" said Freya. "And they smell."

James laughed and said, "Hey you, it's a healthy countryside smell!"

Freya turned up her nose.

George asked Freddie how his investigations were going.

Sarah groaned and said, "Don't start him off, please."

His dad, David, said, "That's all he talks about!"

"Not too bad," replied Freddie.

He put his magnifying glass on top of his backpack rather than inside as he thought he might need it later.

"I haven't found any here yet, though," he sighed. "But I'll keep looking. I did find one clue two weeks ago."

Freya replied that she wasn't sure it was a real clue though. "Freddie thinks it is but I'm not so sure."

"What was it?" asked Mary.

"I can't tell anyone what it is or where I found it until I do further investigating," he grinned looking at Freya. She grinned back.

"What makes you think it's a clue?" asked Anne. Frances said she was just about to ask the same question.

"Because it's something that shouldn't have been where it was found," Freddie answered.

Julie said she had advised Freddie to leave it to the police. She said she had overheard him talking at school in class.

"I want to solve the murders. I'm training to be a policeman," said Freddie as he took a couple of crisps from a dish on the table.

Freya said he wanted to receive a medal from the Queen when he solved them. There were bursts of laughter from the group of adults.

Everyone laughed except one person, but it appeared to go unobserved as there were a lot of people in the room.

"Will you need a suit and tie to meet the Queen?" Freya asked.

"I hope not," said Freddie. "I haven't got either."

Marie said to Sarah that Freddie must be careful because it could be someone in the village who was known to them. Frances agreed and said Sarah should keep him with her as much as possible to ensure his safety. Belinda agreed. She had been relieved that at least the bail jumper had been caught so he was out of the picture.

Sarah said she was doing her best but once Freddie set his mind on something he was like a terrier and wouldn't let it go. Celia said she had also warned Freya.

Freddie and Freya grinned at each other.

George tapped Freddie on his shoulder and said to leave it to the police.

"I've been asking around and haven't really got anywhere and I'm a grownup," he told him as he took a swig of Prosecco.

"Perhaps, you're not asking the right questions. Also, you need a magnifying glass!" Freddie replied solemnly helping himself to an egg sandwich.

Simon clapped his hands and announced it was time to cut the birthday cake. They all sang "Happy Birthday" to Marie who blushed.

She cut the cake after blowing out the candles with some help from the younger children.

It was a fine sunny day and some of the guests wandered out into the yard after eating lunch whilst others remained talking in the kitchen. The younger children, under the watchful eye of their parents, went up to the fence to watch the cows grazing.

Simon looked around at the tranquil surroundings and said to Anne and Frances he would never have believed Merrydale could be in the midst of such horrific events.

Freddie came running out asking if anyone had seen his magnifying glass. "It was on top of my backpack, but it's now gone," he cried.

Simon replied that perhaps one of the younger children had taken it.

Celia asked her younger daughters and Sarah asked Max. They all denied taking it.

Freya said she had seen Freddie put the magnifying glass on top of his backpack when they had returned from seeing the cows in the field. Freddie ran back inside and frantically searched his backpack and the surrounding area.

"It's definitely not here," he said. He looked around at everybody. "One of you have stolen it," he accused.

"Don't be so rude Freddie!" said Sarah to her son.

"It was here and now it's not," he answered. "It didn't have legs. It didn't walk off by itself."

Max laughed.

"Did you take it, Max?" asked Freddie hearing him laugh.

"No, I didn't," Max replied. "I laughed because I was thinking about it growing legs and walking off."

Freya could see how upset Freddie was. She asked her sisters if one of them had taken it, but they said, "No."

The grownups started searching around in the kitchen but it was nowhere to be found.

"I need it to find out more clues. It's too important to lose," Freddie wailed.

Marie said if she found it after everyone had gone, she would be sure to return it to Freddie.

He sniffed and said, "I think the murderer has taken it to stop me finding more clues."

"Freddie!" said Sarah. "You cannot say things like that. You are amongst friends here."

"But we are being told at school that it could be someone we know," he retorted.

"Please, stop saying things like that," said his father, David. "We know and trust everyone here."

Freya put her arm around Freddie and said she would save up and give him her pocket money to buy a new one.

"I want mine back. Can I look in all your pockets and bags?" he cried looking at everybody in the room.

"No, of course you can't!" said Sarah.

Mary, Julia, and Marie tried to placate him but he wouldn't be comforted.

"I know it's been stolen by someone here," he told them. "Come on Freya. Let's go outside."

They left the kitchen and went into the yard.

"I *know* someone's stolen it," he told her. "That means the murderer has got to be one of the people here. They want to stop me investigating."

Freya looked very alarmed. "Who?"

"I don't know yet but I'm going to find out."

"Shall we go back in and have a really good look at everyone's face. We may spot a clue," she replied.

"Alright," Freddie said. "Come on."

They went back into the kitchen. Freddie retrieved his backpack and looked in it again as well as around the area where he had left it. He shook his head at Freya.

The party was coming to an end and people were thanking Marie and wishing her a happy rest of her day.

Sarah and David collected Max and Freddie to head home. They walked with Mary, Celia, Luke and the girls.

"Did you spot anything when we went back in?" Freya asked Freddie as they trailed behind the others.

"No, it was too late. Everyone was talking and getting ready to go," replied Freddie. "But it must have been one of them that took my magnifying glass."

They said goodbye to each other when they reached their houses.

Marie was tidying up after the party. "I haven't come across Freddie's magnifying glass," she told Simon as she started putting crockery in the dishwasher.

"It is a bit odd though, how it just disappeared," replied Simon picking up the black bag holding the wrapping paper that Stan had collected earlier in the to take out to the dustbin.

"Freya said she definitely saw him put it on top of his backpack when they came back inside," she said.

"Do you think someone here did take it?" she asked with a worried expression.

"I don't know, but it is strange. Freddie was very vocal about needing it to find clues. Do you believe someone here took it to try and stop him?" Simon asked.

"If someone did take it then that must mean that they could be responsible for one or all of the deaths," she said. She sat down at the table as she suddenly felt faint.

"It's a terrible thought," she told Simon.

Simon agreed. He went upstairs to change into his overalls and went out to join James for the evening milking. He took the black bag out to the recycling bin. Marie remained at the table deep in thought. She got up from the table and finished clearing up.

*I hope Freddie won't be seeing that magnifying glass again! No one saw me take it and hide it. Careful is my middle name. I wonder what the clue is that he says he has found. I should like to ask him, but that would not be sensible and I am such a sensible person.*

# Chapter Sixty

Simon and Marie received a phone call at eleven o'clock the next morning. Georgina had gone into labour and Gary said they were on their way to the hospital. He would ring when the baby arrived. It was agreed that Marie would come and stay with them for a week when they all arrived home. Georgina had been told she would stay in hospital for a night after giving birth.

Marie packed a bag ready to take with her. She went out into her garden to do some weeding. She was restless and needed to keep busy as she couldn't stop thinking about how things were going at the hospital.

At six o clock the phone rang. Gary congratulated them on becoming grandparents to baby Ben. He had arrived at five minutes past five and all was well. He weighed in at seven pounds seven ounces and had a shock of dark hair. He sent a photo of mother and baby via Marie's phone.

"Georgina was brilliant!" he said.

Marie ran to the milking shed to tell Simon and show him the photo of their new grandson.

They hugged each other.

"Hello, Granny." He laughed.

James was shown the photo and said he looked like a fine lad.

They had a glass of wine with their evening meal and toasted young Ben.

"There are enough meals in the freezer to last you the week," she said to Simon. He was going to take Marie to Gary's house the following afternoon so he could meet his grandson.

"How exciting!" she exclaimed raising her glass.

"At least, it's taken your mind off the events here," he told her.

"Yes, it has for a bit but we still have it hanging over us," she replied.

He told her to try and put it out of her mind and enjoy the week with Gary, Georgina and baby Ben.

Marie rang Anne to tell her the good news.

"That's wonderful news," replied Anne. "George is visiting Frances but I'll tell him when he comes in."

George was at Frances's house having a coffee. It was a fine evening, so he had walked there. She lived in a small detached house on the outskirts of the village. They met up quite often for coffee and chats. They sat outside on the patio furniture. Frances nurtured a small garden. She had some flower beds but grew mostly low maintenance shrubs as she wasn't an enthusiastic gardener.

She was asking him if Freddie's magnifying glass had turned up.

"No," he told her. "It's very strange how it disappeared. We searched the kitchen but it wasn't found. Someone who was present must have taken it without any of us seeing."

"They obviously think Freddie knows something and with him saying he needed the magnifying glass to investigate further it must have worried them," she said.

"Who the hell was it though? There were thirty people at the house!" said George.

"I wish I knew," replied Frances.

"I keep thinking of all the people there and cannot believe any of them could cause someone's death. It's got to be someone who is known to all of us but with a very thick skin to carry on as normal," said George.

"Let's make a list of everyone who was there," suggested Frances.

She went into the house and fetched a pen and notepad.

She asked George of all the names of people who were at the party.

"I can remember some, but not all," she said.

"Let me think. There was Celia, Luke, Julie, Julian, Simon, Marie, Mary, Kerry, Sarah, David, Stan, James, Roger, Fay, Anne, you, me, Harry, Heidi, John, Diane, Len, Connie, Amy, Fred, Ken, Sue, Matt, Heather and Belinda."

He counted on his fingers and she wrote each name down.

"Who would you suspect?" she asked George refilling his coffee cup.

"Absolutely *none* of them. We've known all of them for a long time," he replied.

"But we think one of them took the magnifying glass."

"I just don't know who would have taken it. I can't believe anyone there would have done it," George replied sipping his coffee.

"Damn, the pen's run out," she said shaking it.

"I'll fetch one. Where do you keep them?" George asked as he got up.

"In the kitchen drawer under the radio," she replied.

George opened the drawer. He saw a pen and took it out. The drawer had opened easily and had rolled out to nearly its full length. George was about to push it shut when he spotted something under a pack of blue tack at the very back of the drawer. He took out a magnifying glass. His heart started beating fast. He looked at it quickly and then put it back where he had found it.

"Have you found a pen?" called Frances from the garden.

George went back into the garden and handed the pen to his sister.

George had gone hot and cold. Was that Freddie's magnifying glass in the kitchen drawer? Surely, Frances wasn't involved in any of the deaths?

He looked at her as her head was bent over the names on the notepad.

"We can't rule out any of them. It's got to be someone we know," she said looking up at George.

"No, we can't rule anyone out," he replied with a heavy heart.

He finished his coffee and said he needed to get off. He said for them both to think about all the people who attended Marie's party and speak again in a couple of days.

He wanted to get back to Anne to tell her about what he had found in Frances's drawer.

He walked slowly back home thinking deeply.

Anne was astounded when she heard what George had found in his sister's kitchen drawer.

"Surely, she can't be the one who took it?" she asked. "I can't believe it."

"Neither can I," replied George.

"Should you have asked her about it when you found it? There could be a simple explanation," said Anne.

"I was too shocked to think straight," replied George.

Anne said she couldn't blame him as she would have been too.

# Chapter Sixty-One

Julie and Julian had read the younger children a story and put them to bed. Freya was allowed to stay up later than her sisters, but she decided to go to bed to read. She was reading an Enid Blyton *Famous Five* story and wished she was as brave as the children in it. She knew Freddie would be as brave as them. She was really glad she was his best friend and wished she could find his magnifying glass for him. She would have to save her pocket money for a whole month before she could afford to buy him a replacement.

She put her book down to think about the party. Had she seen anybody go over to the corner where he had put his backpack and magnifying glass down? She recalled it was below the large dresser in the kitchen and had seen several grownups standing nearby. Some had laid their plates and glasses on the dresser and she supposed it would have been easy for one to bend down as if they had dropped something and snatch the magnifying glass and shove it in their pocket.

She remembered people moving around the kitchen. Some had helped out with washing crockery up, some helped clearing up some of the food from near empty plates.

She tried to remember what people were wearing. She usually had a good memory. Who was wearing clothes with a pocket?

She recalled Marie and Anne had cardigans on with pockets and so had Frances. Mary had a check dress on with a patch pocket on the right side on the front. Fay had a pinafore dress on and that may have had a pocket.

Julie's dress may have had pockets but she couldn't remember seeing any obvious ones. The men present would have had pockets in their shorts or trousers.

Belinda had trousers on, so would have had a pocket in the side.

Diane Brown, Amy, and Sue Tarrant were wearing shorts so they presumably would have had pockets in the sides. Freya sighed. Any one of them could have taken the magnifying glass and put it in their pocket. It wasn't a large item to hide.

She lay in bed with her hands beneath her head. She would speak with Freddie tomorrow on the way to school and tell him about remembering who had pockets which thinking about it, was all of them.

There was only one more week left at school before breaking up for the summer holidays. She and Freddie would then have more time to investigate.

She saved her place in the book with a bookmark and put it on her bedside table, switched her lamp off and fell asleep.

# Chapter Sixty-Two

Jane had almost finished the sad task of clearing Sheila's house. A clearance firm had collected the furniture and items that Jane couldn't take to the local tip. She had arranged for a decorator to come in and completely re-decorate the house. She has found them on the internet of local tradesmen.

She visited the house on Monday morning to let the decorators in. They were a local firm and she had heard good reviews. There were two men waiting in their van when she arrived. She let them in and then handed them a spare key so they could come and go without the need for her to be present.

"Nice house, love," said Ted pocketing the key. "It should sell well after we've finished."

"Yes, I hope so," replied Jane.

"Sorry about your sister. I heard what happened here. Terrible business. Have they arrested anyone yet?" he asked.

"No, not yet. I don't think the police have any idea who did it and why," she replied sadly.

"They'll get them I'm sure, it may take time but they usually get someone in the end," said the second decorator Lenny.

They deposited their paints, brushes, masking tape and cloths in the lounge. They looked around the house and decided to start decorating the upstairs rooms first.

Jane hung around for a bit. She had taken a kettle and mugs, coffee, tea and biscuits into the kitchen and told them to help themselves.

She left them to it. She didn't want to get in their way. She had chosen the colours for the rooms.

"We've got your number if we need to call you," shouted Ted when Jane called up to say she was leaving.

"I'll drop back in towards the end of the week," she told them.

"Okay, love," Ted replied.

She could hear him whistling along to a song on the radio as she closed the front door. She was now going into Olehampton to speak to an estate agent about putting the house on the market.

She drove off with a wistful look back at the house.

Celia and Sarah were walking back from dropping the children off to nursery and school. They passed by Sheila's house and saw the decorators van outside.

They looked at the house. The upstairs windows had been replaced and the front of the house had been cleaned and now looked back to normal.

"I wonder who will buy it?" said Celia.

"Hopefully, it will be a family. We need more children at the school to keep it going. Too many village schools have closed," said Sarah.

"I wish the police would hurry up and find out who started the fire," said Celia. "Has Freddie's magnifying glass turned up?" she asked.

"No, he's still very upset about it. He says someone at the party definitely took it and I am inclined to believe him which is very worrying," replied Sarah.

They carried on up the road towards their houses and met Mary coming down. She was going to the shop she told them. She nodded towards Sheila's house and said, "I see the decorators are in. I should think it will then be sold."

"We were just saying we wish the police would find out who started the fire," said Sarah.

"We all want that," said Mary.

"Julie told us this morning when we were dropping the children off at school that Julian thinks he's heard when Beverley's funeral is. Someone came in for his car to be serviced and told him. He knew Julian lived here in the village. Apparently, his wife works for the coroner and her body has now been released. He thinks there's no family involvement so the council will be paying for a quick cremation. It's so sad," said Celia.

"Indeed it is," replied Mary. "I wonder whether anyone is allowed to attend."

"I'm not really sure. If it's a quick cremation being paid for by the council there probably isn't a service involved," said Sarah.

"We'll try and find out. George might know," said Celia. They said goodbye to Mary and carried on back home.

# Chapter Sixty-Three

George had indeed heard from the council that Beverley's funeral would be in a week's time. It was to be a private cremation. "At least she can be laid to rest now," he told Anne.

"Yes, and it's the last of the three funerals, thank goodness. It is almost unbelievable that no one has been arrested yet. I don't know what the police are playing at. Three deaths in one village and no one apprehended," she replied.

George replied that surely there must be a break through soon and then everyone can get back to normal again.

Celia rang him and asked about the funeral. He confirmed that it was a private affair with no service.

She said she would tell people. "I wonder if we could have some sort of short service in the church to remember her by?" she asked him.

"That would be nice. I will speak with the vicar and see if something can be arranged," he promised her. "I will let you know."

He rang the vicar and they arranged for a service to be held this coming Thursday morning at eleven o'clock. He rang Celia back to tell her so she could tell other people.

"It will just be a service of remembrance. We won't hold a wake. I think we've had enough wakes for a time," he said.

Celia said she would let people know and George said he would do the same saying Beverley deserved to be remembered by people who knew her.

The service on Thursday morning was well attended by the villagers. The church bell tolled and people made their way to the church and then into the pews. It was strange without a coffin arriving for all to stare at.

The vicar gave a short sermon and two hymns were sung. Prayers were read and heads were bowed.

"I shall be glad to put my suit away," Simon said to George and Anne as they made their way out of the church. "Wearing it three times in a month is not good."

"Same here," replied George pulling at his tie. "Let's hope we don't need them for a good while now."

People stood around talking. They didn't like to just go home feeling it would be disrespectful to disappear straight after the service.

Simon was asked about his new grandson and when would Marie be back home.

"I'm collecting her on Saturday morning after the milking," he said "She's really enjoyed staying with them and looking after baby Ben. He's got a good pair of lungs by all account," he grinned.

"At least that is some good news for a change," Anne said with a smile. She said she was looking forward to seeing some photos of the baby.

Mary and Frances came up to them. George still didn't know what to do about asking his sister about the magnifying glass he had seen in the kitchen drawer at her house. He felt uncomfortable even thinking that she could have been involved in taking it and even worse, being somehow involved with the recent deaths.

Mary said it had been a nice service and hopefully that was the last one they would be going to for a time. Frances patted her arm and replied she hoped so as well.

Celia and Sarah came up to them. Celia said, "That was a nice service. I hope Beverley was looking over us and saw how many people attended. I'm glad I was able to come. It's the last day before the children break up for the holidays!" she smiled. "I look forward to the summer holidays but am also pleased when September comes!"

"All our children will be at school in September, too. We'll have so much time on our hands," said Sarah. "I was thinking of perhaps getting a part time job but it's difficult finding one around school hours."

Anne said it was indeed difficult to find one with school hours. "Children are bound to be poorly at some point and then there are the holidays to contend with."

"We usually hold a fundraising meeting in September," said George. "We will also need to recruit a new member on to the committee."

Celia shuddered and said perhaps it ought to be postponed until the New Year.

"You may be right. I don't think our minds are in the right place at the moment. Until the police catch whoever did these dreadful things perhaps, we should postpone another meeting," replied George.

"I wouldn't mind being on the committee," said Sarah.

"That's great. Count yourself in, we'll be pleased to have you," beamed George. "We'll hold the next meeting in January, then."

Mary said that it was a good idea to have the September meeting postponed.

Frances said she was leaving now as she was going into Olehampton as she had an appointment. She didn't elaborate and no one asked what the appointment was. George watched her walk down the path and through the church gate. Anne saw him watching and nudged him. He turned to her and shrugged. Mary saw the nudge and shrug and raised her eyebrows. Anne didn't say anything. She just shook her head as she really didn't know what to say. She turned to speak with Roger and Fay who had joined them.

The mourners were breaking away now. Children needed to be collected from nursery and some had work to return to. George walked with Simon down the church path following Sarah and Celia.

"Do you think the person responsible for Beverley's death was here?" Simon asked quietly.

"God, I don't know. I keep looking at people wondering if they have a secret, but everyone looks and acts so normal," replied George. He hadn't told Simon he had seen a magnifying glass in his sister's kitchen drawer. He was trying to convince himself it was just a coincidence that she had one that looked like Freddie's.

They walked towards home. Mary, Roger and Fay joined them as they were all heading in the same direction. Anne pointed out the 'For Sale' sign outside Sheila's house.

"I think Lorna's house will be on the market soon as well," said Mary. "Jack rang the other evening asking how I was which was nice of him. He said he had toyed with the idea of moving in there himself but his wife talked him out of it saying it would always be a constant reminder of what happened there."

"Yes, I don't think I would want to be living in a house where my mother was murdered," said Anne with a shudder.

"I suppose you just have to remember the good times," said Mary. "I don't like passing her house where I was a visitor many times. I do miss her. We had some really good times together."

"It must be awful for you, Mary," said Simon. "We got used to seeing you both going out on your trips together."

"I haven't been to a car boot sale or a fete since it happened. It was something we both enjoyed and it wouldn't be the same going without her."

Mary's house was reached first and they said goodbye to her.

"See you soon," Anne said to Mary. "We'll meet up for a coffee next week if you want to."

"I should like that, thank you," said Mary.

"I'll ring you with a day and time," promised Anne.

Mary went into her house.

"I feel sorry for her," said Anne. "Losing a good friend must be awful plus having someone drop dead in your kitchen. I hope she's coping alright and not just putting a brave face on things."

"Asking her to come around for a coffee will be nice, she'll hopefully feel a bit better knowing someone cares. She doesn't have any family as far as I know," replied George.

Anne said, "I think she has an estranged son from what I can remember Lorna telling me once. I don't know why she doesn't see him though."

Simon, Roger and Fay said cheerio to George and Anne and went further up the road to their farms.

Anne put the kettle on when she and George got in. "Nothing like a good cup of tea!" he said. "Perhaps a nice cheese and pickle sandwich with a bag of crisps and a slice of that fruit cake that I know is in the tin?"

"You and your stomach," laughed Anne as she boiled the kettle and put the tea bags in the teapot. "You could do with cutting down a bit."

"Nothing wrong with this figure," said George pulling his stomach in and patting it. Anne grinned. She loved George just the way he was!

Simon arrived home and got changed out of his suit into his overalls. "I hope you don't come out again anytime soon!" he told the suit as he put it back in his wardrobe.

He would have a quick coffee and sandwich and then find Stan. He saw there was a light flashing on the phone with a message from Marie asking how the service had gone. He would ring her later when he had more time to talk. He was really looking forward to seeing her on Saturday. The house was not the same when she wasn't there. It was too quiet!

# Chapter Sixty-Four

On Friday evening Simon thought he ought to have a quick tidy up in the house. Marie liked things in the correct place and when she was away, he tended to let things slide a bit. He made sure that all the crockery was washed and back in the cupboards. He checked the washing basket in the bathroom and collected some clothes ready for the washing machine. He stuffed the clothes in and then reached down in the cupboard under the sink for the washing powder. He knocked a bottle of washing up liquid over as he was getting the powder out. Something towards the back of the cupboard where the bleach was kept caught his eye. He retrieved a magnifying glass. He held it up not believing his eyes.

How on earth had it got there? Who would have put it in the back of the cupboard under the sink?

He sat down at the table and looked at it. It *must* be Freddie's. As far as he knew there had never been a magnifying glass in the house since the children were little and even if it was a relic from their childhood, it would not have been kept under the sink. Neither he nor Marie had any need for one.

He didn't know what to do. He laid it on the table.

He would ask Marie if she knew anything about it when she came home tomorrow.

He put it on the dresser and tried to forget about it but his eyes kept returning to it every time he went into the kitchen.

He drove over to collect Marie the next morning after he and James had finished the milking.

He was still perplexed about the magnifying glass and couldn't stop wondering how it had got into the cupboard.

He pulled up at Gary's house and got out. He walked to the front door and rang the bell.

"It's Grandpa!" said Gary as he opened the door. "Come in, Dad."

Marie came to greet him with a kiss.

"Nice to see you, I've missed you."

"Not as much as I've missed you," he grinned hugging her.

He could hear a tiny wail from the lounge. They went in and saw Georgina on the settee holding the baby who was grizzling softly. "How are you?" he asked her. "Good, considering the lack of sleep!" she laughed.

Simon crouched down to see baby Ben. "I think he's grown a bit since I last saw him," he said holding a tiny finger. "I'm not surprised with the amount of milk he drinks!" Georgina smiled looking at her son.

She held him up for Simon to take him. "I think I've forgotten how to hold a tiny baby." He grinned.

"It will soon come back to you!" said Marie.

Simon sat down in an armchair cuddling his grandson and looked at Ben. "He's looking good," he said smiling.

Gary came in with some mugs of coffee that he put down on a coffee table.

"How are you bearing up then, Gary?" Simon asked. "Very good. We can't stop looking at him," replied Gary grinning.

"Make the most of this time, they soon grow up!" said Simon.

He handed Ben to Gary who passed him back to Georgina.

"How's everything at home?" asked Marie. "Is there any more news on the deaths?"

"Well, as you know, all the funerals have now taken place but we haven't had any updates from the police."

"It's unbelievable what's been happening in Merrydale," said Georgina jiggling a grizzly Ben. "Gary and I can hardly believe it."

"Same here. Everybody looks at each other wondering if they're the one who did it," replied Simon.

"It must be awful thinking you may know the person responsible. Are the deaths definitely connected?" asked Gary.

"I think they must be, it's far too big a coincidence to have three unconnected deaths in a matter of a few weeks in one village," said Simon.

"At least the bail jumper was caught," said Georgina.

"Yes, and he was definitely connected to Beverley who died first but he's been ruled out of her murder as he was nowhere near her on the night she died," said Marie.

"It's got to be someone who is connected to all three," said Gary.

"I suppose so but all three women were well known in the village. Everyone was friendly with them so in that sense everyone is connected," replied Simon.

"The connection has got to come from outside the village then," said Georgina.

"The police must be looking into all their backgrounds," said Gary. "They must want to find the person responsible quickly before there are any further deaths."

"Don't say that," begged Marie. "I couldn't bear to think someone else may be murdered."

Gary said he would make them all a sandwich for lunch. He asked for their preferences and they all plumped for ham and tomato.

They had an enjoyable couple of hours. At three thirty, Simon and Marie left as Simon needed to get back for the milking. They kissed the baby and said they hoped to see him again very soon. Gary handed Marie a bunch of flowers. Gary and Georgina waved them off, thanking Marie for her invaluable help over the past few days.

They arrived home at four o'clock. James had just arrived for the milking and Simon called out that he would be with him as soon as he had changed. He retrieved Marie's case from the car boot and they went into the house.

On entering the kitchen with Marie's flowers, his eyes went straight to the magnifying glass on the dresser. Marie had gone straight upstairs so she hadn't yet seen it.

He laid the flowers by the sink and went upstairs with Marie's case and got changed into his overalls.

"It's nice to be home," Marie told him.

"Nice to have you back." He hugged her. "I'll see you later," as he went back downstairs. He went into the kitchen and moved the magnifying glass from the dresser into a drawer. He would show it to Marie when he returned. He hoped she may be able to throw some light on how it had ended up under the sink.

He went outside to see James in the milking shed.

He returned to the house at just gone six o'clock. Marie had dinner almost ready.

"It's a cottage pie which was in the freezer," she told him stirring the gravy.

Simon went upstairs to wash and change.

He came down to find the dinner on the table. He sat down and started to tuck in. He needed to tell her about finding the magnifying glass.

"A funny thing has happened," he told Marie.

"What?" she asked looking alarmed.

Simon got up and took the magnifying glass out of the drawer.

"Where did that come from?" she asked. "Is it Freddie's?"

"I found it in the cupboard under the sink," he told her pointing to the cupboard. "I was getting the washing powder out and found it hidden at the back."

"How, on earth, did it get there?" Marie asked him.

"I have no idea, but someone hid it there," he replied looking at her. Marie held the magnifying glass with a puzzled expression.

"Are you asking me if I put it there?" she asked.

"Of course, I'm not!" he replied.

"That's a relief," she grinned. "But it disappeared during my party, so someone who was here must have hidden it in the cupboard."

"But who?" said Simon forking up some cottage pie.

"Well, obviously someone who doesn't want Freddie to have it. They must have been at the sink washing up and slipped it in the cupboard."

"Who helped wash up?" asked Simon.

"A lot of different people. if I remember rightly. There were a lot of people here in the kitchen helping washing up, moving plates to the sink ready for washing up or using the bin which is under the sink," she replied. "It could be anyone of them here at the time."

"I will let Freddie have it back, now it's been found, but I'm not sure what to say about where it was actually found," said Simon. "It's bound to interest him even more and make him want to investigate further which may not be a good thing."

"Do we tell other people it's been found?" asked Marie. "Surely, the person who hid it would know we would find it at some stage."

"I really don't know. It looks like *we* hid it if we tell people it was found in our cupboard or that we hid it to incriminate someone at the party and then, hey presto, we found it. Let's leave it this evening and think about what the best thing to do is," said Simon as he got up and took his plate over to the sink. "That was very nice thanks. I'm going in the lounge to watch the news, are you coming in?" he asked.

"I'll wash up first and bring a cup of tea in," Marie answered taking her own plate to the sink. Simon went into the lounge and switched the television on.

Marie sat down again at the table and picked up the magnifying glass. She needed time to think. Fancy being found at the back of the cupboard.

# Chapter Sixty-Five

Anne rang Mary on Monday morning asking her if she was free to come around for a coffee. "I can't today as Ebony is not very well and I think I may need to take him to the vet," she replied.

"I'm sorry to hear that," said Anne. "What'd you think is wrong with him?"

"He's been sick and he wants to sleep more than usual," replied Mary. "I think he might have eaten something."

"I hope he's okay. Please let me know how he gets on or if there's anything I can do to help," said Anne.

"I will, thank you," Mary replied.

She was worried because she had found her shed door ajar this morning. The kitchen window looked out onto the garden and she had been washing up her breakfast dishes when she noticed it. She didn't let Ebony in there as the shed housed all sorts of chemicals and fertilisers which she used for gardening. She tried to remember when she had last gone into the shed. She thought it may have been yesterday. She had needed some twine to hold back one of her roses against the fence. Perhaps she hadn't closed the door properly. Ebony was a nosy cat and if he saw the shed door open, he may have wandered inside to check it out.

She checked Ebony, who was lying on the settee, fast asleep. She went out into the garden and went to the shed. She opened the door. She saw there was some white powder on the floor. A box had fallen off the shelf and some of the contents had spilled out. Ebony must have leapt onto the shelf and knocked the box down. She picked the box up and returned it to the shelf and then swept up the powder from the floor. Mary went out of the shed making sure she closed the door properly. She went back inside to check her cat. Ebony was now awake and looked a little better. Mary hoped that if Ebony had licked some of the spilt powder, then he would have only ingested a little bit and by being sick would rid his body of it.

She stroked him and he started purring. She lifted him off the settee and took him into the kitchen where she poured some milk into his bowl. He lapped some up which was a good sign. She would keep a really close eye on him today. She would not leave him alone. She would absolutely hate to lose him. Living alone, he was a great comfort and companion to her, a living thing she could talk to.

Anne rang her in the afternoon asking how Ebony was.

"Quite a lot better thank you," replied Mary. "He's eaten a little bit of food but he's drinking well so I think he's over the worst without needing to go to the vet."

"That's a relief," said Anne. "Do you know what may have caused him to be poorly?"

"I found the garden shed door open and I think he may have gone in to explore. Some fertiliser had spilled on the floor and he may have eaten a bit which made him sick. I blame myself because I can't have shut the shed door properly," explained Mary.

"Well, accidents happen but I'm so pleased he seems to be alright now," said Anne. "I know what he means to you."

"It has taught me a lesson to always make sure the shed door is closed," said Mary. She thanked Anne for ringing.

She returned to the settee and sat down with Ebony on her lap. She stroked him and told him how sorry she was and she would be more careful in future.

Anne was telling George about Mary and Ebony. He had been into his office today. He liked to keep in touch and enjoyed the odd days he went in. He had some very good and loyal staff that ran his haulage firm excellently.

"It would have been awful if Ebony had died," she was telling him. "Especially, now she no longer has Lorna about for company." George agreed and said thank goodness the cat seemed to be fine now by what she had told her. "I bet she'll be more careful about keeping her shed door shut."

"I will ring her again in a couple of days, ask about the cat and see if she can come for coffee," said Anne.

"Good, now what's for tea?" George asked. Anne laughed and told him there was a chicken roasting in the oven. He rubbed his stomach in anticipation.

Freddie was delighted to be told he would be reunited with his magnifying glass. Simon had rung his mum up and said it had been found in some paper which had been cleared up after the party.

"I don't know how we missed it," he told Sarah. "I was sorting it out for recycling when all of a sudden it dropped out of the carrier bag that the discarded paper had been in."

Sarah thanked him and said her life would be a lot better now as Freddie mentioned the missing magnifying glass at least three times a day!

Simon said he would pop it around that evening.

Freddie rang Freya to tell her about the magnifying glass being found. "I don't believe it was found mixed in the wrapping paper," he told her. "It wasn't anywhere near any paper."

"No, the presents were opened around the table, not near the dresser." she agreed.

"Why would Simon say it was found in the paper then?" said Freddie. "Someone definitely took it, but Simon must be covering for them."

"Do you think Marie took it?" asked Freya. "She always looks a bit worried when I see her."

"I can't see why she took it unless she is involved in the murders. Also, why "find" it again?" replied Freddie. "I think we need to list her and Simon as some of the suspects. I need to buy a notebook to put all the suspects down in."

"Who else would you put down in your notebook then?" asked Freya.

"All those people who went to the party. It's got to be one of them," he said. "I need to write their names down and give each person a score. A number ten if we suspect them and going down to number one if we don't."

"So Simon and Marie would score a ten," worked out Freya.

"Definitely. Let's see each other tomorrow and ask if we can go to the shop to buy a notebook," said Freddie.

Freya said for Freddie to hold on so she could ask her mum if Freddie could come to her house in the morning for lunch and could they all go to the shop. She called out to Celia and asked if Freddie could come to their house in the morning. Celia said yes, so Freya told Freddie to come around at ten o'clock.

They agreed to both think about who was to be scored ten down to one.

Simon called around to return the magnifying glass that evening. He repeated again where he had found it. Freddie looked at him with an innocent expression and thanked him for finding it but was thinking he didn't believe a word of it.

Simon clapped him on the back and said he could now continue with his investigations. "Are you going to reveal the clue you said you found?" he asked.

"No, I can't tell anyone yet, until I find out more," replied Freddie.

232

Simon looked at Sarah and shrugged. He smiled at Freddie, said goodbye and went home.

"Definitely a number ten for the notebook," he thought.

Next morning at ten o'clock, Sarah stood at her gate and watched Freddie, backpack on his back, run around to Freya's house. The door opened when he rang the bell.

She went back inside her house wondering how to keep Max occupied whilst Freddie was at Freya's.

Freya welcomed Freddie inside and they went up to her bedroom to talk. "Have you been thinking?" she asked him. He got his magnifying glass out of his backpack. He peered at her through it.

He told her about Simon returning the magnifying glass last evening. "I didn't believe him when he said where it had been found, and then he asked me what the clue was that I have already found!"

"A number ten, then," said Freya. "Mum said we can go to the shop in a bit."

"I have been thinking about the scores. As soon as I've got the notebook, we can do the scoring," he told her.

# Chapter Sixty-Six

They all went out to go to the village shop at eleven. The younger girls wanted to walk with Freddie and hold his hands either side of him. He didn't really want to in case Charlie saw him but he did so anyway.

They entered the shop. It was a smallish shop, with a post office, but was well stocked. Celia went to buy a couple of stamps from the post office which was in the corner of the shop and Freddie and Freya went to the stationary section and chose a notebook which cost £1.50. Freya paid for it saying she had been saving her pocket money up to buy Freddie a new magnifying glass and had some money saved. She treated her sisters to some penny sweets.

She took the book and sweets to the counter and paid for it. She handed the notebook to Freddie who thanked her.

They waited for Celia to finish and then they all went out of the shop.

"Do you want to go for a walk?" Celia asked them. They agreed to go for a walk to the park. The children went over to the swings and roundabout.

"Push us, Freddie," cried the younger girls and Max scrambling onto the swings.

He pushed them on the roundabout until he was puffed out. They were leaving the park when they saw Mary approaching.

"Hello," she greeted them. She said she was out for a morning walk and asked how everyone was. "Better, now that Freddie has had his magnifying glass returned. Freya can now stop asking me who I think took the wretched thing," laughed Celia.

"So it's turned up then. Where was it found?" asked Mary.

"It was found tangled up with some birthday wrapping paper at Simon and Marie's house," said Freya.

"Really?" she replied "That's very good news then," she said looking at Freddie.

"Yes, it is. Freya and I can continue investigating and perhaps, find some more clues now," he replied.

"What was the clue you found?" she asked him.

"We can't tell anybody yet, it's a secret," he replied looking at Freya.

"Let's go home and get some lunch now," said Celia as they said goodbye to Mary and made their way home.

Once back home, Freddie and Freya disappeared to her bedroom.

Freddie opened the notebook and asked Freya for a pen. She found one in her bedside drawer and handed it to him.

"We now need to remember who was at the party," he told her tapping the pen against his teeth.

He looked at her ready to write down the names of all the people they remembered being present at Marie's party.

Freya recited, "There was Mum, Dad, Julie, Julian, Simon, Marie, Mary, Kerry, your mum and dad, Stan, James, Roger, Fay, Anne, George, Frances, Harry, Mr and Brown, Mr and Mrs Davies, Miss Fry, Amy, Fred, Ken and Mr and Mrs Tarrant," said Freya.

"Gosh, what a good memory you've got," said Freddie looking amazed. "I can't believe you've remembered everybody who was there."

"I lay in bed last night trying to remember everybody," she replied with a grin. "I have a good memory."

Freddie told her she certainly had, and then asked her to repeat them as he wrote each name down.

"Now, we have to score them," he told Freya.

This was hard. They didn't know some of the people very well. They tended to score the lesser-known people with a one. Neither Freddie nor Freya had seen any of them behaving suspiciously they told each other.

"We know Simon and Marie are a ten. I suppose George and Anne should be a ten because they always seem to know village things that are going on. Frances is a ten as she is related to George, and she also wanted to know what your clue is," said Freya. "Belinda must score ten as she knows Frances. Mary should be a ten because she asked what your clue was, as well. We can't score our parents surely."

"They can be a one," said Freddie writing it down.

"What about our teacher and her husband?" asked Freya. "Let's score them a seven, we know her but not him very well," said Freddie.

"Roger and Fay?" asked Freya.

"They have to score a ten because they know Simon and Marie. They could all be involved," wrote Freddie.

"Kerry, Stan and James?" asked Freya. "At least a seven, I think," said Freddie. She wrote their score down.

He looked at the list. "Top scores go to Simon, Marie, Belinda, Mary, George, Anne, Frances, Roger and Fay."

"That's a lot of tens. I can't believe one of them could be a murderer," said Freya.

"Nor me, but you never know," said Freddie. "It could be someone who is perfectly alright on the outside but evil inside."

Freya looked at the list. "I don't think we're getting anywhere, do you?"

Freddie said no he didn't think they were.

He opened his backpack and showed Freya the clue again.

"I need to find out about where this came from before finding it at Sheila's," he told Freya. "I think it's a very important clue."

He put it back in his backpack.

"Lunch is ready." called Celia up to them from downstairs.

Freddie sighed and put the notebook in the backpack and they went downstairs to eat.

# Chapter Sixty-Seven

Julie was talking with Stan. She was out for a walk in the village and saw him leaving Simons at the end of his working day. They walked along the road together. He was asking if there were any updates on the three deaths. "I don't like to keep asking Simon."

"None that I know of," she told him. "The police are not around anymore in the village. I suppose they are working behind the scenes though."

"Any main suspects?" he queried.

"None that I know of. There are some theories going around but no concrete evidence," Julie replied.

"Is young Freddie still investigating?" he asked with a grin.

"I believe so," she replied. "He was beside himself that he couldn't investigate without his magnifying glass."

"Perhaps he had a point. Someone may not want him poking his nose in. We all know what Freddie's like if he sets his mind on something. It's strange how it just disappeared though," said Stan.

"Thank goodness Simon found it," she replied.

"I didn't know that," said Stan looking amazed. "He never told me it had been found."

"Yes, he found it in a bag for recycling. Apparently, it was caught up in some paper that the presents had been wrapped in," Julie informed him.

"I wonder why Simon never mentioned finding it," Stan said. "That's a bit odd though. I collected the paper up and put it in a black bag ready for the recycling bin. I'm certain it was not in there then. I can't see how it could have become mixed up with the paper. The magnifying glass was nowhere near where the presents were opened. I'll have to ask him tomorrow."

"I'm only repeating what Marie told me," said Julie. "I saw her yesterday in the shop. Is she alright? She always looks quite worried."

"I think she was worried about her daughter-in-law when she was expecting but that's over now so I don't know what she might be worried about now," said Stan as he said goodbye to Julie as they reached his cottage. She continued with her walk towards the end of the village.

On her way back, she passed Sheila's house. She saw the 'For Sale' sign. There were two cars parked outside. The front door opened and a man of around forty stepped out followed by a young couple. They looked to be in their mid-twenties. He closed and locked the door behind them. He turned back to the couple.

"We do like it," the young man was saying to the older one as they walked down the short path. "And we can see it's been painted recently," smiled the young lady.

"We will be in touch when we've discussed it," said the young man to the other man who Julie presumed was an estate agent.

The man shook hands with the couple, got in his car and with a wave drove off.

The young couple saw Julie passing and said hello to her. Julie stopped. "I see you've been looking at the house," she said.

"Yes. Did you know the lady who lived here?" her husband asked.

Julie wasn't sure if they knew about the fire and subsequent death so she wasn't sure how much to say.

"Yes. I did know her," she answered hoping they would not ask any more about her.

"It's a very nice village to live in," she told them trying to change the subject.

She told Julian later that she had told them it was a nice village to live in but didn't blurt out that there had been three murders in the space of three weeks. She didn't want to frighten them off.

She bade them goodbye and continued up the road. Mary was walking down from her house. Julie told her she had just spoken with a couple who were looking at Sheila's house.

"I didn't know what to say when they asked if I knew the lady who had lived there as I didn't know if they knew why the house was up for sale."

"Yes, I can see that would be awkward," Mary replied. "Surely, an estate agent would need to tell a potential buyer something about the previous owner."

"I would have thought so," agreed Julie.

"Is Lorna's house going up for sale?" asked Julie. Mary said it was. Jack kept in touch with her which she appreciated.

Julie replied, "Hopefully, no one will say what happened there to potential buyers. Look well if the couple I just saw at Sheila's look around Lorna's and then they find out what happened at both houses. We probably wouldn't see them again for dust!"

Mary agreed that it would indeed be unfortunate.

Julie carried on up the road and went home. Mary had a half hour walk and then she too returned home. Ebony was fine now and greeted her at the front door wrapping her warm furry body around Mary's lower legs.

# Chapter Sixty-Eight

The August weather was being very kind. It was sunny and warm and many people went off on their summer holidays. Freddie missed Freya when she and her family went off to Devon for a week. His own family summer holiday to Cornwall was not for a couple of weeks.

He spent one morning at Charlie's house but he had an annoying younger brother who insisted on being with them even when Charlie told him to "shove off." Charlie's mum told him off when she heard this and said to let William play with him and Freddie.

"We can't talk properly when he's around," complained Charlie. "He can't keep anything to himself."

"What are you talking about that's so secret?" she asked Charlie.

"Freddie is telling me about his investigations into the village deaths. William might open his mouth to one of the suspects and it could be dangerous for him," he told her.

"I think you should stop this nonsense, Freddie," she told him. "Talk about other things instead."

"Alright," said Freddie with a discreet wink at Charlie.

They played a card game with William who then went crying to his mum saying Charlie and Freddie had cheated.

Freddie was collected by Sarah at one o clock which he was quite pleased about. Max could be a bit annoying at times but William was ten times worse.

He had his lunch and then went to his room to look at his notebook. He hadn't written anything else in it apart from the people who had been at the party and their scores.

He wondered whether Freya had thought any more about them. He would ask her when she returned from Devon.

Stan had asked Simon about finding the magnifying glass in the bag holding the party wrapping paper. He thought Simon was a bit sheepish and wondered why. He asked Marie about it as well but she said it had obviously been collected up by mistake.

He didn't believe either of them. It had obviously been found somewhere else but they were not letting on where. It puzzled Stan as normally they were very open and honest. He had known them for a long time and had never doubted their word before.

He began to wonder if either of them knew more about the deaths than they were letting on.

It was a sobering thought.

George had also wondered about the way the magnifying glass had been found.

"It's very odd," he said to Anne. "It wasn't anywhere near the presents if Freddie had laid it on his backpack like he said he did."

Anne agreed it was strange but what reason could they have for fibbing where it had been found?

A sold sign had gone up outside Sheila's house. Anne told George she thought it might be the young couple that Julie had seen coming out of it a few weeks ago. She wondered when they would be moving in. Lorna's house had still not gone on the market.

# Chapter Sixty-Nine

Anne decided to hold a coffee morning. She rang around and invited the usual crowd. She baked a large cherry cake and laid out the coffee cups ready for ten thirty when her guests would arrive. Fay arrived first as she lived the nearest.

Mary, Celia and Sarah and David arrived together. Freddie and Max came with Freya and her sisters. Freddie and Freya were pleased to be together again. He told her about going to Charlie's house and how annoying young William was.

Julie and Kerry arrived together and then Frances came with Belinda. It was a lovely day, so Anne decided to hold it outside on her patio. The children could play in the garden.

Marie arrived and apologised for being late. She said Georgina had rung up for a chat just as she was leaving. Anne said it didn't matter at all. Hearing news about baby Ben was more important than arriving on time!

Anne brought out the coffee and cake and orange juice and biscuits for the children.

There was lots of chat and laughter.

Inevitably, the conversation came around to the deaths. No one had been apprehended. No one had any updates.

"I don't think they will ever find out who is responsible," said Celia sipping her coffee. "If the police had any evidence, then they would have arrested someone by now."

"I agree," said Mary. "Someone has clearly got away with it."

She took a slice of cake and complimented Anne. Julie said last time she had made a cherry cake all the cherries had been at the bottom!

Celia said it was very worrying not having updates with the investigations. She asked Anne if George had any intention of further investigating.

"Well, he came to a full stop before," replied Anne. "So, I don't think he's planning on doing anything else, he's leaving it to the police now."

"I agree he ought to leave well alone," said Marie. Fay agreed.

"I see Sheila's house is sold," Anne announced.

"Yes, I have seen the sign," said Mary.

Frances asked if anyone knew who had bought it.

"A young couple, I believe," said Julie and told them she had spoken to an interested couple coming out of the house with an estate agent.

Freddie overheard the conversation. He had come to the table to refill his glass with orange juice.

"When are they moving in?" he asked. "I need to see if I can find out another clue to go with the one, I've already found there before anyone moves in, now that I have my magnifying glass back."

He clapped his hand over his mouth. He hadn't meant to say where he had found his clue.

"What was the clue you found there?" asked Marie. The conversation around the table stopped. All were waiting for Freddie's reply.

"I-I-can't tell you," he stammered.

"Come on, Freddie," said Mary. "You can tell us."

"No, I can't," he replied and rushed off to see Freya in the garden. He told her about blurting out where he had found his clue.

"That was silly," she told him. "I know," he replied, "it just came out. I didn't mean to say it."

"The murderer may go to the house and look for another clue now they know one was found there," Freya told him.

"I know," Freddie sadly replied. "I was stupid saying it."

The conversation around the table resumed. "I wonder what Freddie's clue is?" asked Anne.

"I should love to know exactly whereabouts he found the clue and what it is," said Mary.

"So would I," said Frances. She sipped her coffee. "Do you know, Sarah?"

"Don't ask me what it is," said Sarah. "He hasn't told me anything."

"Perhaps, you ought to try and find out?" suggested Frances. Marie agreed saying the clue could be important in finding out about the deaths.

"I don't think he would tell me even if I asked him," said Sarah. "Freya may tell you though, Celia."

"Not a chance," said Celia with a grin. "Thick as thieves those two!"

"But they are only ten years old and parents should be in charge and if they suspect their children know anything that needs to be told then they should be made to tell them," said Marie.

"That's easier said than done," said Sarah feeling a bit miffed at being spoken to like that. She liked Marie but thought it out of order being told what to do about her own child. She looked at Celia who shrugged.

"Freya probably wouldn't tell me anything either," she said.

The coffee cups were refilled by Anne and the last of the cherry cake eaten. The conversation turned to holiday destinations. Murders and clues were put on temporary hold.

*I'm disappointed the wretched magnifying glass was found so quickly. I thought I had hidden it well out of sight at the back of the cupboard.*

*I need to find out what Freddie's clue is. Freddie has obviously found something, but what can it be? He is an interfering boy and needs to be stopped. I must be very careful and think very carefully about what to do next.*

# Chapter Seventy

The rest of August passed pleasantly. The weather had been very warm with above average temperatures and there had been very little rain. The Bank Holiday Monday was enjoyed by all. Roger was telling Fay that he needed some good rain for his crops. "I may have to get the sprayer out on the fields."

They had just finished their breakfast and Fay was washing up the dishes. She looked out of the window and said "George is coming up the drive."

She dried her hands on a towel and went to the front door.

"Hello, George," she said as she let him in.

"Hi, Fay, is Roger in?"

"Yes, come in," she said and led him into the kitchen.

"I thought I'd run something by you both," he said removing his cap as he sat down at the table. He accepted Fays offer of a cup of tea.

"What can we do for you?" asked Roger.

"It's about Simon and Marie. I think they have something to hide," he said thanking Fay as she handed him his tea.

"What, on earth, do you mean?" asked Fay as she sat down.

"Well, I suppose I didn't think anything odd after Simon told me about finding Freddie's magnifying glass in the wrapping paper. I was pleased Freddie would get it back," he replied. "But I went to the pub a couple of evenings ago and Stan was there. We got talking about Marie's party and the missing magnifying glass and he was adamant that the glass had not been in the bag with the paper. He said he had cleared up the paper and put it all in a black bag ready for the recycling bin."

"But why would Simon lie about where it was found?" asked Fay.

"I really don't know," replied George. "I did say to Stan that perhaps he was mistaken and he said no it definitely was not in the bag. He would have felt it amongst the paper if it had been in there. He said he tied the bag up with the drawstring as well. He also said Simon hadn't let on that it had been found until

Julie told him when he met her in the street. Stan thought it was strange Simon hadn't said anything as they spend a lot of time on the farm together and had talked about the missing magnifying glass and the uproar at the party when Freddie discovered it was missing. So why didn't he let on to Stan it had been found?"

George didn't mention that he had suspected his sister Frances of being involved in the deaths after finding a magnifying glass in her kitchen drawer. He was just relieved Freddie's had now been found. He hadn't asked Frances about it and still didn't know why she had one.

"It *is* odd," said Fay.

"We can only presume the magnifying glass was taken because Freddie was going on about finding clues and he needed to be stopped," said Roger. "I really can't believe Simon and Marie are involved in what's happened in the village."

"I can't believe it either," said Roger. "We've known Simon and Marie for years. There's never been anything dodgy about them, as far as I know. They are good neighbours. They've just become grandparents as well!"

"Marie does seem worried lately but then I suppose we all are, due to the events that have gone on in the village," said Fay.

"Stan said Julie said she thought Marie looked worried as well," said George.

"Let's have a think," said Roger. "Marie and Simon hosted a starter course for the Safari Supper so had access to prawns. Both Simon and Marie were at Mary's house when Beverley died and they both appeared at the scene of Sheila's house fire and Marie was walking past Lorna's house when the neighbour was knocking on the door. The turning up of Freddie's magnifying glass is suspicious as Simon didn't tell Stan."

"But other people were also present at both Mary's house when Beverley died and at the house fire," said Fay, "also, anyone at the party could have taken the magnifying glass. It must have been found somewhere in their house though, so why didn't they say where it was really found rather than saying it was in the black bag caught up in the paper."

"But was it coincidence that Marie just happened to be walking past Lorna's house at the time her body was about to be discovered or was it planned to throw people of the scent of suspecting her?"

"Why on earth would one or both of them be involved in the deaths? They have been just as shocked as the rest of us have. What possible reason could they have for killing the three women?" asked Roger.

"I don't know. We need to think very carefully about this," said George.

"I can't believe we are talking about friends of ours!" said Fay with a trembling hand over her mouth. "I've been to a couple of coffee mornings where the deaths have been discussed and Marie appears just as concerned as the rest of us that no one has been arrested yet."

"Don't forget Simon came with me when we went to Haleton to try and find out about Beverley's past before coming to live here and he was just as interested as I was in what we discovered. He didn't appear to be hiding anything," said George.

"But whoever has done these dreadful things would need to have a very thick skin. They are not going to say or do anything to bring attention to themselves are they? They will be carrying on as normal and being very careful," said Roger.

"I think Simon may be covering up for Marie," said George. "He would do anything for her."

"But covering up a crime?" said Fay. "Surely not."

"Would it not be better if we rang up anonymously on Crimestoppers?" asked Roger. "It would then be out of our hands and no one would know who rang them."

"It might be the best way forward if we all agree," said George.

"I think it would be the best thing to do, however much it hurts us naming Simon and Marie as suspects," said Fay.

They all looked at each other.

"All this could hopefully be just a horrible list of coincidences and they may have nothing to hide but can we risk it?" asked George.

"Well, when the police investigate and find they are innocent, at least we would know for sure, but how I'm going to look at them in the face again, I just don't know," said Fay.

"So shall I inform them?" asked George.

Roger and Fay replied in the affirmative.

"I've never had to do anything like this before," said George getting out his mobile phone.

He googled "Crimestoppers" and found there was an online form that he could complete on his phone. He showed it to Roger and Fay.

He started filling in the details and mentally crossed his fingers that his phone number would not be made available to them. It did say it did not store mobile phone data from completing the form so he hoped it was true. He didn't want the police coming around to his house asking why he had not informed them personally.

"This is just awful," Fay said.

George completed the form, took a deep breath and submitted it. He looked at Roger and Fay and grimaced. He then got up, shook his head, put his cap on and left.

The following morning a police car arrived outside Simon's farm. He had just come in from milking the cows and was looking forward to a good breakfast. Marie was frying a couple of eggs and a rasher of bacon and two sausages were waiting on a warm plate. She put two slices of bread into the toaster and switched it on. She had eaten toast and marmalade earlier.

Simon washed his hands and sat at the table. Marie was just sliding the eggs onto the plate when the doorbell rang.

"You sit and eat and I'll see who it is," she told Simon putting the plate on the table.

She opened the door to two police officers. One male and one female. They showed Marie their warrant cards and introduced themselves.

"Is your husband in?" the male officer asked.

"Yes, he's just eating his breakfast after the morning milking," she replied "What's all this about?" she asked.

"May we come in and talk to you both please," said the female officer.

She led them into the kitchen where Simon was eating his breakfast. He looked up and appeared very surprised to see the two police officers.

They introduced themselves to Simon. Marie asked them to sit down.

"We have had some anonymous information relating to the recent deaths in the village," said the male officer. "Your names have been given to us so we need to ask you some questions. We can do this here or you could come to the police station."

"What sort of questions?" asked Marie looking worried.

"Can you tell me where you both were on Saturday 15$^{th}$ June of this year, please?" asked the female officer looking at her small notebook.

"We have already spoken to the police when they came around the village asking questions after Beverley's death," said Simon. He pushed his half-eaten breakfast to one side.

"Just answer the question please," said the male officer.

"That was the Safari Supper evening. It was the night Beverley died. We hosted a starter course and had about thirty people around here," replied Marie. "We did go along to Mary's house a bit later to see if she needed any help with the coffee course."

"Did you see her handbag that contained her sandwich in the kitchen?"

"Yes, I did," admitted Marie.

"I saw it in the kitchen too but wasn't sure whose bag it was," said Simon.

"But Beverley's handbag was red so it was quite noticeable, and she also took it to the fundraising meetings where you were, so surely you would have recognised it as hers when you saw it in the kitchen at Mary's."

"I saw it, yes, but I don't take much notice of women's handbags and I certainly didn't touch it," said Simon.

The officers looked at him but didn't comment on him admitting to not recognising the red bag as Beverley's.

"Where were you both on Wednesday, 19th June?" the male officer asked.

"That was the night Sheila died in the house fire?" Simon said to them. "We saw the house on fire and went to see if there was anything we could do. We were seen by lots of people."

The female officer looked at her notebook. "Where were you prior to going to look at the fire?"

"At home all evening," replied Marie.

"Can anyone verify that?" asked the officer.

"No, no one came around as far as I recall and no one rang up that evening," said Simon.

"Can you tell me about finding your friend Lorna's body in her house?"

"I have already spoken to the police about what happened," said Marie. She was looking very worried. "They will have a record of my statement. I went into Olehampton station."

"We will check on that again. What can you tell me about a missing magnifying glass?" asked the male officer.

"What???" said Marie with her hands on her face "What on earth has a missing magnifying glass got to do with anything?"

"We have been reliably informed that it was taken from your kitchen when you were holding a birthday party. The suggestion is that it was taken to stop its young owner from finding clues relating to one or all of the deaths. He told people at the party he needed it to investigate. Someone needed to stop him investigating further so they took the magnifying glass," said the male officer reading from his notebook.

"But it was found!" said Simon.

"Yes, I know, but it is implied that it was actually located in a different place from where you told people it was found. We were informed that you told people it was found with the discarded wrapping paper in a black bag but from what we have been told it was not in there at all," said the female officer.

"Who, on earth, has been saying these things?" asked Marie looking at Simon.

"We cannot tell you that," she was told.

"Alright, I can tell you we actually found it in the back of the cupboard under our kitchen sink," said Simon. "We fibbed about where it was found because we may have been suspected of putting it there ourselves because it was such a strange place to hide it."

"But why should it matter? As long as it turned up then it shouldn't matter where it had been found?" said the female officer. "It's suspicious because you lied. Perhaps, one of you put it in the cupboard yourselves. Making out it was found in the bag of paper people would assume it had been accidently caught up in the wrapping paper. By admitting it was under your sink would mean it had been deliberately hidden, possibly by either one of you."

"Of course we didn't put it under the sink but someone at the party must have done," said Marie. "We didn't know what to think when we found it."

"Who actually found it?" interrupted the male officer.

"I did, a few days after the party," admitted Simon looking at Marie. "Marie was away at our sons at the time. Our son and his wife have just had a baby and she was staying with them for a few days."

"Who else, apart from yourselves, would have had the opportunity to hide it under the sink?" asked the male officer.

"Any number of people at the party," Marie told them, "we had around thirty people here and some of them helped wash up or cleared dishes putting them ready for washing up by the sink, plus our small waste bin is under the sink so anyone could have shoved the magnifying glass at the back of the cupboard without being seen."

"Do you have any ideas as to who was at the party and may have hidden it and ultimately would cast the blame on yourselves with a view to the police investigating whether you had anything to do with the village deaths?" asked the female officer.

"None at all, but we *were* worried that it was someone present at the party who had something to do with the deaths. Someone who wanted Freddie to stop looking for clues," admitted Marie. "We lied about where it was found, so the guilty person would think we didn't suspect anyone who was at my party."

The two police officers looked at each other.

"But the person who hid it would know you lied about where it was found," pointed out the female officer.

"I'm sorry, but we obviously weren't thinking straight," said Simon. "It was my idea to say we found it in the bag of paper. Once we did find it, we just wanted to return it to Freddie and get it out of our house."

"Even though he could continue with his "investigations", which could be dangerous for him if indeed the person responsible of one or all of the deaths was present at the party?" asked the male officer.

Neither Simon, nor Marie knew what to say. They hadn't even thought about whether Freddie could be in danger once the magnifying glass had been returned to him.

The police officers stood up and thanked them for answering their questions. "We will need to speak with you both again," the female officer said. "We will be in touch."

Simon showed them out.

He went back into the kitchen and sat down at the table where Marie was still sitting. "Who would report us to the police making out we have something to hide?" Marie asked.

"I have absolutely no idea," replied Simon. "I will ring George this evening and ask if he has heard anything about who may have it in for us."

He patted Marie on the shoulder, told her not to worry as the police were only doing their job and said he would see her later. She stayed at the table deep in thought. She was frightened.

# Chapter Seventy-One

George and Anne had just finished their evening meal when the telephone rang. It was Simon asking if he could call around as he needed to talk with them.

"Of course, you can," Anne replied. She told George that Simon was coming around. She cleared the table and put the kettle on. George hadn't told Anne that he had been in touch with Crimestoppers. He wasn't sure how she would take it.

Simon arrived ten minutes later, and Anne made him a cup of tea. They sat down at the kitchen table.

"What's up, Simon?" George asked knowing what the answer would be.

"Someone is pointing the finger at me and Marie. The police came around this morning asking all sorts of questions," he told them.

"What on earth do you mean, Simon?" asked Anne.

"First of all, they were asking where we were on the night of the deaths. They asked Marie if she could remember any more about the morning when she found Lorna and to cap it all they started asking us about young Freddie's missing magnifying glass!" replied Simon. He took a swallow of his tea. He looked really worried.

"What in earth do they want to know about the magnifying glass for? It's been found, hasn't it? You said it was caught up in the rubbish bag. It's hardly a police matter!" asked Anne.

"Well, I wasn't being entirely truthful about where it was found. Someone contacted the police and suggested that we knew what had happened to it so we could stop Freddie investigating," George replied.

"So where was it found then?" asked George. He felt awful knowing he was the reason the police had called to see Simon and Marie.

"I found it at the back of the cupboard, under the kitchen sink," Simon told them. "It had obviously been hidden there by someone at the party. We thought if we said it had been found with the wrapping paper, then the person who had hidden it under the sink wouldn't have anything on us should the police search our house for any reason."

"But why would they want to search your house, George?" asked Anne with a questioning look.

"If there was an anonymous tip off suggesting either Marie or I had anything to do with the deaths then they could come with a search warrant. Someone obviously thinks we're guilty of something or the police wouldn't have come around this morning. Once they heard about someone taking the magnifying glass to stop Freddie investigating and it was found under our sink, they could say we deliberately took it and hid it there as we had done something that we didn't want Freddie finding out about," Simon explained. "We decided to say it was found in the bag of paper so we could be said it was found without us explaining we actually found it under the sink."

"Blimey, Simon! Surely, that's all a bit farfetched," said George.

"So you think the person responsible for the deaths was actually at the party. They took the magnifying glass and planted it under your sink so if the police found it, it would look suspicious for both of you, and then that person tipped the police off," said Anne. "You said they asked you about where you were at the time of all the deaths. But why are they pointing the finger at you two all of a sudden?"

"I don't know, I wish I did know. I have no idea why we are suddenly in the frame. We've done nothing wrong," said Simon.

"What do you think about all this, George?" Anne asked.

George felt dreadful. He needed to think how to answer. Simon was understandably upset.

"I really don't know, Simon." He was thinking he had made a huge mistake in talking to Roger and Fay and then contacting Crimestoppers. He wished he'd kept his mouth shut. He could lose Simon and Marie as friends if they ever found out about this. Thank goodness he hadn't confided in Anne; she would never forgive him. He needed to make sure Roger and Fay never told anyone.

"The police have nothing on you for the deaths, only about lying about the magnifying glass," he said.

"Yes," said Simon, "but it's why we lied about where the magnifying glass was found that interests them now. It looks suspicious to them. They obviously know Freddie was saying he couldn't investigate without it and by taking it, would stop him finding more clues into the deaths."

He put his head in his hands.

"If I'm going to be honest, I did wonder whether Marie had taken it and hidden it under the sink. How awful is that? Suspecting my own wife of possibly killing three people! Not that I told the police that, of course! Also, they suggested that Freddie could be in danger because he's now got his magnifying glass back."

Anne patted him on his arm, "We know that you are not involved in any if this," she told him. "Don't we, George?"

"Of course, we do," he replied.

"Marie has looked worried for a while but I've put that down to Gary, Georgina and the baby," said Simon. "Now baby Bens arrived safely she should be much less worried but it appears something is still on her mind. I've asked her but she says she's fine so I have to believe her."

Anne asked if he wanted another cup of tea but Simon said he needed to be getting home. He thanked them for listening to him. Anne saw him out and then returned to George.

"Poor Simon," she said. "He's really worried. I hope everything's going to be ok." "Me, too," replied George. He needed to ring Roger without Anne knowing.

A lot of the villagers had seen the police car outside Simon and Marie's farm. Gossip was rife. Questions were being bandied between people but no answers were found.

"Surely, Simon and Marie can't have had anything to do with what's been going on in the village? We have known them for ages," was on many people's lips.

Simon and Marie were mortified thinking that they were under suspicion "I daren't go out in the village, even for a walk," said Marie.

Simon told her to hold her head up high and she should still go out and about as she normally would. They had nothing to do with the deaths and she should tell that to anyone who asked her.

"It's easier said than done," she told him. "People always say there's no smoke without fire."

"'We' know that we have nothing to hide and the police will soon realise that," replied Simon. He said this to Marie but was still worried.

George had spoken to Roger the evening before. Anne had gone up for a bath so he knew he wouldn't be overheard. Roger agreed with him that no one must ever know they had contacted Crimestoppers. He said Fay would keep quiet too.

Anne had asked George if he had any idea who may have pointed the finger at Simon and Marie.

"I can't believe they would be suspected of being involved in the deaths," she told him.

"No idea at all," replied George.

*I must think very carefully about my next step. I want this whole nightmare to be over, so everyone can carry on with their normal lives. If someone gets hurt in the process then so be it. As long as it's not me!*

# Chapter Seventy-Two

School resumed in the first week of September.

In assembly, the head master welcomed the children back and said he hoped they had enjoyed their summer break. He said a new term was starting and everyone should settle down to their lessons.

He welcomed the new intake of children and asked the older children to look out for them as they may be feeling bewildered at starting big school. He smiled at the small group of new pupils and introduced the teachers to them. They sang "Morning has Broken".

After assembly, the children went into their classrooms with their children.

Julie was still the teacher for the pupils in their last year of school. She looked around the class and said how nice it was to see them again. She asked if anyone would like to share what they had been doing in the holidays.

Freddie raised his hand.

"Yes Freddie?" she asked wondering what he was going to come out with.

"I have done some investigating and found a clue but no one's caught the murderer yet and it's been a while now. Do we still need to be careful or do you think they have stopped murdering people now?" he said.

The children sniggered. *Good old Freddie*, they were thinking.

"Everyone should be careful at all times. The police will catch the person or persons responsible but it does take time," she replied. "Now, let's start with an English lesson. Hands up who has heard of JK Rowling?"

All the class raised their hands.

"So, let's start discussing her books."

She told the other teachers during break about Freddie and his questions.

"It *is* very worrying that no one has been arrested yet," Sally said. Julie was making a cup of tea. The headmaster remarked he had heard there were a couple of suspects.

"There's no way those two would be involved," Julie replied knowing he was referring to Simon and Marie. "I know them quite well. They are a lovely couple."

Sally said, "But the police must have thought they had something on them. I heard they visited them a couple of times."

"Nothing came of their questioning though and they were not taken to the police station," replied Julie handing Sally her mug of tea "No, I cannot believe they had anything to do with it."

"No smoke without fire," said Sally stirring sugar into her tea.

"No, it's got to be someone else. Someone who is definitely lying low, thinking they have got away with it," replied Julie. "Now, let's change the subject," as she handed around the mugs of tea.

She returned home about five o'clock. A new term was always stressful to begin with until the children settled down to lessons again after the long summer break. She started preparing the evening meal. Julian would be home in about an hour.

The phone rang. It was Celia asking if she had heard the news.

"What news?" asked Julie.

"The police have taken Simon and Marie into the police station for further questioning," Celia told her.

Julie was shocked. "Simon and Marie? No, I haven't heard that. When was this?"

"This afternoon about half past four. A police car turned up at their farm and the next thing Simon and Marie were being put in the back of the car and driven off."

"How awful. Did you actually see it happen?" asked Julie.

"No," said Celia, "but Mary did. She was out for a walk and was passing the farm and saw it. She said she couldn't believe her eyes."

"I bet she couldn't," replied Celia. "Surely they can't have anything to do with what's happened."

"The police must suspect Simon and Marie of something, though," said Julie "They have spoken to them at their house a couple of times."

"If I hear any more, I will let you know," said Celia and rang off.

Freya had overheard the end of the conversation. "Is that true?" she asked Celia. "Are Simon and Marie the murderers?"

"No, of course not," her mother told her. "There's obviously been a mistake."

"I need to tell Freddie; can I ring him up?"

"I suppose so but I expect his mum might already have told him if she's heard what's happened," Celia said.

Freya rang Freddie who said he had heard about it just a few minutes earlier "I was going to ring you. Mary just rang Mum and told her. This is so exciting; people actually now being arrested!" he said.

"No, it's not. I like Simon and Marie and I don't want them to go to prison," said Freya.

"I don't think my clue was anything to do with those two though," said Freddie. "I need to think about this."

"Perhaps, it wasn't a real clue about the murders after all," suggested Freya.

"It was, I'm sure," replied Freddie. "I've got to go now; Mum says tea's ready."

Freya put the phone down.

She told her mother that Freddie already knew as Mary had rung his mum to tell her the news.

# Chapter Seventy-Three

Simon and Marie were sitting in an interview room at Olehampton police station. They were clutching each other's hands tightly. They had been shown into the room and were told someone would be with them shortly.

"Why have they brought us here?" Marie whispered. "We don't know any more than what we have already told them which isn't much."

"I don't know. Let's wait and see what they say," replied Simon. He looked at his watch. James would have to manage the milking on his own.

The door opened and two men walked in. They smiled at Simon and Marie and thanked them for coming in. The younger one went to a table in the corner of the room and switched a recorder on.

"We didn't have a choice," Simon remarked looking at Marie.

"I am Chief Inspector Morris and this is Detective Sergeant Smith," said the older man who sat down and opened a folder in front of him on the table. "Can you tell us your names and dates of birth for the tape please?"

Simon and Marie did as they were asked.

"We need to ask you some more questions about the deaths of the three women in Merrydale," said Inspector Morris.

"We have told the police everything we know," replied Marie.

"We have had some more information since we last spoke with you," said Detective Sergeant Smith.

"Are we under arrest?" asked Simon.

"No, you are not under arrest and are free to go anytime but I wouldn't advise it. It's best to stay so we can clear these things up," said the Chief Inspector.

"So, how can we help you?" asked Marie.

"Let's talk about the night when Beverley died. We know you were hosting a starter course for the Safari Supper event at your house so would have access to prawns. You then both have admitted to going to Mary's house where

Beverley was helping out. You admit you saw her sandwich in her bag in the kitchen," said the Inspector.

"But we didn't touch it and also there were lots of other people there who would have seen the sandwich in the bag as well," said Marie.

"We have had an anonymous phone call directly to the police station here yesterday, saying you were seen going over to the red bag in the kitchen," he told Marie.

"But that's a lie!" she gasped. "Who would say something like that? It's just not true," she said tearfully. "Why on earth are we being blamed for something that we didn't do and why would Simon or I want to kill Beverley? We liked her. She was a friend. We had no reason to kill her or anyone else!" She gripped Simon's hand tightly.

"It has also been suggested that you were seen walking near Sheila's house about an hour before the fire was discovered," said Inspector Morris looking at his notes.

"I can't believe we're hearing this. This is ridiculous. We were both at home watching television and only left the house when we saw the flames and heard people shouting. We had absolutely no reason to kill Sheila," said Marie. She wiped her tears away with a tissue. Simon was pale and really didn't know what to say. How often could they keep defending themselves? He shook his head in disbelief.

"Where do you do your shopping?" the Inspector suddenly asked Marie. Her head shot up in amazement.

"My shopping? I shop weekly in Tesco's, but why on earth do you want to know that for?" she asked.

"We have established that the ready meal that poisoned Lorna came from Tesco's," he replied.

"I should think half the village shop at Tesco's," said Simon. *He was in a dream,* he thought. *I will wake up in a minute and be at home in bed.*

"Did you shop in the week that Lorna died?"

"I shop every week on a Tuesday afternoon," Marie said. "But that *does not* mean I bought a ready meal, laced it with arsenic and sent it to Lorna."

"It has been reported to us that you were seen in Tesco's on Tuesday afternoon looking at the ready meals section in the store."

"Marie makes all her own dishes. We do not have ready meals in our house," said Simon.

Marie nodded her head. "I do make all my own dishes so I would not need to look at the ready meals in Tesco's."

"Who is saying all this about us?" asked Simon. "You must have some idea. There is absolutely no evidence we are involved but how can we defend ourselves against these wicked allegations? All we are doing is telling you the truth."

"I told you, we received an anonymous phone call yesterday so we need to follow it up."

"So on the strength of an anonymous phone call you were able to take us, in full view of the village, from our house, put us in the back of a police car and bring us here," said Simon.

"That's right sir," replied the Inspector. "We have three murders to solve and we intend to catch the person or persons responsible."

"I think you are clutching at straws. You have not made any real progress since June and it's now September," said Simon.

"We have made some very good progress but cannot discuss it with you," was the reply. "Can we now go over the events of the missing magnifying glass which was found under your kitchen sink?"

"We have been through this before," said Marie with a sigh.

"Let's go over it once more," she was told. Simon repeated what had happened at the party with him finding it a few days later under the sink but telling people he had found it in the rubbish bag.

"I know it sounds odd but I thought it was better than the truth about where I found it," he concluded.

"It is indeed extremely odd sir that you made up such a tale," said the Inspector "but we will leave it there for now except to say the anonymous caller suggested you hid it yourselves to stop the young lad investigating, but then you thought better of it, and later announcing it was actually found in the rubbish bag, it would be presumed by everybody to have been mislaid in entirely innocent circumstances. The caller said you needed to have it innocently found so as not to bring attention to yourselves."

"What happens now?" asked Marie dreading the answer. She could already see a prison cell looming.

"You are both free to go for now but I must stress you are not to leave the village. No doubt we will need to speak with you again."

The Inspector and his colleague rose. "We will take you home now," the Inspector said.

"Don't bother, we will ring a friend to come and collect us. We do not want to go in a police car again," replied Simon.

"As you wish sir," was the reply.

Simon and Marie were taken back through to the foyer. There were a couple of ladies at the desk talking to a policeman about a lost purse. They looked up as Simon and Marie passed by.

Simon rang George who answered his phone quickly.

Simon asked if he could come and collect him and Marie from the police station and said he would tell him all about it on the journey home.

George said he would set off straight away saying he would see them in about half an hour.

Simon and Marie waited outside as they didn't want to spend another minute inside the police station.

"What an awful experience that was," she told Simon holding onto his hand. "Who would do this to us?"

"I don't know but My God, I'm going to find out," he replied.

George arrived and pulled up outside the station. Marie got in the back seat leaving Simon to get in the front passenger seat. She would leave it to Simon to tell George about what had happened.

Simon relayed to George everything that had gone on. "Someone's got it in for us, or, the most likely explanation is that someone wants the blame shifted from them to someone else and for some reason it's us they've chosen," he said.

"Blimey, what a horrible ordeal for you both."

He met Marie's eyes in the rear-view mirror. She wiped a tear away.

George dropped them off at the farm. He asked if they wanted him to come in but they said they would rather be on their own. They got out of the car, thanked him for collecting them and made their way to their front door. George sighed and drove home.

Anne was very upset when she heard what Simon and Marie had gone through at the police station.

"How absolutely awful for them," she shuddered. "I will ring Marie in the morning and suggest we meet up for a coffee. She may want to talk."

# Chapter Seventy-Four

Saturday morning Celia was asked by Sarah if she could mind Freddie and Max for a couple of hours in the afternoon as she and David wanted to go and buy a new three-piece suite. She said the children wouldn't be interested in furniture shopping and it would be better if they didn't come along. "We'll be a lot quicker without them!"

"Of course I'll look after them. It's a nice day so we can go for a walk in the park," replied Celia.

She told the girls who were pleased. It was a nice sunny day and they would look forward to going to the park and playing on the swings and slide.

Freddie and Max were dropped off at two o'clock by Sarah and David. "We'll be back in a couple of hours."

"Its fine, no problem at all," replied Celia.

Freddie and Freya immediately rushed to her room where they could talk without the younger girls and Max overhearing them.

"Come on," said Celia after fifteen minutes "Let's go to the park."

She herded them all out of the door calling out to Luke they would be about an hour or so.

"Don't hurry back on my account," he grinned. "I'm going to do some gardening."

He enjoyed his Saturday afternoons in the garden. When the children were there, they side-tracked him and he couldn't always get on with his jobs. He had found a wasp nest in his shed as well that he needed to sort out without the children around.

He mowed the lawn first. He took pride in his mowing and enjoyed the look and smell of nicely mown grass. He preferred to use a push mower to get the stripes. He listened to the sound of his neighbour's other mowers doing their job.

He finished mowing the lawn after half an hour and returned the mower to his shed. He looked into the top corner of the shed and saw the wasp nest hanging. He looked around to see what he could use to destroy it. He thought he had some wasp disposal foam but he couldn't find it. He decided to walk to Mary's house and see if she had some. He knew she had a shed where she kept all her gardening equipment and thought she kept chemicals and fertilisers as well so hoped she may have something for destroying wasps.

He locked the door and walked to her house. He rang the bell but it wasn't answered. He could hear the lawn mower being used so assumed she was in the back garden. He walked around to her side entrance and found the gate open. He called her name but there was no reply.

She obviously couldn't hear him over the sound of her mower. He walked up the side entrance and turned into her garden. He called her name again. She heard him this time and turned around from her mowing.

"Hello, Luke," she said smiling.

"Hi, Mary, I wonder if you could help me," Luke replied.

"If I can," she said and turned the electric mower off. "I rang your front door bell but you couldn't hear me," he explained.

"No, I didn't. These mowers are quite noisy, aren't they?" she replied.

"They are, indeed. I have a push mower," he answered. "I like to get the stripes which you can't always do with the electric ones."

"They are a bit heavy to push so that's why I have one of these," said Mary. "What can I do for you?"

She listened to why he had called around. "I think I do have some foam," she replied. "Let's go and see," Luke told her how nice her garden was looking. "I wish my garden looked as nice but with three children and their paraphernalia it's hard!"

They walked to the bottom of the garden to her shed. The door was closed. "Ever since Ebony wandered in and knocked some fertiliser off the shelf and licked some up which had spilled out that made her sick, I'm obsessed with keeping the door shut," she said as she opened the door. Luke followed her inside. He was impressed. It was a very tidy shed. She had a large range of gardening equipment, all stacked neatly along the sides of the shed and different packets of fertilisers and gardening chemicals on shelves. "I have something for most things," she pointed out to him. "This is for black fly, another one for whitefly, this is for roses, slug pellets for those dreadful slimy creatures, and these small granules are excellent for putting around shrubs in pots. Now, let's see if I have any of that wasp foam you are after. I'm sure I have some."

She looked carefully along the shelves and suddenly pounced. "Here we are!" she said holding up a canister for him to see. "I thought I had some."

"I will replace it for you," he promised. He took it from her and took it outside to read the label in the light. "This should do it," he said to Mary. "Thanks very much." She closed the shed door firmly.

"You're welcome." She smiled. "Would you like a cup of tea?"

"I'd better get back, thanks. I want to sort the wasp nest out before Celia and the children get back from the park. She's looking after Freddie and Max as Sarah and David have gone furniture shopping."

They walked back down the side entrance towards the front of the house. "Too late!" he said. "I can hear them coming back."

They could hear the sound of children coming up the road shouting and laughing.

Celia and the children stopped when they saw them at Mary's front gate.

"Hello, Mary. Goodness, I turn my back for five minutes and he's off visiting another woman." Celia laughed. Mary laughed too.

Luke held up his hands, "Guilty as charged," he grinned.

Luke showed Celia the canister of wasp destroying foam. "It's for the wasp nest in our shed. I thought I had some but couldn't find it so I came along to see if Mary had some."

Freddie was staring at Mary. Freya nudged him as she'd asked him something and he hadn't replied. The younger children were dancing around him but he wasn't taking any notice of them either.

"Are you alright, Freddie?" Freya asked him. "Yes. I'm fine." He grinned turning to her. She shrugged wondering if anything was wrong. They had enjoyed the trip to the park and she was now thirsty and wanted to get home. "Can I have a drink please, Mum?" she asked Celia. "I'm really thirsty."

"Yes, we will all have one at home, come on everybody, cheerio, Mary," she said herding the children up the road. Luke thanked Mary for the wasp foam and said he would buy another to replace the one she had given him. "No rush for it." She smiled as they headed off.

Mary watched them all go up the road. She sighed and then went back to finish mowing her lawn. There was always so much to do in the garden to keep it looking its best.

# Chapter Seventy-Five

Another anonymous phone call was made to the police station. Inspector Morris held a meeting with his team of officers.

"We are definitely closing in now," he told them after discussing the investigations so far, the most recent anonymous phone call and the previous one. "I believe we will soon be in a position to make an arrest. We have now been made aware of something we were not aware of before." He detailed what the phone caller had said.

An officer raised his hand. "From what you have been telling us there is now more than one person having the finger pointed at them."

"Yes, as you all know we have spoken twice to one couple, who are still persons of interest, but we do not have enough to charge them but now we have another name in the frame. This latest phone call is naming the person we have wondered about earlier in the investigation but have had no evidence to question further." He pointed to a name on the board behind him. He had written other names on the board with arrows surrounding the three dead women. "As I said earlier there was some useful information in this latest phone call that we had not been aware of."

"So have we now got enough to make an arrest?" asked an officer from the back of the room.

"We need to move quietly and quickly and make sure of our facts first," said the Inspector. "We do not want to arouse their suspicions. Someone is feeling safe and believes they have got away with what they have done."

"So what's the next step?" asked the officer from the back of the room.

"We will be investigating into this person's background," he said tapping his finger on a name on the board. "There must be some connection with this person and what has gone in Merrydale but it's not yet apparent what it is. I will meet up with you all again here in two days with an update with what has been found out. This investigation is hopefully soon coming to an end but we need real evidence not just anonymous phone calls with possibly malicious intent."

"But at least this phone call has put another name in the frame," said the officer.

The Inspector agreed with this and ended the meeting.

He left the room and went to speak to his superior. He needed to inform him of intending to investigate the latest person being named from the anonymous phone call. He was given permission to go ahead and contact a neighbouring police force.

He was now going to get in touch with the Burford police.

He went into his own office and made the phone call. It was arranged that he would meet up with an Inspector in the morning. In the meantime he gave them the name of whom he wanted to have enquiries made into their past.

He really hoped this would all be at an end soon. It had now been over four months since the first death. The villagers needed answers and the police needed to put a murderer behind bars.

# Chapter Seventy-Six

Simon and Marie were anxious. They were frightened the police would pay them another visit. Simon carried out his usual jobs around the farm but was distracted wondering about what could happen next. Marie did her daily chores but couldn't stop thinking about their recent visit to the police station. She couldn't believe that someone was making anonymous phone calls about her and Simon. She hadn't plucked up the nerve to walk into the village because she thought people would be pointing fingers of suspicion about them after hearing about them being taken away in a police car.

She stayed inside the farmhouse not even wanting to speak with James or Stan.

Anne had rung her up asking if she was alright and did she want her to call around. Marie had assured her she was fine but in reality, she wasn't but couldn't face talking about it.

Inspector Morris travelled over to Burford police station to meet an Inspector Tarrant. He was told that his officers had made some enquiries regarding the person of interest. Some interesting facts had been discovered. There was definitely a connection between the person of interest and Beverley Kingston. Inspector Tarrant told him what had been found out.

"I can't believe we didn't discover this connection before," said Inspector Morris. "This throws a whole new light on everything," he said.

"It certainly makes a valid reason for at least the first death in your village," said Inspector Tarrant.

"I can't see a connection between the other two deaths though."

"But if either of them suspected that this person was responsible for killing Beverley than they needed to be silenced," replied Inspector Morris.

"That's true," replied Inspector Tarrant.

"The latest anonymous phone call suggested a clue had been found which would place the person we suspect was at the house of Sheila before the house was set on fire, but didn't elaborate as to what it was," said Inspector Morris.

"You need to try and find out who made the phone call," said Inspector Tarrant.

"That's easier said than done," was the reply.

He thanked him for his time and investigation and said he would return to his own station with the new information.

He travelled back to Olehampton police station and immediately spoke with his superior about the new information.

"Bring this person in," he was told.

"But shouldn't we find out who made the phone call first?" Inspector Morris asked.

"If you can do that," his superior said. "It's difficult finding out who makes anonymous calls."

Inspector Morris listened carefully to the anonymous phone call again. He called in a couple of officers who had interviewed the villagers at the time.

"Listen very carefully and see whether you recognise anything."

The two officers listened to the recording. They heard an adult female voice and could hear something in the background. "I can hear a child calling out something," said one. "This means it could be a mother who made the call?"

"Listen carefully again," said the Inspector.

They all listened again to the recording. "Definitely a child asking something but I can't make out what it is being asked," one said.

"Right. Revisit all the people we originally interviewed who have children," the Inspector said.

The officers groaned and said that could take some time.

"I don't care how long it takes, just do it," they were told. "Have another couple of officers to take with you."

The two officers left and sought out two officers who had already interviewed the villagers.

Police presence was seen around the village again which unnerved the villagers. Were they closing in?

*Why are the police around the village again? What have they discovered?*

# Chapter Seventy-Seven

The police consulted the record of whom they had originally spoken to after Beverley's death. They made a list of all people who had children and decided who would go to which house. There were about twenty-five families they needed to visit.

It was time consuming and the anonymous phone call was completely denied by the families visited so far.

One officer called at Sarah's house. She denied phoning the police station. She was a bit hesitant when asked if she knew who could possibly have made the phone call.

"My daughter Freya and her friend Freddie have been intrigued about the murders but they wouldn't ring up the police station. You said it was an adult female who made the call anyway."

"Where does Freddie live?" she was asked. Sarah told him and he thanked her for her time.

Freya had been listening behind the door to the conversation but hadn't made her presence known. She rang Freddie to warn him a policeman was on the way to his house.

Freddie put the phone down just as a knock sounded on his front door. He heard his mum open it.

"May we have a word please?" he heard a policeman ask.

He went into the hall and saw a policeman entering the house. His heart was thudding fast.

Celia took him into the kitchen.

"Do you know anything about an anonymous phone call made to the police station yesterday?" he heard him asking Celia. "It relates to the recent deaths in the village."

Celia asked him to sit down.

"Yes," she admitted. "I did make the phone call."

"Can you tell me why you made it?"

Freddie entered the kitchen. "I asked Mum to make the call because I think I know who killed the ladies."

The policeman turned to him. Celia sighed and explained.

"Freddie has been investigating. He says he has found a clue and now he's saying he knows who is responsible," she said. "He kept going on and on about it and I didn't know what to do, so I thought if I rang up, then the police would investigate further and it would keep him quiet."

"And what is the clue, young man? And why do you think you know who has done these awful things?" asked the officer.

Freddie told him about the clue he had found and why he believed he knew who was responsible.

"That's very good detective work Freddie." he was told. "That's useful information. Thank you. I will take it from here, you can now leave it to the police."

He got up to leave. "What are you going to do now?" Freddie asked.

"I will go back to the station and report your findings to our Inspector," he was told.

Celia showed him out. Freddie looked at her and said he needed to ring Freya.

# Chapter Seventy-Eight

A police car pulled up outside a house in Merryvale. Two officers got out.

One officer rapped on the front door. The door was opened.

"What can I do for you?" they were asked.

"May we come in, please? We should like to ask you some questions relating to the deaths of Beverley, Sheila and Lorna."

They were shown into the lounge and were asked to sit down.

"How can I help you?"

"We have some information relating to the three deaths and have discovered a connection between yourself and the death of a young boy in the village of Haleton. Can you explain the connection please?"

There was a long silence. Then words started pouring out.

"I certainly can. He was killed by the nurse who did not take his condition seriously. She got off because of her wicked lies. She deserved to be punished but oh no, she carried on as if nothing had happened. Call herself a nurse? She was nothing more than a murderer. She killed my grandson. My son and his wife couldn't cope, so they split up and I have now lost all contact with them. She also had her husband's death on her conscience."

"So you decided to do something about it?"

"I certainly did, and I don't regret it for a minute."

"What about Sheila and Lorna?"

"I thought Beverley would have told Sheila about what had happened in Haleton, so I couldn't let her tell anyone else after Beverley died, but somehow Lorna suspected me. I could see it in her face. I must have let something slip and she then sent me an anonymous card saying she knew I had done it. I didn't want to kill either of them, but I had to do it, I didn't have any choice but I was very careful how I did it as I didn't want Sheila or Lorna to suffer, only Beverley." she shrugged.

The policemen stood up.

She was read her rights.

"Mary Oliver, I am arresting you for the murders of Beverley Kingston, Sheila Davies and Lorna Miller. You do not have to say anything but it may harm your defence if you do not mention when questioned something you later rely on in court. Anything you do say may be given in evidence."

She was then taken out to the police car and driven to Olehampton police station where she was formerly charged with three counts of murder.

When interviewed she admitted everything. She held nothing back.

She admitted to slipping a prawn into Beverley's sandwich and taking the adrenaline pen from her handbag.

"I had a small bowl of prawns in my fridge ready for my cat's tea the next day. He likes a little treat, bless him! What an opportunity! I had been waiting for nearly three months to get her once I found out she was the nurse responsible for my grandson's death. I received an anonymous phone call in March asking how did I like having the nurse who had killed my grandson living in the same village as me? I don't know who rang me, they wouldn't give their name, just a person from Haleton they said, who said I ought to know she was now living in Merrydale. I knew then I needed to plan my revenge. I didn't know how at the time, but her bringing that sandwich in that silly, little red bag to my house during The Safari Supper event was perfect, as there were so many people at my house that could be suspects. I think I played my part of the grieving friend very well! No one would ever suspect me as I was so upset. I can still see her lying dead on my kitchen floor." She smiled at the Inspector as she said this.

She admitted she walked in the late evening to Sheila's house and thrust a lit rag through the letter box. "I took the risk of being seen but I would then have had to think of something else but luckily no one was about. It was a shame as I liked Sheila but I couldn't risk her talking to people after Beverley died so she had to die. Now you tell me my button was found near her path which put me on the scene. I later realised the damn button was not in my jacket pocket but wasn't sure where it had dropped out. I should have put it safe somewhere in my house rather than leaving it in my pocket after it was ripped off my jacket a couple of days earlier. Then that blasted Freddie Carter found his clue. Obviously, I didn't know he'd found my button as I didn't know where I'd actually lost it. He kept going on and on about the clue he'd found, without telling anyone what it was, so I took his magnifying glass at Marie's party as he was saying he needed it to investigate further. Not having it, I hoped he'd shut up about his silly investigations. I ask you, he's ten years old and thought he was in a position to find out who had killed Beverley, Sheila and Lorna. Interfering stupid boy!"

She then admitted to seeing Marie in Tesco's on the Tuesday afternoon when she was going to buy Lorna's fatal ready meal and thought she would cause trouble for Marie.

"Taking Freddie's magnifying glass and shoving it in the back of Marie's sink cupboard would cause more suspicion to fall on her and then they lied about finding it in the bag of rubbish!" she laughed. "It was good when she and Simon got taken in for questioning after my anonymous phone call to you, but not so good when they were released. The one I was most sorry for killing was my good friend, Lorna. We had some really good times together, but I think she guessed my secret. I have all sorts of chemicals in my garden shed and found one that contained arsenic. I added it to the ready meal and put it on her doorstep for her to find. I thought it would be a quick death. I hope she didn't suffer. I thought it would be quite a nice way to die. It was good news when I heard Marie was first on the scene when Lorna was found. Another reason for the police to question her! I was very upset my cat was ill after licking some of the arsenic powder off the shed floor. That would have been terrible if he had died. I would never have forgiven myself. I love that cat. I wonder what will happen to him now. I hope he goes to a nice home. I need to write a list of his favourite food as he's quite fussy. Have you some paper and a pen, so you can give the list to whoever takes him in?"

*She's quite mad*, thought Inspector Morris.

# Chapter Seventy-Nine

The villagers were astounded when they heard. They couldn't believe it. "Mary!" was repeated over and over. "Unbelievable!" "I can't believe how she could have been so brazen."

Simon and Marie were very relieved to be off the suspect list and were given an apology from the police. Marie told Simon she had had a feeling about something being not quite right about Mary and some of her comments, but couldn't put her finger on the reason why, which was why she had been so troubled lately.

George discovered that Frances had the magnifying glass in her kitchen drawer as she was having trouble reading the small print on some food labels. She was astonished he hadn't asked her about it when he had found it.

"I hope you didn't think it was Freddie's and you suspected me of taking it!" she teased him.

"Of course, not," he replied feeling a pang of guilt.

Freddie and Freya couldn't stop talking about it.

"I knew it was Mary!" said Freddie. "As you know, I found the button on Sheila's path and then I saw her wearing a jacket with a blue button missing when your dad was coming out from her house with the wasp killer. I knew then she was the murderer as the other two jacket buttons matched the one I found."

"Well done, Freddie!" Freya said. "I thought something was up when we were standing outside her house and you had gone very quiet. You were just staring at Mary."

Freddie beamed broadly.

He was the talk of the school. He was clapped on the back by his friends.

In assembly, he was asked to come to the front for a round of applause as a policeman presented him with a certificate.

"Your clue was invaluable to wrapping up the investigation," he was told. "I shall look forward to you joining the police force when you are older."

The school children cheered. Good old Freddie. He never let them down.

Patricia Bevin's third novel *The Final Chapter for Some* will be published soon.